CRAFTING *for* SINNERS

a novel

Jenny Kiefer

This is a work of fiction. All names, places, and characters are products of the author's imagination or are used fictitiously. Any resemblance to real people, places, or events is entirely coincidental.

Library of Congress Cataloging-in-Publication Data
Names: Kiefer, Jenny, author.
Title: Crafting for sinners / Jenny Kiefer.
Description: Philadelphia : Quirk Books, 2025. | Summary: "When Ruth is caught shoplifting from the megachurch-owned craft store in her small hometown, she is locked in and attacked by employees who seem to have a secret and sinister plan for her"—Provided by publisher.
Identifiers: LCCN 2025008583 (print) | LCCN 2025008584 (ebook) | ISBN 9781683694700 (paperback) | ISBN 9781683694717 (ebook)
Subjects: LCGFT: Horror fiction. | Novels.
Classification: LCC PS3611.I396 C73 2025 (print) | LCC PS3611.I396 (ebook) | DDC 813/.6—dc23/eng/20250311
LC record available at https://lccn.loc.gov/2025008583
LC ebook record available at https://lccn.loc.gov/2025008584

ISBN: 978-1-68369-470-0

Printed in the United States of America

Typeset in Adobe Garamond Pro, Proxima Nova, and Rough Cut

Designed by Andie Reid
Cover crochet art by Nicole Nikolich

Quirk Books
215 Church Street
Philadelphia, PA 19106
quirkbooks.com

Quirk Books' authorized representative in the EU for product safety and compliance is Easy Access System Europe, Mustamäe tee 50, 10621 Tallinn, Estonia, gpsr.requests@easproject.com.

10 9 8 7 6 5 4 3 2 1

For my best boy

For all the empathetic fighters

New Creations

~ STORE MAP ~

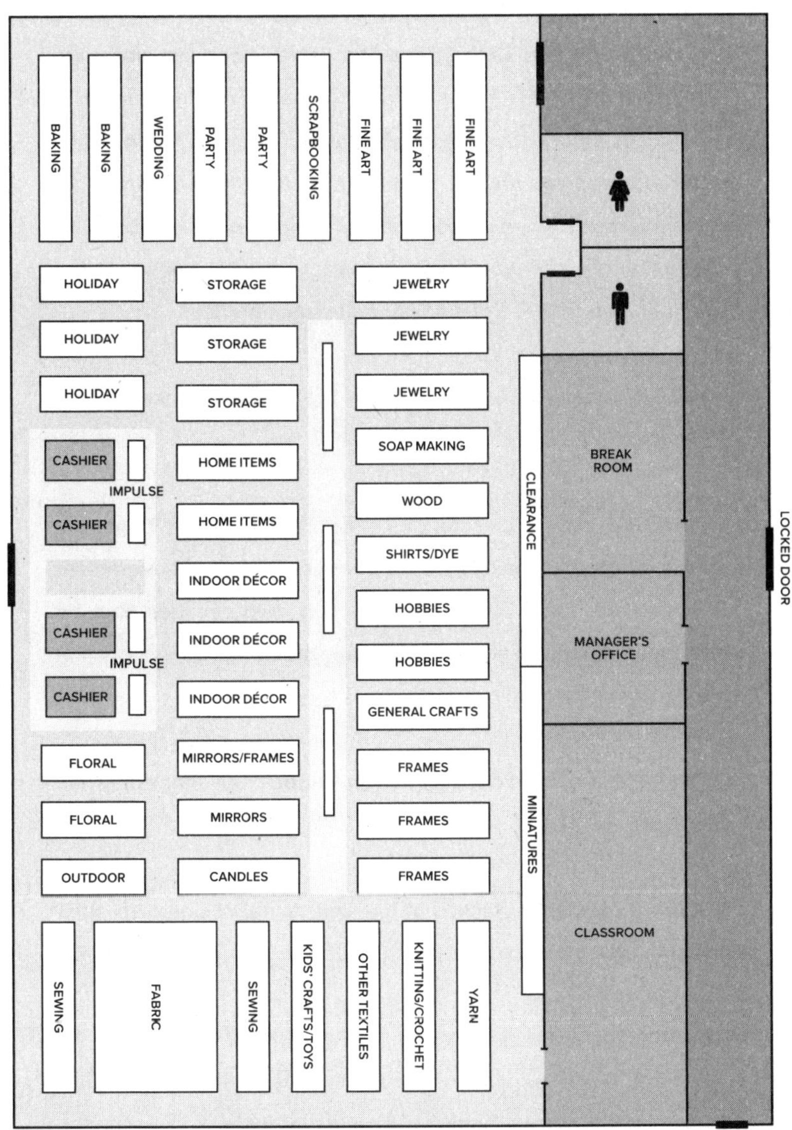

COLD CASES, LOST FACES

Season 3, Episode 7

SARAH: Welcome to *Cold Cases, Lost Faces*, a podcast where we explore cases that went cold almost immediately. I'm Sarah and my co-host, Lindsey, is here to tell us about today's case. And this one's a doozy, you guys! The deeper we dove, the crazier it became. We'll post more information and artifacts on our website, so check that out after you listen. To start, as always, we speak the victim's name to give them power and remembrance.

LINDSEY: Today, we're looking into the disappearance of Tom Torrence.

SARAH: This case is ice cold, y'all. We only heard about it because one of our fans' uncle bought Tom's house when the government finally seized it and put it up for auction—two decades after he disappeared without a trace. All of Tom's belongings were still in the house, untouched.

LINDSEY: Bills spread out next to a checkbook, the check only half filled out.

SARAH: Dirty dishes stacked in the sink. A loaf of bread so old it had shriveled into moldy dust.

LINDSEY: The sheets askew from Tom's last night of sleep.

SARAH: Mildew-laced laundry rotting in the washer.

LINDSEY: Our listener's uncle inherited all of this, and more. But unfortunately for us, he gutted Tom's house and threw out all of Tom's belongings, and probably a lot of clues, too.

SARAH: But there's a small bit of luck—our listener discovered an overlooked box in the basement with some of Tom's things. Mostly photographs and some trinkets, which our listener scanned and sent to us.

LINDSEY: The photographs are so intriguing. They show Tom across his entire life span, from a little boy playing in the snow to a teenager working at an ice cream shop.

SARAH: Oh, my God, his smile is *so* contagious in that one!

LINDSEY: So let's tell our listeners a little about Tom—at least what little we do know about him.

SARAH: Tom lived alone in a small town called Lovelace near Paducah, Kentucky. From the photographs and artifacts, we can tell that Tom was a sentimental person, and overall he seemed happy. He wore a broad grin in almost every photograph.

LINDSEY: We couldn't find any official records on Tom, like a birth certificate, but based on the dates on the photos, we think he was born somewhere between 1945 and 1950 putting him in his fifties when he disappeared. We tried searching for Tom on the internet, but his name doesn't come up with any relevant results. It was the early 2000s—not everything was as well documented as it is now.

SARAH: Again, when we say "cold case" here, it's *ice cold*, y'all.

LINDSEY: And back then, nobody used their real names on the internet! Even if he was active in chatrooms or forums, he would have used a screenname. It was truly a different time.

SARAH: And when we searched for articles printed in newspapers, not much came up.

LINDSEY: There were only a few short articles in the local paper about his disappearance, which was overshadowed by another news story, which we'll get to in a second. First, we want to talk about *why* Tom may have gone missing.

SARAH: Since we couldn't find any information about Tom via the usual methods, we took an unusual route. We actually looked up old phone books from the time he went missing and we *cold-called* some of his neighbors to see if they could tell us anything at all.

LINDSEY: This is probably the wildest thing we've done yet, but we owed it to Tom to try to learn more about his case.

SARAH: Honestly, it was a lot of work to try to track down current phone numbers and addresses, but luckily, a lot of his neighbors still live in the same houses. Some said they didn't know Tom, but we were able to get some information that we don't think anyone has uncovered yet.

LINDSEY: The neighbors who talked to us described Tom as a very nice, quiet man. They said he was a bit of a loner and rarely entertained or had visitors. He kept to himself most of the time, but was always friendly, with a pleasant hello. About a year before he went missing, a young family moved in next door to him. A couple with a baby girl—this will be important later.

SARAH: Most of the neighbors we talked to pretty much said that same thing. Tom was nice and quiet, but ultimately, they didn't remember much about him. We thought we'd reached a dead end, until we got on the phone with a man we'll call John—he didn't want us to use his real name.

LINDSEY: Like we always say, names have power! So we will honor John and not use his real name.

SARAH: John was the only person we spoke to who knew Tom well. According to John, the two were more than friends. They were dating. But, sorry, guys, there's no happy ending on this one. John and Tom did not run away together and live happily ever after. John said he wouldn't be surprised if Tom's disappearance had to do with his being gay. It was the early 2000s, and being gay wasn't as accepted as it is now, especially in the small town of Lovelace, Kentucky.

LINDSEY: John said that Tom was exceptionally kind, and a great cook. When they'd have date nights, Tom would always cook and John would do the dishes. Then they'd snuggle on the couch and watch movies from Blockbuster. They didn't tell anyone they were dating because they didn't know what their conservative neighbors would think. They usually met up at John's house, which was a bit more secluded than Tom's. But a few weeks before Tom went missing, they had a date night at Tom's house.

SARAH: John said after Tom went missing, he was pretty much the only person who was trying to look for him. The local police department didn't seem to care, or maybe they just didn't have the money or resources to look for a missing person. But John says he does wonder whether Tom's disappearance was somehow tied to that one date night at Tom's, because of something strange that happened around the same time.

LINDSEY: And here's where the disappearance of Tom Torrence starts to get really, really weird. So we mentioned earlier that a young couple with a baby daughter had moved in next to Tom. Well, about a week after Tom went missing, the mother and daughter *also* went missing. Her husband said he went to work that morning and when he came back, they were gone. Her car was missing, and he thought maybe some of their valuables were gone, too, but it was hard to tell because they were in the process of moving, so everything was in boxes.

SARAH: So the question is—are the two disappearances related? Did they run away together? Or was there foul play involved?

LINDSEY: Why would Tom—a gay man—run away with a young woman who, by all accounts, he barely knew? And with her newborn?

SARAH: Unless there was something sinister in Lovelace, Kentucky, they were both running *from*.

LINDSEY: We'll dive into it right after this brief break to talk about our sponsor.

Chapter 1

Stab.

Strangle.

Pull out the guts.

Ruth repeated this refrain in her head as she worked her stitches across the row. Her knuckles ached from the repetitive motion, but she had a deadline.

Her phone buzzed on the couch next to her.

"It better not be another message from Charlie," she muttered under her breath. He'd been sending her text messages all week, saying he was sorry about how things went down, that he had a daughter now and it made him re-evaluate. That he wanted to *make things right*—whatever that meant.

He'd been her fiancé, and they'd broken up just a few months before their would-be vows, but that was years ago—and *felt* like a lifetime ago. She'd ignored every single one of the fifteen messages he'd sent so far.

Would it be possible to get the blanket tomorrow? I can pay extra.

Shit. Not Charlie—her client. Holding the stitches in place on the needles, Ruth lifted the partially finished blanket aloft. It wasn't even at the halfway point. Not only did the commissioner want it by tomorrow, but just last week she'd asked if it would be possible to make the blanket larger. The woman had asked for a baby blanket, but then decided she wanted something the kid could grow into. Of course she'd pay extra, she'd said. Ruth had almost been finished with the thing. It took her nearly an hour to unravel the work she'd already knit, rewind the skeins, and cast on with three times the number of stitches.

She could *maybe* finish by tomorrow if she knitted literally every second up to the moment it would be picked up, assuming she had enough yarn. But she had to try. She really needed the money.

The "moving fund" mocked her from the mantel: an oversized ceramic jar with only a few crinkled bills and pennies in its belly. On the outside, thorny, fruit-bearing vines had been hand-painted. Inscribed on the lid were foreign characters of some unknown language. Ruth and her girlfriend Abigail had started the fund soon after Abigail's mom passed, both hoping to move to a more progressive area, one where they didn't have to pretend to be roommates or keep the curtains closed if they wanted to dance in the kitchen or kiss each other goodbye. Instead, they were stuck in a town of twelve thousand that boasted the largest Christian congregation in the entire state, some flashy new sect calling themselves New Creationists.

The jar became a chicken-and-egg situation. It would be easier to fill it if they could move away and get higher-paying jobs in a place with more opportunities—but they needed the jar to be full in order to move away and get those jobs. So they were stuck in Kill Devil, taking temp gigs, odd jobs, and the occasional crafting commission, the internet too slow to do anything remote. And Ruth constantly had to pull painful paper guts from the jar to pay for insulin or syringes or test strips.

"How's the blanket coming?" Abigail asked, sitting on the couch next to Ruth.

"I'm making a dent, I guess," Ruth replied. She leaned against Abigail, lifting her face for a kiss.

But Abigail didn't lean back. Instead, her eyes flitted across the room, lasering in on every window. A habit she'd inherited from her mother. Ruth followed her gaze as Abigail leapt from the couch. One set of curtains was not fully closed, a sliver of midmorning light poking in, a glimpse of a single tree trunk from the untamed land that lined their yard in view. Abigail pinched them shut.

Ruth rolled her eyes. "Like mother, like daughter."

Abigail's mom, Judy, had always been deeply paranoid—the insane column of locks that still lined the inside of their front door was a testament to that. Now Ruth had begun to notice some similar inherited qualities in Abigail.

"One of us has to be cautious," Abigail said. "There's always that weird birder hanging out by the woods. What if he sees us kissing through the window? What if your old manager from New Creations finds out where you live? Didn't they fire you over it?"

"He's known for ages and hasn't done anything," Ruth said. She'd been let go nearly three years ago. "Why would they start now?"

"I don't know, Ruth," Abigail said, her tone like knives. "But last week that new boutique a town over was burned to the ground because they put a rainbow in the window. The largest building in a fifty-mile radius is a fucking church that preaches that being gay is a sin, and it's very likely that whoever started the fire goes there every Sunday. Doesn't that scare you?"

Ruth turned back to her knitting, working the yarn in silence.

Abigail scoffed. "I can't believe you can be so comfortable living here, knowing that every face you pass in the grocery store might hate you if they knew you loved another woman."

"I've lived here my whole life," Ruth said. "My parents are among those people."

Ruth had been raised under their so-called *traditional beliefs*, shoots of bigotry sprouting in the soil—but they had loved her. But then the New Creationists came, and the vines grew, mutated. So much so that the moment the word *bisexual* left her lips, they instantly disowned her. They shoved her out of their house and slammed the door in her face, like a leper. That was nearly five years ago, and she hadn't spoken to them since.

"I'm not comfortable with it either," Ruth continued, "but nothing bad has happened to us. We haven't even had a neighbor yell at us or give us a dirty look. Plus, we don't have any money to move anywhere, so what's the point in worrying?"

"We'll figure out a way," Abigail replied.

"How? We don't have any family to lean on. No friends anywhere else. We only have each other. If we just keep saving, we'll get there eventually."

"I don't know how much longer I can stay here, Ruth," Abigail said.

Ruth's needles froze, midstitch. One dropped away, the loop hanging loose in thin air. "What does that mean?"

"I don't know," Abigail replied, picking at the skin around her cuticles. "I just—I'm scared. I know we don't have much money or any family or friends to fall back on. And you can't help it that insulin is fucking expensive. I get that. But every day there's some new insane thing happening. There's been a slew of vandalism. They've already banned tons of books in schools and in the library. Just a couple towns over, someone was hospitalized because they didn't look a certain way and went into a bathroom. We know that giant church here sends kids away to who-knows-where if they don't perfectly conform to what they think a person should look or act like. The one gay bar in a fifty-mile radius closed its doors due to threats of violence and a fucking Proud Boys demonstration."

"Those things happen in big liberal cities too," Ruth protested.

"Don't play devil's advocate with me," Abigail shot back. "You know we're not going to be safe here forever."

What could Ruth say? She knew Abigail was right, but some part of her didn't want to fill the jar. Some part of her wanted its belly to gurgle and starve. Daggers of anxiety went shooting into her chest when she imagined it stuffed to the brim, imagined shoving all of their things into boxes and heading out into the wilds of some unknown place full of unknown challenges. A small sense of relief actually bloomed in her stomach when she needed to empty the jar, had to push back the timeline of leaving. Sure, they had to hide their love, but they were happy, weren't they? Moving might not even solve anything. It might create more problems.

What if they moved away and Abigail found someone new? Someone better? What if she was with Ruth for the same reasons Ruth had been with Charlie—convenience, naivete, and no other available option? There wasn't a large chance she'd meet another out queer woman in Kill Devil. Whenever Abigail added a new bill or clattery handful of coins to the moving fund jar, Ruth's chest hitched, stealing a breath, the same scenario always looping in her head: Abigail, in their new city, working, or grocery shopping, or perusing a bookstore—the venue rotated, but the story stayed the same—and she met someone else, another girl who was brave enough be open and free and *out.* Every time, in Ruth's mind, Abigail chose this new girl, leaving Ruth alone. Again.

Now, Abigail slumped against the doorway. Tears welled at the corners of her eyes, a storm cloud hovering behind her irises. Ruth dropped the blanket, stitches and deadline be damned, and wrapped her arms around her girlfriend. Abigail scanned the room again, checking the windows for closed curtains, before settling her weight onto Ruth.

"It'll be okay," Ruth assured her. "You're right. We'll figure it out."

Abigail's words emerged between choked, heaving sobs. "I don't want to wait around here until something happens to *us*. It never stops. It feels like each incident is inching toward us, like the walls are closing in."

"We'll be okay. Let's make a plan, okay? Let's set up goals and deadlines and get really meticulous. Then we can get the fuck out of here."

Abigail sniffed, her breathing normalizing.

"Actually, I just got a text from the woman who commissioned this blanket," Ruth said. "She said she'll pay a premium if I can have it done by tomorrow. That's a start, right?"

"Yeah," Abigail replied, pulling free from Ruth's arms. "Thanks. I'm going to take a nap. I'm suddenly exhausted."

Abigail slipped out of Ruth's embrace, wiping at her eyes with the heel of her palm, heading for their bedroom—the one they actually slept in, not the second bedroom that had once belonged to Abigail's mom and had become more like a storage unit for Ruth's craft supplies after her death.

The familiar knot gnarled and twisted itself into a tight wad inside Ruth's chest, the same movie with the same ending starting up behind her eyes. She'd try to finish this commission on time if it would calm Abigail's nerves. It wouldn't be enough to leave, and a part of Ruth hoped Abigail's anxiety would calm after a while. As long as they didn't ever quite reach their goal, they could stay in this little snow globe, trapped—but together—in Kill Devil.

Ruth finally texted the woman back: *Sure, I can have it ready for you! What time would you need to pick it up?*

Her phone dinged almost instantly with the reply: *Thanks so much! My friend went into early labor, and I'd love to be able to gift it to her at the hospital tomorrow – can pick up at 9am.*

Ruth had a little under twenty-four hours to complete it. She could do it. Knitting feverishly, she moved across the row of stitches, so quick that she often had to backtrack, carefully unraveling the stitches she'd just knit that she should have purled, scooping up the stray ones that dropped off the needle like a person free-falling off a cliff. For the next two hours, she knit through her aching knuckles until the skein ran dry, a little six-inch tail hanging into thin air in the center of the row.

The bag with the rest of the skeins was somehow empty. Shit. She needed more yarn. And that meant another trip to New Creations, her former employer and the only craft store within fifty miles, not counting Walmart's aisle of scratchy Red Heart or stiff dishcloth cotton. It was owned by the megachurch across the street, some new-look-but-same-traditional-flavor Christians calling themselves the New Creationists.

They'd arrived in town around the time Ruth graduated high school, cutting away a chunk of the forest to build a giant monstrosity of a church the size of a mall, asphalt stretching in a halo around it. It was around this same time that she started to question her sexuality—and her fiancé started to be drawn deeper into the rabbit hole of the New Creationists, their tendrils pulling him tighter and tighter as he raised their walls, working with his family's construction company. Ruth had watched as the giant eyesore emerged from the ground piece by piece like a pale cicada, wings and random features jutting from every angle like the Winchester mansion.

Once construction was complete, the righteous flocked to it like moths to a flame, whole congregations leaving their stuffy, moldering church buildings in the surrounding area—some even with the blessing of their pastors, many of whom retired or joined the ministry of the New Creationists. Each

Sunday morning, the lot filled, only a few spots near the edge of the halo unoccupied.

Even Ruth, at the time, had entered the doors, hand-in-hand with her ex-fiancé, starry-eyed and mouth agape at the vast, almost cavernous sanctuary with giant screens, a balcony, and plush seats. The preacher was passionate and charismatic. The well-practiced choir sang modernized, up-tempo gospel songs. It couldn't have been more different from her childhood church, with its flaking exterior paint, a preacher as decrepit as the building itself, and a tone-deaf choir droning hymns they'd never bothered to practice. If the glitz and glam weren't enough to lure people in, the New Creationists worked to build a community through potlucks, singles events, school supply drives, youth groups, and ticketed plays that turned out to be pious re-imaginings of Broadway shows. When the craft store opened a year later, adding dozens of jobs to their various admin positions, they were one of the largest employers in the small town.

By that time, Ruth had already shed herself of religion, having been abandoned by both her soon-to-be hubby and her own flesh and blood. But the thought of being able to purchase actual wool yarn or quality paint without driving an hour one way or waiting a week for packages to find their way to her doorstep was enticing. She'd even worked there for a stint, before the bigoted owners somehow managed to deduce she was dating a woman. They fired her for "going against their values," forcing her out of the one steady job she'd been able to find after cutting ties with Charlie. It didn't matter that it was likely illegal—who was Ruth going to complain to? Who would enact justice for her, when every authority figure in town was an upstanding member of the very church who had discriminated against her? God would judge her, the manager had said, smirking as she'd handed over her employee badge.

As nice as the employee discount had been, ever since she'd been fired from New Creations, Ruth's craft budget was unlimited. She remained a frequent shopper, using her five-finger discount, sometimes raising a singular digit as she peeled out of the parking lot.

She even had a little game: she'd never take anything more than would fit in her tote bag, but she always tried to outdo herself, palming something progressively more expensive each visit. Tiny tubes of oil paint. A full set of interchangeable knitting needles. Some type of framing tool she didn't even know how to use. The rush of adrenaline and spite she felt on her way out the door with a tote full of stolen merchandise was worth the risk.

"Hey, babe, I need to run to the craft store," Ruth called, poking her head into the bedroom.

"Oh boy," Abigail said, calm now, lying in bed with her eyes closed. "What will you bring back this time to add to the collection of crap you won't ever use?"

"I ran out of yarn. On a tight deadline for this commission."

"You know one day they're going to catch you and throw you in jail. Maybe worse."

"Over taking less than one hundred dollars of merchandise?"

Abigail scoffed, eyes still closed. "You know they would. They're that petty. They might even be tallying everything you've taken, and are waiting for you to hit a certain amount so they can *really* fuck you over. Can't you just pay for it this time? Isn't the cost of materials included in your commission rate?"

"Yeah, but I make more if the materials are free," Ruth replied with a grin. "That's all the more to add to the jar. And if they'd been counting, I'd already have reached that limit. Plus, I think they want people to steal from them. They don't use barcodes. They have no inventory system! They don't even know what they have or what got sold or stolen."

"No barcodes?" Abigail asked.

"Nope. They say something stupid about barcodes being the mark of the devil, but I bet they're just doing something shady with their taxes. If you don't inventory anything, you can claim whatever losses you want."

"So you're helping them by stealing?" Abigail replied with a coy smile, her eyes finally cracking open. "Isn't that the opposite of what you want?"

Ruth shrugged. "It's the same either way. So I might as well take it—at least with this arrangement, I get free stuff."

"And I suppose the end goal is to clutter our house with unopened supplies that you'll never touch."

"You never know what artistic venture I'll take up next," Ruth replied, matching her girlfriend's smirk. "Hell, maybe we can sell it online and fill up the jar even faster."

"Just—seriously. Be careful," Abigail replied, sitting up. "I always worry when you go there that you're going to call me from a jail cell. Then we'll have to empty the jar to get you out."

"I'm always careful," Ruth said. "Plus, if they gave a shit they'd have already caught me. I'll be okay. It's not like I'm heading into untamed woods like those hikers over in Livingston."

She'd seen theft on each of her shifts, but nobody seemed to care. There were cameras all around the store—she remembered the spread of TV screens in the manager's office, bisected by multiple views, all showcasing mothers picking out the perfect pink fleece or a budding artist plucking glitter glue from the shelf. But she'd never heard of them stopping anyone for shoplifting.

Ruth scanned the knitting pattern and measured how much she'd already knit—now almost halfway done. She'd need a lot of yarn, so much that she'd need to get creative with this steal. A ballooning tote bag would be a dead giveaway—a little too obvious even for her. Maybe she could throw on an oversized sweatshirt and try to stuff the bulk of the skeins beneath it.

Sweatshirt on and tote in hand, she kissed Abigail goodbye behind the safety of the curtains.

"Seriously, be careful," Abigail said. "How's your blood sugar level? Do you have your Dex4?"

"I'm fine. I'm just going to run there and back—an hour and a half, tops. Plus, they have candy and icing and stuff if I really have an issue."

She pulled on her shoes and groaned, thinking about the drive ahead. As the crow flies, it was just a couple of miles away, but a tangle of undeveloped land and the creek, bizarrely named Hell for Certain, stretched between her house and the store. She had to drive a mile down the road and make a big loop around the woods and the creek.

Ruth threw open her front door, nearly colliding with two bodies. On her porch stood a man and a woman in starchy-stiff clothes. The man wore a crisp, short-sleeved button-up and pleated pants and the woman wore a plain blue dress, the hem reaching her shins and the top buttoned up to her neck, a little Peter Pan collar settling on her shoulders. She held a clipboard to her chest. The man's right hand hovered, poised in the air, ready to knock. He pulled back, just as startled as Ruth.

"Hello there," the man said, a little chirp in his voice. "We're here with—"

"Yeah, I know where you're from," Ruth said, shutting the door behind her. "We're not interested."

"Well, maybe you can just take one of these," he said, pulling a little booklet out of his briefcase and pushing it into her hand. Her fingers wrapped around the paper before she realized she'd even taken it. Crinkling it inside her fist, she automatically shoved the thing into her tote bag. "You can look at it at your leisure."

Ruth was laser-focused on her task: drive to store; take yarn; return and knit until her fingers grew blisters and the blisters popped; hope the blister goo did not soak into the blanket and ruin it. And these dumbasses were in her way.

"Do you have a moment to talk about the Creator and how He can save you?" the woman said, standing at the top of the porch stairs, blocking Ruth's exit.

"No, I don't," Ruth replied, barreling past her without stopping.

"He can save you," the woman replied, wincing like a brittle bird as Ruth's shoulder collided with her own, leaving a little dent in her crispy sleeve.

"I'll read all about it later in that pamphlet you so graciously gave me. Is it different than the hundreds of others you've already mailed to us?"

The woman turned around to face Ruth. Staring directly into Ruth's eyes, unblinking, she pulled a small crucifix from beneath her high neckline, holding it in between her thumb and forefinger.

"Thy blood will make us white as snow," she said, dreamily, almost transfixed. A strange emphasis on *thy*. Still she did not blink. "No other tide can cleanse us so."

What the fuck was that supposed to mean? It sounded vaguely familiar, but Ruth couldn't pull the origin of the phrase from her subconscious. She'd been raised in this town under religious parents—had at one time had dozens of religious songs and slogans and verses memorized.

Whatever. Ruth didn't like to think about that time in her life. As she closed the car door, the pair remained on the porch, now both staring at Ruth. They looked ghostly, pale and ominous. Their eyelids appeared glued to their eyebrows, wide and unblinking. The woman's lips parted as if she was going to spout more prophetic nonsense.

This wasn't the first time these overly starched zealots had attempted to convert them, and it wouldn't be the last. They had received so many of the group's pamphlets and newsletters in the mail that Ruth and Abigail joked their beloved Creator would be forced to come down and save them from the uninhabitable planet created by all the trees these weirdos killed to print their propaganda. Once, they'd giggled at the ridiculousness inside: a pamphlet page bearing a clock face pointing to eleven o'clock, stating simply, *THE CREATOR IS COMING.* For a week afterward, they held their breath twice a day, waiting to see if He would suddenly materialize in their living room. Maybe He'd bring destruction upon just them, at eleven o'clock sharp.

But, all too quickly, the jokes dried up. The pamphlets started advertising *help for troubled youth*—the pair hadn't read much further, their guts churning, their appetites destroyed. That night, dinner sat forgotten in the oven, chicken breasts blackened to ash. After that, the pamphlets became shredded fodder for their compost or embers at the bottom of their fireplace.

Ruth tossed her tote bag into the passenger side and started the engine. Her phone erupted into a cacophony of noise, the tones shrill even through the canvas of the tote.

"Shit," she said, fishing it out. *CHECK YOUR GLUCOSE!* read the scheduled reminder on the screen. Ruth had never been able to afford a monitoring device, instead relying on regular reminders and learning her body's signals. She'd always had to do old-fashioned prick tests, the cheapest method possible. She could barely afford the little test strips most months after all their bills and her insulin and syringes and other meds.

The testing kit was inside. She hazarded a glance toward the house. Sure enough, the two starchy saviors continued their staring contest through the windshield. The thought of having to sneak past them twice more made her want to vomit. She felt fine—the insulin could wait another hour.

She reversed out onto the road. The man's and woman's wide eyes panned in their sockets, following her car's path.

It wasn't until that moment—as they remained still as statues in her own front yard—that it occurred to her their actual, physical presence was odd. This was the first time that anyone had actually shown up on their doorstep. She'd never heard of the church being that aggressive about recruitment. Even when she'd worked at the craft store, she'd never heard anything about sending missionaries to people's houses. Since when did they send out soldiers to knock on doors? Weren't their seats full enough?

Maybe it was a new initiative, Ruth pondered. Flyers couldn't answer questions, could only be so persuasive. Envelopes could be ignored, thrown away, sight unseen. But a body at your door? Can't throw them in the trash or burn them in the fireplace. Maybe others had politeness that Ruth didn't, imbued with automatic Southern hospitality that would force them to hover in their doorway and hear these weirdos out, or face the ultimate consequence: being seen as rude.

But as Ruth twisted down the road, moving closer to the main highway, another odd itch wormed its way into her head. The missionaries hadn't driven to their house. There was no car. She would have noticed—they lived at a dead end to a mile-long, narrow street. Either the stiff duo would have parked in her driveway, or she would have had to swerve around a car parked on the street. So where had they come from? Had they hiked through the forest and crossed the creek from the church? She'd never found any trails in the trees lining the end of the street, though they'd seen the occasional birdwatcher hanging out there.

She pulled off to the side of the road and dialed her girlfriend. Her nerves grew as the phone rang, some deep anxiety welling up from her gut. Something didn't sit right about the pair outside their house, but she couldn't figure out exactly what. Even the no-car thing—it wasn't that strange for churches to drop off a whole busload of missionaries and make them walk a million miles, right?

Ruth was ready to turn the car around when Abigail finally answered.

"Sorry," she said, "I was in the bathroom. What's up? Forget your wallet?"

Ruth exhaled in relief.

"Everything okay?" Abigail prompted.

"Yeah," Ruth replied. "Sorry. When I left, there were two people outside the house from the megachurch, trying to convert us, I guess. Something just seemed off about them."

"Looks like they left. I don't see anyone outside—but they stuck one of their stupid booklets in the door."

"Okay, good. I'll be back as soon as I can. I really need to finish that blanket."

Tossing her phone into the passenger seat, Ruth pulled onto the main highway.

Chapter 2

Flying down the highway, Ruth saw no other evidence of holy misdeeds: No nondescript passenger van that might have dumped a horde of missionaries out into the streets. No other starched pairs walking along the road, clipboards in hand and pamphlets spilling out of their totes. Where the fuck had they come from?

Whatever, she thought. She needed to make sure she got ample supply in one trip: at least six more skeins, and probably one or two extra just in case her math was wrong. She'd hate to run out again in the middle of the night, and besides, it was Saturday. The Good People of the New Creations Craft Store did not sell their wares on Sundays.

She'd thrown on her largest sweatshirt to help conceal the bulky skeins, a dingy, worn thing buried at the bottom of her dresser, a relic of her ex-fiancé. The thing had once fit him, but after he'd joined his father's construction company after high school and any lingering baby fat transformed into muscle, he was bursting out of it. He'd wanted to throw it out, but Ruth stole it instead. Before their relationship ended, it'd been an endearing thing, something cozy and warm that she'd wear around the house. She wasn't sure why it had remained in the bottom of her dresser. She hadn't remembered keeping it. But hopefully it was baggy enough to conceal all the yarn she needed.

Ruth cringed at the sudden, unwelcome thought of bumping into Charlie at the craft store. She was lucky that it had only happened once before. In a town this small, the odds were extremely high, but she'd managed to avoid him besides one encounter just after she'd started working at the craft store. Just six months after they'd broken up, there he was. Still muscular with a dimpled smile. Already with a new fiancée, a heavy diamond slipping off her slender finger.

A harried Ruth nearly ran headlong into them, carting an oversized broom and dustpan, on her way to clean up a broken jar of glitter. Sweat slithered down her face from making the trek across the store two or three times—she'd retrieved the heavy vacuum with a stuck wheel just to be informed that using the only nearby outlet would plunge the store into darkness for days, some wiring issue that had never been resolved. She'd just retrieved the broom and was hustling through the wedding aisle, her hair wild and frizzy like a crony old witch, when the pair appeared in matching unwrinkled linen, not so much as a single flyaway buzzing around their skulls.

"Whoa, Ruth," Charlie had said. "Haven't seen you in a while."

"Uh," she replied.

"This is my fiancée, Jessica. We're here to get invitations for our engagement party. Can you show us where they are?"

Jessica beamed beside him, a cutesy blonde with neat, hair-sprayed locks.

"They're right over there," Ruth said, pointing. "Sorry, I have to go clean something up."

She'd managed to make it to the scene of the exploded glitter crime before her chest unhitched and tears threatened. She'd thought she'd gotten over their breakup, but seeing Charlie with her replacement so soon, treating her as if they'd been mere acquaintances, felt like an invisible dagger trying to wedge its way through her intestines. Charlie seemed so happy. He'd accomplished what she couldn't—or refused to—give him. She was sure by now she didn't want that life, but running straight into it still ate at her, sharp teeth stripping away little tendrils of her skin.

His fiancée's perfect face had contorted, just for a moment, when he'd said hello to Ruth. Like she couldn't believe he was speaking to someone so inferior, that he had ever once been engaged to someone like her, someone so unkempt. Someone who had to sweep up glitter and glass. She wanted to shrink to the size of a mouse and scurry beneath the shelves when they'd appeared.

Ruth shuddered at the memory as a new fear emerged. What would Charlie think if he and his perfect family ran into her while she was *wearing his old sweatshirt*? The thought made her sweat. He'd probably think she still secretly loved him. He'd probably think she wore it all the time. He'd probably chide her for not answering his constant texts with his broad, toothy smile. Maybe he'd even try to have whatever conversation he wanted to have then and there. Suddenly the oversized fabric seemed to shrink, to curl up against the soft skin of her neck and wrists, constricting, cutting off all circulation.

The flame in her heart had long since extinguished, though sometimes she still missed Charlie's friendship. She'd lost her whole life in the breakup, everything gone in a matter of hours: her family, her home, her job, her social standing. Thinking of him didn't make her pine for what she could have had, but what she could still lose. What happened with Charlie was proof that relationships were tenuous and temporary—a reminder of how quickly she could be abandoned. If it happened once, it could happen again. It could happen with Abigail.

The sweat now reached her hands, making the steering wheel slippery. Just the thought of running into him made her want to turn around, go home, and text the lady that she wouldn't be able to finish the blanket early after all. She still didn't know what to make of his text messages asking to chat or hang out or *talk* after all this time—each one had seemed to get more desperate after she'd ghosted him.

She pulled up to a stoplight. She could turn right and continue on to the store, or she could turn around. When the light turned green, she remained stationary. This was stupid, she thought. He wouldn't even be there, and this woman was offering a lot of money for this blanket.

Ruth turned right. Abigail was more important. They needed the money more than Ruth needed her pride. She pressed on the gas, trying to make up for lost time.

After another two right turns, Ruth reached the new pavement that led to the craft store and the big-box church that owned it. The black asphalt was still smooth and new. Trees lined either side, like someone had paved a route through the middle of Daniel Boone National Forest, like she was in the most remote area of Kentucky.

The illusion ceased as the trees parted on her left, revealing a two-acre parking lot surrounding the largest building in town, the church: an ark in the middle of a roiling sea of pavement, boxy in the front with odd, disjointed architecture in the back, on the side that couldn't be seen from the road. Once she'd witnessed the mayhem of the parking lot for latecomers on a Sunday when she forgot that the craft store was closed. Minivans and monster-sized spotless pickups circled the aisles like vultures, trying to seize a space before the service started. People traveled from all over to come to the church—no way the sparse population of Kill Devil could fill this lot. Why attend service at the tiny church in your own town when you can drive a little farther to this one, which has air conditioning, food, a whole daycare and Sunday school wing? It was practically its own economy.

Ruth buzzed past the enormous building, heading for the craft store. New Creations did not have such an awe-inspiring reveal. In fact, the trees on the right parted just enough to accommodate a small access road that wound its way through the trunks to the parking lot. Ruth had always found it odd—and still did, the same thought popping into her head as she turned off the main road and onto the access—that the store wasn't visible from the road. It was tucked at the back of the dead end. If not for the fading sign mounted on a 4x4 post, it'd be all but invisible.

Ruth passed the sign, unchanged since the store's opening: *New Creations! NOW OPEN!*

She slowed on the access road, knowing all the twists and turns of it, knowing that it was narrow and irregular. Knowing that at any moment another car could appear going the opposite direction, too fast, ready to smash into her. The first time she'd driven down this road, the trees were still full of changing leaves, and it was already dark. She'd felt more like she was driving on a tiny mountain road than a path to a craft store. It was eerie, and she hadn't worked there long enough to get used to it, to shake the odd feeling that something ominous was going to pop up around the blind curves. Even now, in the afternoon, something sinister crept up her spine, some awful premonition: Like she'd pull around the curve and there'd be a clown with a machete, dripping with blood. Or a big truck barreling straight for her.

Today, as always, nothing waited for her as she pulled around the blind curve. And there was nothing awaiting her in the parking lot, either. There were a few cars stationed in the employee spots, but otherwise the lot was an empty sea of black—odd for a Saturday afternoon. Was there a football game on or something? She didn't pay attention to that kind of stuff, but she guessed that was probably it. If there was one thing about this town, it was that everyone loved a ball game.

She parked in a spot close to the front doors, having no spare time to even walk across the pavement. She had to be in and out. Moving quickly, she grabbed her tote bag and headed toward the store.

Only when she had entered the double doors at the front, the air conditioning blowing an icy breath into her face, did she realize that it would be harder to slip under the radar without any other customers around to bother the staff.

Shit.

Chapter 3

Through the doors was a ghost town.

Not a single apron-clad soul haunted the cash registers. A stray garland of plastic roses lay on one of the checkout counters, like an offering at a gravestone. No customers wandered in view of the shiny impulse shelves, full of glitter and candy and miniature travel Bibles and books written by the New Creationists themselves. Not even the low hum of smooth jazz or Christmas music played over the buzzy, ancient speakers. Goose bumps rose along Ruth's arms in the staticky silence. Although it was August, a muddle of red and green garlands poked around the corner of an endcap. The sect refused to acknowledge Halloween, which meant Christmas merchandise in July.

The sticky weight of unease settled on her shoulders, sinking through the worn fibers of the sweatshirt and through her skin to her bones. There was some electricity in the air that tugged at the hairs on her arms, something she couldn't quite pinpoint, something that sent a primordial alarm pinging through her whole body. She'd never seen the store so empty, even at closing time. There had almost always been shoppers who rushed in two minutes before they were allowed to lock the doors, and policy was that staff had to stay until those customers left. There was also a policy that two staff members, dubbed "Mustard Seeds" and clad in bright yellow aprons, must be stationed at the front of the store at all times: one working a register, and one at the door to greet every customer who entered.

She didn't encounter anyone as she moved farther into the store. Ruth tried to recall if she'd ever worked on a game day, when the townspeople of Kill Devil were collectively glued to their televisions. She could only remember one shift when she'd arrived and been greeted by a completely empty parking lot, the rain-filled potholes free to reflect the clouds. She'd thrown her bright apron over her head like a good little Mustard Seed, tossed her shit in her locker, and plucked her manual time card from the rack to clock in. Before its teeth could notch the paper, the manager had snatched it from her fingers and told her to go home.

"We don't need you today," he'd said. Little circles of sweat from his fingers bled into the paper. Beads of it dotted his forehead like a crown of tears. "It's been really slow."

"But I'm already here," she replied. "And I really need the money."

"Sorry. When we're not making money, we can't just give it out for you to stand around doing nothing."

"I could do inventory or stock—"

"We've got everything taken care of," he replied, cutting her off. He grabbed her arm, somehow latching on and pinching her skin despite his slick, oily sweat, and steered her toward the break room. "Gather your things. You need to leave. *Now.*"

The manager had watched her pack up, fidgeting in the doorway like she was keeping him from something important, his eyes constantly darting down the hall. He'd escorted her back to her car, holding both her shoulders in a meaty vise. He even stood outside the employee entrance until she disappeared from view, her car turning that first corner into the trees.

A sickly-sweet stench assaulted Ruth as she pushed farther into the depths of the store, past the aisles of artificial flowers and outdoor décor. A thousand intermingled scents filled her nostrils as she passed shelves packed with candles and diffusers and essentials oils, but not a single match in sight. Another Mustard Seed had once explained the reasoning to her—something about hellfire—but she'd forgotten the specifics. She'd been too distracted by the passage emblazoned across the row of glass jars: *Be Pure, for those who give themselves to immorality will suffer the punishment of eternal fire.*

She spied that same candle from the corner of her eye now. Crossing to the other side of the wide central aisle, attempting to evade the olfactory onslaught, she nearly collided with a display, a square stand in the middle of the thoroughfare. At her approach, a wooden sign clattered to the floor, the sound of it like a scream against the silence. Ruth plucked it from the ground to set it back in its place, an automatic gesture left over from her days as a Seed.

A miniature painting of a rifle hovered at the bottom beneath a quote printed in gritty capital letters:

WHOSOEVER ATTEMPTS TO ENTER, I WILL TREAD THEM IN MINE ANGER AND TRAMPLE THEM IN MY FURY, AND THEIR BLOOD SHALL BE SPRINKLED UPON MY GARMENTS—ISAIAH 63:3

The rest of the display held more of the same, all crammed together in an overflowing, overwhelming cornucopia of bloodthirsty kitsch. On another placard, two vintage handguns that might have been lifted from a John Wayne western formed an X with their barrels overlapping, beneath a declaration that read:

Righteous judgment will be revealed on the day of His wrath.—Romans 2:5

Piled in a basket were drawer pulls in the shape of bullets. On planks of rough barn wood were paintings of crosses, each one enveloped with coils of barbed wire. Bottle openers were screwed to boards declaring *God Is Great. Beer Is Good.* Ruth released her fingers from the sign, a sudden taste of bile in her mouth. Did people really buy this stuff?

She swallowed it, the acidity singeing her throat, and continued on toward the yarn. Still, she had not encountered a single customer or Mustard Seed. She quickened her pace, hoping she would be lucky enough to stuff the skeins into her sweatshirt and evade the yellow aprons entirely.

Seven skeins. Seven skeins. She just needed to grab seven skeins and get the fuck out of there.

On her left were more stacked stands of tchotchkes in the *live, laugh, love* genre. Dainty ring dishes urged women to submit to their dear hubbies; pink ceramic holders for sponges instructed the buyer to *scrub the bad out.* Placards proclaimed the household as *#blessed.* Little silver crosses and angel's wings encased in resin collected dust: a pile of things her ex's seamless wife would fawn over, the glittery knickknacks cluttering their shelves and walls. Ruth could envision their pristine house—new construction through Charlie's family's company—with its clean light gray walls and unmarred white sofa despite now having a newborn. Could that really have been her life? It almost made Ruth gag.

She knew exactly what her life would have been like if she'd stayed. She'd be expected to mother his children, both bearing and rearing while he followed his father's footsteps in the construction business. She'd join the women's group at the church and take shifts of Sunday school duties. She'd attend services every week with Charlie and their 2.5 children. She'd be Little Ruth Stepford, content to cook and clean and hardly eat, while her husband did the *real* work of earning a living. At one time, she'd accepted this as not only natural but inevitable. She'd never imagined there was any other way to live.

Charlie had proposed during prom, bending a knee against the waxed gym floor, right in the middle of the roiling sea of tulle and rented tuxedos. She'd slipped the simple diamond onto her finger without hesitation. They'd dated since freshman year—the next logical step was to make it permanent, even if it functioned more like a promise ring than anything else. She'd never had any second thoughts about the future that lay before her—not until Abigail had scoffed at the ring, wrinkling her face when Ruth had presented her bejeweled hand. Only then did the seeds of doubt begin to germinate.

"We're not even eighteen yet," Abigail had said, dropping Ruth's hand. "Do you really want to jump out of your graduation gown into a wedding dress?"

Flustered, Ruth had twisted the ring, the diamond orbiting her finger. "Why not?" she'd asked, the cracks already seeping through her conviction. "We love each other. We won't have the ceremony for a year or so, but why wait on something you know is going to happen?"

"If your love is so true and strong, surely it can wait a little longer. Don't you want to travel? To see some place other than Kill Devil, Kentucky?"

"Married people can travel," Ruth mumbled. "Charlie wants to go to Gatlinburg for our honeymoon."

"Of course he does," Abigail replied, her eyes rolling back into her skull. "Ruth, come on. We're so young. We don't even know who we are yet. I mean, do you even want kids? Do you want to stay at home all day while Charlie goes off and builds houses?"

Ruth clamped her teeth together, spinning the ring around and around, the diamond disappearing beneath her finger. She didn't have an answer.

Abigail put her hand on Ruth's, quelling her fidgeting. "I'm being serious, Ruth. You know I'll support you if this is what you really want—I just want you to think about it, okay? And really think about it. Don't blow it off. That ring's not permanent. There's still time to give it back with only a bruised ego."

Ruth had promised. And once that little seedling poked its head from the soil of doubt, once Ruth truly started to consider what it was she wanted from life, she couldn't stop the sprout from growing into a monstrous weed, flourishing and mutating until it became something unrecognizable.

Leaving the twee trinkets behind, Ruth shook the ghosts of her past from her mind, noting bald spots around the notions shelves in the sewing section. They were still terrible about keeping things in stock. Nothing had changed there. The complaints of customers past rang faintly in her ear, as if she had been the one in charge of orders, as if she were personally responsible for the lack of two-inch wired-ribbon spools. Or that she could have magically made a box of felt appear in the fabled "back of the store." But there was no overstock, no back of the store at all—only a steel door that had remained locked during the entirety of her tenure as a Mustard Seed. Not even the manager seemed to have a key.

Your problem now, she thought, finally reaching the edge of the yarn aisle. The coiled gray skeins she needed sat on the bottom shelf.

Shit.

Shit, shit, shit.

There weren't enough. There were only four skeins.

Still, she stuffed them into her baggy sweatshirt, keeping one out in the open as a color gauge, hoping to spot a near match. Her client wouldn't know the difference, and she could start splicing and interchanging the skeins every other row to make it even less noticeable. But her options were sparse. Between her fingers, she twisted a stray strand sticking from the correct yarn as if memorizing the fibers could make a twin suddenly appear. This was taking too much time.

"Shit," she mumbled. She just needed to pick something.

Finally, she settled on an alternative and stuffed the skeins inside her tote.

Now, to transform these fluffy balls into a blanket.

As she turned to leave, a glint caught the corner of her vision, a glimmer beckoning her to investigate. A set of iridescent pink knitting needles hung on the shelf, polished and gleaming beneath the fluorescent bulbs. They seemed too long to be practical, almost longer than her forearm. The label boasted that they were "light as air," made from a proprietary carbon fiber shell.

Sharp tips for smoother knitting! the label promised. Printed on the package was an image of a polished infomercial hand pushing the sharp tips beneath unruly stitches. *Perfect for tight tension, lightweight yarns, and more!*

Maybe they'd help her finish the job faster, she thought. They, indeed, felt light as a cloud as she pulled them from the shelf. She pushed the pointy ends to her fingertip, so sharp that the nerves beneath her skin seemed to hold back a shriek. If she pressed any less gently, she might have drawn blood. She slipped one from the cardboard sleeve to gauge how it felt in her hands, how it might feel to knit with them, whether they might bend or warp beneath the weight of all the yarn.

Ruth wasn't sure if the needles would help, but she might as well slip them in the tote bag. They were long and skinny and—weirdly expensive. Not quite enough to beat her shoplifting record, but close.

So mesmerized was Ruth by her shiny new toy that she did not notice the man at the end of the aisle. He wore the bright yellow apron, a blocky radio in the left pocket, a cord snaking up to the earpiece clipped over his ear. A standard-issue Mustard Seed. A little golden shepherd's crook sat pinned to the apron where the name tag should have been. A small grin pulled at the edges of his wormy mouth.

"Ma'am, I'm going to ask you to come with me," the man said, sending a jolt of electricity through Ruth's spine. She turned toward him, the little sizzle of surprise shifting a skein beneath her loose sweatshirt. Before she could respond, could feign ignorance, the evidence of her deed spilled to the floor. It sat between them like a coiled mass of gray intestines, like Ruth had literally spilled her guts.

"This way, please," he continued.

"Why?"

"I think you know why," he said, his eyes darting down to the skein on the floor.

"I just forgot to grab a cart when I came in. I couldn't carry all of them in my arms."

"Fools mock at making amends for sins," he replied, a too-nice smile creeping across his face. "You and I both know you did not intend to pay for those. We've been watching you on the security cameras for months, cataloging each and every item you've stolen. As of your last visit, you've officially stolen enough merchandise to amount to a felony of the highest degree."

Ruth's heart disconnected itself from her chest and smashed into the bile of her stomach. Of course that was what they'd been doing—waiting for her to walk into their trap. Why go through all the trouble, all the official reports and paperwork and submitting footage, to charge for petty theft if you could simply wait a little longer and hit the thief with a felony?

"So, let's not turn this into more than it has to be, and come with me, please," he said.

What could she do? She could run—she imagined she'd be faster than him—but then what? They had footage. They knew where she lived. The end result would be the same, merely delayed. She didn't know what the highest degree of felony for shoplifting entailed, but she imagined it must involve some time in jail, especially when the case is Sinner Ruth v. Poor Upstanding and Charitable Craft Store Who Has Done No Wrong Ever.

"Okay," she said, exhaling, placing a foot in the man's direction.

He turned his back to her, leading her toward the end of the aisle. She put one begrudging foot in front of another, a death march of her own making. How could she have been so stupid? Of course they were paying attention. Of course they were merely waiting until the best moment to strike, lying in wait while their prey became complacent, became lazy and comfortable. And of course, Abigail had been right. She'd been caught, just like Abigail had warned.

"Shit," Ruth whispered. *Abigail.* When would she be able to see Abigail again? Every television show she'd ever seen informed her that she'd get one phone call, but then what? There was no way they'd be able to afford bail. Ruth had no idea what to expect. The most trouble she'd ever found herself in was getting kicked out of her parents' house after coming out.

Ruth slowed her pace. The Mustard Seed ahead of her reached the end of the aisle and disappeared around the corner. At that moment, Ruth pivoted and ran back down the aisle. If the end result was going to be the same, if she was going to rot in jail for who knows how long, perhaps for the rest of her short life considering her medical needs—would the local cops dispense insulin at proper intervals? Would they know how to store it? Or would they give her too much, too ignorant to know what they were doing, or at least feigning ignorance? If her fate was sealed, if the prophecy could not be changed, she would at least see Abigail one more time. She refused to go quietly, to be swallowed or slaughtered or forgotten by the justice system without spending even one more second with Abigail.

She ran on the very tips of her toes, nimble and quiet as a mouse, weaving through the displays of disturbing knick-knacks, careful to leave enough berth to not knock them to the floor. But, rounding the corner from the wide path toward the registers, her feet stopped dead, her body nearly toppling from the forward momentum.

"Fuck!" she swore, the syllable muted, barely bubbling out of her throat.

The entrance to the store had been sealed. They'd rolled down the metal gate that blocked anyone from breaking in through the large windows, with little steel bars that she imagined she'd soon become all too familiar with, and locked it.

Fuck.

Before she could move, could process a single other thought, a meaty hand snapped over her arm, squeezing like a vise and heaving, twisting her tiptoed feet beneath her. On pure instinct, her arms lifted to brace for a fall, and she did fall: Ruth toppled onto the Mustard Seed, both bodies slamming onto the concrete.

But in one hand, she still gripped the knitting needle with its sharp, shiny tip.

Before she realized what would happen, what was already happening, what had already happened before she could stop it—the tip of the sharp needle pierced through his flesh. The pink carbon fiber pierced his eye, and continued its trajectory as if it were pushing through gelatin. The rubbery resistance of his pupil reverberated up through the lightweight shaft and into her fingers. Ruth might have imagined the bubble-popping sound as it pushed through and continued past the eye, plunging deep into his brain, but she could not ignore the stuff that oozed out like a runny yolk. Through sheer momentum, the needle continued its path into the man's head until there was a faint crack, until it met some sort of crunchy resistance.

His fingers went limp at her arm, sliding away from her skin with gummy slowness. Her own fingers released the needle and covered her mouth, holding in a silent scream.

Oh shit.

Oh shit.

Oh fuck.

What had she done?

Chapter 4

"*Ohmygod*," she finally said, every word merging into a single syllable, scrambling off his body.

The man lay on the floor, a moan bubbling out of his throat, a gurgling sound that was more disbelief and surprise than pain. Goo leaked from his socket—some mixture of blood and eyeball—rolling down the side of his face and plopping into the crook of his ear, sliding into the canal like a worm. On the other side of this spectacle oozed a dark, sticky red, little tacky tendrils stretching out from the back of his head, inching across the concrete. One of his hands, shaky and tentative, reached toward the needle jutting from his skull, long and straight like a flagpole. Grimly, Ruth wondered whether it still felt light as air when smashed into your socket.

"*Ohmygod. Ohfuck*—I didn't mean to. It was an accident. Are you okay?"

Obviously not.

Another gurgle rose from his throat, something closer to words but still not entirely decipherable. "For—written, vengeance . . . mine . . . repay, the Lord" was all Ruth could stitch together.

The man's hand swiped for the needle, grabbing fistfuls of air before his fingers finally settled around the pink shaft. With the added weight of his hand, the end of the needle dipped downward toward his crooked grimace. The tip—the way-too-sharp point that must be lodged in his brain, Ruth realized with horror—scraped upward, tearing through more gray matter. She wondered if it had hit the back of his skull, scratching crazed doodles on the bone.

In what felt like slow motion, his hand clamped down over the needle and pulled. More eyeball spilled out, a pink pulpy mess that leaked down his face, some splattering onto the floor with a wet *plop*.

"Oh God," Ruth said. "Stop. Just—don't pull it out! You're making it worse!"

The man seemed to have not heard a word. He continued to struggle with the needle, managing to slap his other hand over the shaft, the whole thing slick with blood and plasma and smoothied cornea. His meaty fingers slipped around, straining to gain purchase, spinning the needle around and around and around.

The pink shaft slid out, inch by inch, the man's unsteady hands shifting the sharp tip upward, slicing through more gunky flesh, before it finally exited his skull. It hooked a vein or a nerve like a loop of yarn, like a dropped stitch, the dark, slick strand stretching with each yank until it snapped, the needle finally swinging free of his face. Like a slingshot, the exiting needle splattered blood across Ruth's face and chest, polka-dotting her threadbare sweatshirt.

By the time his arms released the metal and fell to the floor, his body unmoving at last, his brains must have been scrambled eggs.

The whole event lasted mere seconds, too quickly for Ruth to have done anything but try to warn him. She stood in shock, the twin needle still clutched in her hands.

"What the fuck," she whispered. She could only stand and stare at the man's limp body. She had forgotten entirely about the commission, the yarn beneath her sweatshirt now soaking up her nervous sweat. She'd stabbed someone in the eye, and now they were—what? Unconscious?

Dead?

What the fuck was she going to do?

"Uh, are you okay?" she asked, knowing she'd receive no response.

Her thoughts spun, panicking and reeling, coiling around and around, overlapping until they knotted together and settled like a boulder in her chest. She'd just come in for yarn. Did she really just kill someone? Was this really happening?

In her spiral, she stood frozen, unable to will herself to even reach down to feel for a pulse. The man lay there, her stationary mirror, the only movement being a stream of blood trickling away from the dark lake around his head on the unlevel floor. His snapped vein flopped over his cheek like a downed power line. The remnants of eyeball and goop had already started to dry in a chunky brown rivulet.

The evidence, too, remained on her own face, little globs of gummy goo in her eyelashes, flecks of blood dripping from the tip of her chin. She could smell the coppery tang of it, and the stubble of gore at the end of her nose tickled the little hairs there with her terrified tremors.

Ruth knew how this looked—she'd stuffed stolen merchandise under her sweatshirt and then stabbed an employee who'd tried to apprehend her for shoplifting. He had grabbed her first, and gravity had acted as a malicious force. But would it be evident in the security footage just how forceful he had been, how his fingers had wrapped tightly enough around her wrist to cease blood flow? How he'd yanked so hard she'd tripped over her own feet, throwing out her hands to brace for the fall? With the store's outdated, potato-quality cameras?

Or would it look like she pivoted on purpose to plunge the needle in?

The owners of the store were powerful members of the community. Everyone knew them. Everyone loved them. Ruth? She was known mostly for having broken the heart of the son of a prominent business owner. At the time, nasty rumors had flown that she was promiscuous, or a gold digger, and that Charlie, a nice, upstanding boy, had been blindsided by her betrayal. And now she was an odd duck, a spinster. Who would believe her story over theirs?

She'd just needed yarn today. How had this gone so sideways? If only she'd listened to Abigail, had just taken the skeins to the empty register to pay for them. How many times had Abigail warned her? If she wasn't going to rot behind bars before, she was definitely fated to that life now. No one would believe that it had been accidental; no one in their right mind would replay that overhead footage and truly believe that she had simply tripped, unlucky to have had her fingers wrapped around the world's sharpest knitting needles. Murderers weren't usually granted bail. That one moment, that one slip of her foot—a moment lasting less than a second—had sealed the rest of her lifetime.

Her greatest anxieties had come true. For the second time in her life, she would lose everything: her home, her freedom, and worst of all, Abigail. Maybe she'd stick around for a little while, but Ruth could more accurately predict the path forward: Ruth would be sentenced to decades in prison, if not life. Abigail would pack up her things, move out of Kill Devil, and find someone new.

Ruth stood frozen, several skeins of yarn suffocating her beneath her sweatshirt, a man's hot blood turning cold against her cheeks, standing over his bleeding and probably dead body. He still hadn't budged, and she still hadn't checked. She knew what she would find if she did, and she didn't want to make it real. Tears bubbled at the edges of her eyes, and she reached up to wipe them away, scraping a trail of blood and chunky viscera across her cheeks. A few more skeins of yarn fell out of her sweatshirt as she moved, quickly lapping up the pool of blood still expanding around the man's head.

What the fuck was she supposed to do now?

Chapter 5

Call for help, stupid.

The thought filled her brain, the other worries finally emptying down the drain, and she dug in her tote bag for her cell, her fingers painting the man's blood across the canvas. She tossed out the skeins she'd stuffed there, the gray coils landing in the growing blood puddle. Each yarn missile splattered more red onto her shoes. She needed to call an ambulance. Where the fuck was her phone? Why couldn't she find it in her bag?

Shit.

Shit.

It was in her car. She'd left it in her car. She'd pulled it out of her bag to call Abigail about those fucking weirdos at their doorstep and then she'd just tossed it into the passenger seat. She'd never put it back into her bag. Her arms dropped to her sides.

"Hello?" she called into the eerie quiet of the store. On tiptoes, she dodged the growing puddle and hurried down the aisle. Where the fuck was everyone? If they'd been surveilling close enough to catch her in the act, surely they had seen what had happened next, right? Shouldn't they be rushing to help? She tried again, louder, peering around into other aisles. "I need some help! There's been an accident! Is anyone else here?"

She had to find another person. She was trapped inside by the metal gate, and she knew the phones at the registers were useless. Each one had an old-fashioned telephone, coiled cord and all, but no buttons. They were merely conduits for the Mustard Seeds to spread their knowledge, but only if a customer dialed in asking for it. The only other phone she ever remembered seeing hung on the wall next to the mysterious locked door in the back, where it collected dust. She couldn't recall whether there had been one in the manager's office or whether they'd simply used the company-issued cell phones strapped to their waistbands, fellow soldiers in line beside the headsets.

Her feet twisted beneath her, spinning her in the direction of the employee-only door. Finally, another yellow apron appeared before her, striding toward her as if magnetized to Ruth's location. Like the first one, he also bore a golden shepherd's crook where his name tag should be. She didn't want to think about how she must look—wet with someone else's blood.

"What happened?" the man said.

"There was an accident," she panted, pointing back down the aisle. "Just over here."

"Come with me, and we'll sort it out," the Mustard Seed said, grabbing her arm. Was it her imagination, or was this guy also squeezing like a vise? Maybe she was just in a state of shock. Or maybe it was the simplest explanation—they were not merely apprehending her for shoplifting. Now they were dealing with a murderer.

"But he's back there," Ruth said, a lump forming in her throat. "Shouldn't you make sure he's okay?"

"Someone else is assisting," the man said. "Just come with me, and we can get this all figured out."

She walked willingly behind him, a stoic death march through an aisle lined with mirrors, each square inch covered with gilded frames or reflective glass. Two dozen Ruths stared back at her, each one with the same gore-freckled face, the red contrasted by her pallid hue, her own blood fleeing from her cheeks. Thirteen globs of gelatinous goo hovered on thirteen foreheads, an equal number of ragged, stained sweatshirts moving past the wall of glass.

The ghostly visions of herself churned her stomach. Beads of sweat eroded the blood on her face. Her legs transformed into gelatin, tremors wobbling through her knees and up to her torso. Against his grip Ruth's skin grew cold. Was it her ghostly reflection and her ghastly deed weighing on her, or had the adrenaline spike lowered her blood sugar? When the Mustard Seed pulled her out of the hall of mirrors and into the wide center aisle, the heaped displays there blurred together, the items becoming a slurry of biblical soup.

"I think my blood sugar is dropping," she said, her feet stumbling underneath her, threatening to trip her again. "I need some food—some sugar."

"When the police get here—"

"No," Ruth blurted. "I can't wait that long. If I don't eat

something—I could pass out or—die."

The man stopped, turned his face back to her. Was it her imagination, her hypoglycemic fog, or did the grimace inked through his wrinkles waver, his expression shifting into fear—eyes widening, his lips parting, his eyebrows twitching closer together like fuzzy caterpillars?

"She says she needs something to eat or she'll pass out," the man reported into the microphone of his headset. A buzzy reply returned. The man nodded. "There's some brownies in the classroom," he said to Ruth. Then, as if reading the confusion on her face, he added, "From a birthday party."

Something felt *off*. Alarm bells rang inside Ruth's head, but she couldn't quite pinpoint why. Sweat dribbled down her scalp. Since when were parties hosted in the classroom? When she worked there, it had only been used for occasional knitting tutorials or group painting classes. But the gravity of the past ten minutes slithered back into her consciousness—*you killed a man*—and she gulped. There were greater worries now.

The Mustard Seed kept her arm in a firm vise until he sat her in a chair. On the paint-speckled table sat a neat plate of individually wrapped brownies, six stacked in a pyramid, all polka-dotted with colorful chips. Ruth unwrapped one and started chewing, the carbohydrates slowly solidifying her jelly legs back into bone and flesh.

"Please remove any merchandise you've taken and place it on the table," the man said once she'd slipped the final bite into her mouth. Ruth complied, spilling the remaining skeins from beneath her sweatshirt like coiled intestines and stacking them before her.

"Is that everything?"

"Yes."

The Mustard Seed sighed. "Lying lips are an abomination; those who deal in truth shall be rewarded. This is your last chance to be truthful—is that all you have stolen?"

"Yes," Ruth repeated. Hadn't they seen what she'd taken on the cameras? Isn't that what the other guy said? "There's some others that fell out already."

"I'm going to check for any other stolen merchandise," he said. Kneeling, he started by her feet, patting along her socks. It reminded her of Jesus washing the feet of the disciples. The man's touch was surprisingly gentle, almost reverent, as if she were made of porcelain and he might break her. Ruth remained still, hoping that her compliance would indicate innocence.

The classroom hadn't changed since she'd worked there, beyond the layer of rainbow patina that seemed to cover every surface. Six fold-out tables, each with six fold-out chairs. Cubbies and off-kilter drawers and cabinets lined the walls, full of overflowing cardstock and cups of paintbrushes. Across the wall, right beneath the ceiling, a painted declaration read: *Let the Greatest Among You Become a Servant.*

Ruth had almost forgotten about the store's stupid slogan, the phrase that had been plastered all over the break room, recited to her countless times by management to quell any staff complaints. The eight words had even been printed on their paystubs.

Her thoughts continued to stray from the bloodied mess she'd made. As the Mustard Seed reached her knees, she scanned the room, trying to memorize it, trying to focus on anything besides the fateful moment she'd have the rest of her life to ponder from behind bars. She noticed an assortment of chunky clay creations on a nearby shelf—oblong pieces with odd, patterned scratches in rows. Crumbling at the edges. What class had that been? What were they trying to make?

A faded flyer tacked to the wall advertised some sort of camp project. *Use the talents your Creator gave you to help us build New Creations Camp!* A little cartoon campfire sat in front of a log cabin. Beneath that was another flyer, its words concealed except for *Tell a Good Shepherd.*

The Mustard Seed crested her knees, hesitated at her thighs. Crackling erupted from the man's earpiece, feedback snaking up the little cord that connected it to the standard-issue radio that every employee was required to wear at all times, even on breaks. A working headset was almost as important as the *customer-is-always-right* regulation, the *always-be-a-servant* mindset.

If he hadn't had the volume turned up to the max, if he hadn't been patting up her legs, putting his earpiece right next to her face, Ruth might not have heard the voice on the other end. The voice that she was definitely not meant to hear.

"Make sure she's contained," it snapped, distorted with static. "She's special and precious. We need her."

What the fuck?

What did that mean?

Ruth's head spun with thoughts, each one worse than the last, all screaming and yelling and overlapping until she couldn't distinguish one from the other. They *needed* her? For what? The inevitable trial?

"We've made sure there's no interference," the voice said. "We are ready to receive her and her gift."

"I've got her secured in the classroom," the man replied.

"Good," the crackly voice said. "And make sure she eats. It won't work if she's dead."

If she's *dead*? What the fuck? Why would she be dead? Was it related to her diabetes? Were they just making sure she'd gotten her blood sugar up? Ruth's muscles tightened. Her instincts told her it was more than that. Whatever was happening here was not related to her shoplifting. And it didn't even appear to be related to the man she'd stabbed—the man she'd *murdered*. She didn't know what the fuck they wanted with her, but she knew she needed to get away from this person immediately.

When the man reached her jean pockets, bending over her, she jerked her knee upward, connecting right between his legs. He folded like a square of cardstock, kneeling in front of her, groaning in pain. Before she could do more than push her chair back, before she could even register the reality that she was trapped with nowhere to run, the man clasped his hand around her ankle.

Ruth thrashed, squirming, kicking, anything she possibly could to extricate her leg from his meaty vise. As she fell off the chair and onto the floor, he squeezed tighter and tried to snatch her other ankle. She kicked and clawed and yanked. With a final burst of force, she finally freed her ankle.

But though she left him on the floor, ego and body bruised, somehow he still managed to squeeze his hand around her arm as she reached the door, as if he'd teleported to her. The

Mustard Seed shoved Ruth against the wall, trying to pin her down, to cease her flailing. He tried to capture her free hand, which fluttered like a bird trapped on the wrong side of glass. Then he moved toward her throat. And started to squeeze.

Feeling her breath shrink, constrict, Ruth threw her free hand back against the wall, scrabbling until it found the row of clay chunks on the shelf. Her fingers clasped around one, nearly dropping it from the unexpected weight. She swung the thing at the man's head, the divots and scratches of the tablet creating imprints on her fingertips as she squeezed it tight. She missed a couple of times, the blows pinging off his shoulder, until, finally, the thing connected with his face, a cracking blow. Blood spouted from the man's nose and lips, staining the unglazed clay, and the sudden pain forced him to release Ruth, just long enough. She didn't hesitate. She ran.

Ruth could not let him take her. Something in her gut assured her she might be alive when they received her, but she wasn't going to leave that way.

Ruth pumped her knees, her shoes slapping against the concrete floor, autopiloting to the front of the store. Her eyes remained alert for anyone else who might be there to try to capture her.

Capture her? Even as she ran, the thought seemed odd. Was she really being hunted? Why did they want—*need*—her?

If she could get to a register, she could press one of the panic buttons that was installed beneath each—and pray that they were actually connected to something. Too late, she realized the direct path there would take her to the scene of her crime, right to the holey body, and surely there would be someone there, someone tending to the man, someone who could easily hear her coming and jump out to grab her. Cutting away from the main pathway, she ducked back into the mirror aisle, cursing at her many selves staring back at her, wrinkled with blood-streaked stress lines, until she realized her luck—she could use one of the mirrors to peer around the corners.

The glass revealed . . . nothing. Not even the body lay there. Only the pool of blood was left. Like the man had vanished. Maybe someone really had come to help him. Maybe he was on his way to the hospital. But nothing in this town happened that quickly, especially not at this location, backed into a dead end at the bottom of a narrow, curved road.

She hadn't heard any sirens. And if they didn't want the police to show up, they wouldn't have called an ambulance there, either.

The store sat in the perfect isolated location. Even if the panic button sent the police, it could take them over an hour to show up, and then they'd still be obstructed by the locked metal gate, each two-inch gap mocking her, revealing the freedom just beyond her reach. Realization sank into Ruth like a leaded stone. There was no other reason why they'd lower that in the middle of the day.

They wouldn't have lowered the gate unless Ruth was the only one in the store, unless they really needed to make sure she couldn't leave.

Not unless they really were hunting her.

Chapter 6

It didn't make sense. Why the fuck would the employees of New Creations, a craft store, be *hunting* her?

What could they possibly want with her?

Ruth could fabricate precisely zero logical explanations. They'd lowered the gate *before* she sank her knitting needle into the man's eye—and it seemed too extreme a reaction for shoplifting. She'd seen her fair share of shoplifters during her employment, but the managers seemed to shrug it away when she tried to be a Good Girl and report it. Their official policy had seemed to be report, document, but do not engage.

How stupid she'd been to think they'd never take action, that'd she'd be safe to continue her prolonged *fuck you*, taking whatever she wanted after losing the one steady form of income she'd been able to find after breaking up with Charlie. How stupid to have thought New Creations could be a fresh start, a place with managers and colleagues she didn't recognize, people who hadn't lived in Kill Devil their whole lives, whose opinions of her hadn't been marred by rumors of promiscuity or gold digging. She should have known it would only be a matter of time before the church-owned store would figure it out and choose discrimination, choose to take one more thing away from her.

They'd waited until she came in for her shift to do it. Her eyes had glazed over when they told her she was fired.

"Why?" she'd asked. "Was my work not satisfactory?"

"Well," the manager said. A fully-sprouted Mustard Seed, he wore a clean button-up instead of the gaudy apron. On his collar was a gold pin—a small shepherd's hook. "We discovered something."

Goose bumps prickled her arms. A tight knot formed in her chest. The air suddenly felt thick and soupy, and her breath hitched. She prided herself on being a Good Worker. This was the only place that had given her a chance since her scandalous breakup. She needed this job.

"What did you find?" she pressed, her palms sweating oval stains onto her jeans.

"We discovered something that proves your values do not align with ours," the manager replied. "Our company has chosen to terminate your employment. Effective immediately."

"What does that mean? That my values don't align with yours? Did I do something wrong?"

Silhouetted by the eerie white wall of screens behind him, the security feeds, the manager shifted in his seat, hesitating, like he was searching for a way to cover up the real reason. "We can't have someone like you working for us," he said finally. "Our ownership believes in good, traditional values, and we cannot sacrifice that."

Emphasis on *traditional*.

"What, exactly, are the *traditional values* I'm going against?"

The manager sighed, as though she were a stupid, petulant child who couldn't see the neon elephant in the room. "We discovered that you are dating a woman."

He said nothing more. Period. Full stop. As if that made any fucking sense. As if that had anything to do with her ability to type in prices at the ancient registers or put paintbrushes on a shelf.

Ruth's heart dropped into her stomach. She and Abigail had been so careful. How could they have known?

"You can't be serious," she said, almost laughing. "That can't really be the reason. You're joking, right?"

"No, I'm afraid it is not a joke."

"That's illegal," she said. "That's discrimination. You can't do that."

"There's just the two of us here," the manager said, a smirk settling on his face. "Kentucky is an at-will state. We can fire you for any reason we like."

"But not discrimination," she persisted.

"We're not discriminating," he replied, the smirk deepening, carving deep dimples in his cheeks that transformed into cavernous black holes in the light of the screens. "We're upholding our values."

Tears threatened, little pearls pooling at the corners of her eyes. She stared at the security monitors, rotating views, each screen split in four. The crying child she'd seen as she made her way to the back of the store was still screaming, had relocated from the seasonal décor to the baking aisle. Someone looked both ways and stuffed a tiny tube of oil paint into their pocket. Yesterday, she might have said something. Today? Fuck them. Then the screen shifted, showing views from four new cameras.

One showed a view of a space she couldn't place. A small room with a few tables, doors on opposite sides of the room. The view shifted before she could discern more.

"Your values are shit," she said, sniffing back the tears. "I can sue you."

"You can certainly try," the manager said, turning back to the screens, "but we both know you wouldn't win. That is, if you could even afford a lawyer in the first place."

She'd stormed out, still wearing her apron. Snatching a craft knife from its hook, she'd stabbed a hole in it and ripped until there was a large, fraying mouth in the center, tossing it onto the floor in the middle of the aisle. She left and cried in her car. Only months later did she feel bold enough to return to take some five-finger discounts.

The memory boiled inside her. First they fired her, and now they were *hunting* her. She was sure of it. Maybe it was part of their missionary work, to round up all the gays and convert them. Take them to the fucked-up conversion summer camp they wanted to build.

"Fuck," she whispered. Even that didn't seem right. Surely there were easier ways to convert people.

Everything seemed hopeless, unless she could shrink to the size of a pebble or somehow snip through the metal grate. There were no emergency exits—a flagrant violation of building code that she had only just now processed. The only possible exit was through the sole remaining door, the one that led to the back, to the break room and the manager's office, and eventually to the employee entrance—but surely that door was guarded by the man on the other end of the headset, and who knew how many other Mustard Seeds. There was also that weird steel door, if she could even find a way to get it open. But she had to try. The distance between Ruth and the back area would be just a quick speed-walk through the knickknacks, back through the arts-and-crafts aisles, and then to open air. It would take a couple minutes, maybe less. But stuck in the front with a bounty on her head, it might as well have been the length of three marathons, one right after the other.

Who knew how many Mustard Seeds were lurking in the aisles right now, waiting to pounce and ensnare her—*alive*, at least. A headache sprouted between Ruth's eyebrows. Ruth rubbed her temples, trying to will away the throbbing that had settled there. If she could press the panic button, there was a chance authorities would show up, villains of a lesser degree. Even if they spelled the end of her freedom, at least they might spare her life. The small mirror she angled around the end of the aisle contained no aproned bodies within its gilded frame. Like a rabbit, Ruth darted into the open space, the hunting ground with a clear line of sight for her predators, speeding straight for the nearest register. Her fingers found the button beneath the counter. She pressed it, and pressed it three times more for good measure, as if that might transmit some sort of panic-laden Morse code.

Even if the button had actually sent out a distress signal, even if the corroded knights in blue were on the way, it would take them time to arrive—minutes or even hours that she'd be alone with the Mustard Seeds. She'd encounter more of them before anyone could possibly rescue her. She couldn't remain empty-handed.

The obvious weapons of choice: the blades lining the sewing shelves—the ones that had borne bald patches, the notions nearly barren. Now she realized why. Scissors, rotary blades, even the tiny packs of pins had all been missing. Every type of blade had been removed, their pegs hosting only thin air. The absences were conspicuous enough to churn her guts now.

Just in case she fought back.

An added contingency plan.

But then, why had they left those knitting needles on the shelf, the ones sharp enough to stab through flesh? She supposed they only removed the obvious choices for weaponry, not thinking about the thousands of other items in the store that could be used with hazardous intent. Not thinking she was smart enough to reason beyond blades. Maybe they'd forgotten to take the scissors from the register drawers, the never-replaced ones that surely were dull by now, their blades so full of sticky gunk they could barely open their sharp mouths, each pair inscribed with *Cut from the Cloth of the Creator*.

Ruth tugged on the handle, but the drawer stuck, the wood swollen or cracked, yet another broken thing in the store that nobody cared enough to fix. The moment she lifted her head to find the next nearest register drawer, her eyes instead locked upon one of her apron-clad foes, barreling toward her with uncanny silence. His feet smacked against the floor with each oversized step, yet the accompanying *slap* was absent, like a muted television. If he had arrived mere seconds earlier, he might have been able to catch her by surprise.

No time to hop registers. Ruth yanked the drawer one more time, thrusting her foot against the base of the counter for leverage. The drawer poked out an inch. Scissors rattled inside, shifting and scratching at the wood, a terrible tease. The metal of the blades glinted beneath the fluorescents.

The man had nearly reached her, a slimy grin curling his lips. He zagged between the staggered counters.

Shimmying the drawer in the frame, hoping to loosen it, she gave one final, mighty wrench—one last attempt to arm herself.

The drawer sprang from its perch like it was slick with oil, bolting away too fast. Its contents crashed against the floor, the sound like a booming cannon cutting through the fluorescent hum. Drawer still in hand, she swung it at the man, just steps away from her now. The wood crunched against his cheek, his mouth releasing a howl—the only sound Ruth had heard from him since he appeared. Staggering back from the blow, he knocked the drawer from her hands and tripped over his feet, hurtling to the ground as Ruth untangled herself from the register's alcove and sprinted away.

At best, she'd cracked his jaw, loose molars rattling around on his tongue, but she imagined she'd just bruised it. The scissors had flown away in the commotion.

What was she going to do now? Choke him with plastic roses?

Chapter 7

Shit. She sprinted to the floral section, the closest cluster of aisles to the checkout counters.

She had nowhere to hide—not unless she could somehow camouflage herself into a plastic bouquet. Scanning the shelves, she sought something to gouge, to maim, to poison. But these shelves weren't familiar; even when she'd worked here, she rarely perused this section, the land of tacky plastic petals, each one with its own price tag, each one coated in shedding glitter.

Time was running out—the man had been stunned, nothing more. She plucked a pair of wire cutters from the rack, but they were too tiny to do much damage. She slipped them into her tote bag.

She couldn't hear anything but the buzzy electricity. No footsteps, no heavy breathing, no raspy wheeze from a broken or bruised jaw. She hadn't heard him coming before—he'd merely appeared, arms spread wide to snatch her. He could round the corner at any moment.

On the bottom shelf sat a cylindrical can. She picked it up and read the label. It was some kind of cleaning spray, heavy in her hand. Along the bottom of the can was printed the warning *DANGER! EXTREMELY FLAMMABLE! INJURIOUS TO EYES.*

She uncapped it as quietly as possible. She hoped the man pursuing her had darted into the next aisle over, the one closest to the registers, stalking through the stems. Or that she'd stunned him just long enough to get her bearings.

Shit, she thought. The can needed to be shaken to release its toxic potion. Of course the one thing she could use to defend herself had to rattle and screech. She froze, listening for the location of her hunter. Still she heard nothing but the steady fluorescent scream.

Pressing the nozzle released a hiss of nothing. She really would have to shake it, and if it was anything like spray paint, it needed a full minute to activate.

Before she could calculate the best move, the man appeared at the end of the aisle. A dark spot was purpling the skin around his chin. Ruth began shaking the can. Never letting her eyes leave the approaching man, his footsteps eerily silent, she nabbed something from the shelf—a bag of glass rocks used to fill up floral vases—and shuffled closer to the man, aiming for his face once more. She readied the bag in her hand and launched it, but he knocked it away, easily, like swatting a pesky bug, the rocks flying behind him and across the aisle, where they collided with a mirror, which shattered into a thousand glittering shards.

"I have her," he said into the headset's microphone, curling his lips into a lopsided grin.

Ruth began to frantically launch floral projectiles at the man, whatever she could reach—spools of green wire and useless, squishy foam blocks and fake bouquets. She shuffled backward, the Mustard Seed moving in tandem, slow and steady. On his breast was pinned the same golden hook.

He rubbed his jaw, as if trying to wipe away the aching pain settling there. Ruth's eyes widened in sudden recognition. He'd shaved his mustache and his hair had transformed into a mostly-salt-and-some-pepper gray, but this was no ordinary Mustard Seed—it was *him*. It was her fucking former manager, Christopher—the one who'd fired her.

"I know you're scared and confused, Ruth," he said. "Come with me. We'll figure it all out."

Ruth growled, still shaking the can. "I don't trust you," she said. "I heard it over the radio—*it won't work if she's dead.* What does that mean?"

His mouth curved into the shape of a smile, a pitying one, a condescending semicircle.

Ruth backed toward the front of the store, right up to the metal grate. Between the metal bars, the wan sunshine still shone over the parking lot that housed only her car—or should have. Her car was gone. They must have towed it. And her phone was gone along with it. Even if she could get out of the fucking building, she wouldn't have a quick escape, still couldn't call for help.

"What the fuck do you want—*need* me for?" she asked.

"It's okay," he said again, raising his hands beside his face, as if to show he was unarmed. "I just want to help."

"I know there's something else going on—this isn't just about shoplifting." Her finger hovered over the nozzle, ready to spray. But when her feet paused, so too did his, three linoleum squares apart.

"I remember you, Ruth," he said, his hands still raised, fingers splayed. "When you used to work here. It really was a shame that we had to let you go. You were one of our best workers. You always wanted to do what was best for our customers and for the store. I know, deep in your heart, you are a good person. That you want to do what's good and right and true. Please, come with me. Do what's good."

He smiled at her, earnest and toothy. He lowered one of his hands, held it out to her. An invitation that Ruth rejected, squeezing both hands around the spray can and holding it up like a pistol.

"I'm not going anywhere with you. Not until you tell me what's going on."

"We just want to help you," he said. "I know you. I know you're a good person. You're better than the sin you chose. If it had been up to me, we wouldn't have let you go. We would have let you redeem yourself. No one is beyond reform. Come with me, and we can help."

She marched backward again, until her heels rattled the metal gate.

"Be sensible, Ruth," he continued, favoring the unbruised side of his mouth. "There's no need to do this the hard way. There's nowhere for you to go. We can track your every move. Please, let us help you."

Fuck, the *cameras*.

"I'm not going anywhere with you," Ruth spat, moving parallel to the bars. "The police are on their way right now."

"I don't think we have to worry about the police." He sighed, a deep hiss of disappointment. Then he lurched toward her, a dark silhouette against the bright windows. When he was close enough to grab her, his fingers skimming her sleeve, she crushed the nozzle and sprayed him in the face. In the air, the scent of a thousand bouquets bloomed, the fine mist settling in his eyes.

With a grunt, he released her and stumbled back, rubbing his eyes. "Why do you insist on sinful behavior?" he said, the words slithering through his clenched teeth.

Ruth held the can in front of her, ready to spray again. The fumes singed her nostrils, a headache sprouting between her eyes.

He staggered toward her, squinting his sore eyes, his sclera matching the red of his face, anger and disappointment boiling beneath. Each heavy step was still, somehow, silent—as though he were stomping his feet against pillows. Ruth wasn't sure how that could be possible. Even her own tennis shoes made a *clap* against the floor. How were this man's heavy work boots absolutely silent? Were the bottoms coated with something that dampened sound? Was that how he'd snuck up on her both times, seeming to appear out of nowhere?

She sprayed the nozzle once more, but he was too far away for the honeysuckle-sweet cloud of toxic chemicals that ate dust—and men's eyes—to have much effect.

"Ruth, please see reason," he entreated. The harsh sunlight cast half his face in shadow, elongating the purple bruise along his jaw. "Why do you resist the love and light of the Creator?"

Ruth needed a better weapon, something that would do some real damage, something that would at least fell him long enough for her to get some distance. She dropped the useless can, hurling ceramic pots at him as she retreated. Even with squinting, burning eyes, he dodged or swatted them away. His heavy boots made easy work of the shards, crunching them into sand. She sprinted to the end of the aisle, to the far corner of the store. Ahead of her was the useless, emptied sewing department. To her right, more useless pots.

"You are only increasing your sins," he called, his voice careening around the corner. "I know you're better than this, Ruth."

To her left sat a stand of corrugated metal yard signs. *USA PROUD*, they declared, the text emblazoned atop an American flag. Beneath the sign, a post ended in a pair of sharp metal spikes, meant to pierce the ground. But they'd probably do well on flesh, too.

Ruth grabbed a sign and aimed the pointy part toward the end of the aisle as her former manager rounded the corner. His red eyes bulged. As soon as he came into view, Ruth rushed toward him until she felt the thick metal prongs penetrate his apron, two twin divots settling against his chest, not nearly as quick or fluid as the knitting needle had been. As her body collided with his, he fell heavily to the floor. His hands felt around the post, trying to get a grip on it so he could pull the sign away. But Ruth pounced on him, holding it in place, the entire weight of her small body settling on his chest. The prongs had not yet split his skin; they had merely unraveled the fibers of the thick canvas of his apron, little yellow hairs poking up around the spikes.

"What's going on?" she demanded. "What the fuck do you all want with me?"

The man grunted as Ruth's weight settled into his lungs. "We want to help you."

"Help me how?" Ruth persisted.

"We want to save you from yourself," he gurgled. "We want to absolve your sins, make you pure and clean."

"So this is some kind of conversion thing?" she asked. The little golden pin scraped against the crude metal. "You're going through all this trouble just to get me to join your church? I already tried that once; I'm not interested."

Beneath her, the man made the motions of a cough, void of sound, choking on his own saliva. "It's bigger than that," he grunted, his voice low. Ruth leaned in, bringing her ears closer, the prongs meeting resistance before breaking through his skin. Small pebbles of blood bubbled up, soaking into the yellow apron.

"What will you do, Ruth, once you have slain me?" he asked. "Where will you run? You can't outrun what's good and right. What will you choose? Sin or truth?"

Ruth gritted her teeth. "Fuck you," she spat.

"I still do not believe you to be this far gone, this lost inside the devil's grasp," he continued, closing his eyes. "But should I leave this realm at your hands, I will ascend to my rightful place with the Creator. All my trust is in Him and He will relieve me of my pain, of all that is this world, for I am in this world, but I am not of this world. He will forgive me, that I have failed in gathering a sinner like you to Him. That I have failed to help rid you of your evil. Evil people beget evil. Are you really evil, Ruth?"

Was she? Ruth imagined what it might feel like to stamp her foot down on the horizontal bar of the metal sign, as if depressing it into dirt. How the vibrations might shiver up to her hands as the prongs plunged deep into his flesh, scraped against his rib cage, the jolt of pain forcing his muscles to clench, his legs springing up to his chest. She imagined him buried in a grave, sucked down into the earth, truly silent, forever, no Creator come to resurrect him. A part of her wanted that. In her mind, she increased the pressure against the bottom of the sign, blood spurting from the punctures.

But she hesitated. She didn't contain evil. She just wanted to go home to Abigail.

"If you are lucky, you will meet Him yourself, tonight," he said. "He is the ultimate judge on high, and you would do well to listen to us, so that you may meet Him with a clean slate. If not—you'll have one more mortal sin added to your tally."

Ruth left him there, heading again toward the front of the store.

"You cannot run from your fate," the man called after her, his voice growing dim as the distance between them increased. "Another Shepherd will come to collect you, to prove his worth to the Creator, to the mission. His army is exceedingly great."

He was right. What the fuck was she supposed to do when they could track her path across the store through cameras and headsets? It seemed hopeless. They'd know where she was no matter where she went. There was no way out for her, even if she continued to fight. She kicked the shelves in frustration, the metal vibrating and shaking. A jar of floral glitter rattled and fell to the floor. The glass shattered, the noise sharp and loud. She didn't care. She kicked the shelf again, swiped the toe of her shoe through the shimmer and glass.

She nearly slipped on the glitter, and as she twisted around, catching herself on the shelf, she realized.

This was where she'd been rushing to sweep up when she'd run into Charlie and his then-fiancée. A grin spread across her face.

The outlet.

The outlet that meant certain doom for the store, and yet, in Ruth's entire tenure there, nobody had bothered to fix it. Warnings of it spread from coworker to coworker like a whispered ghost tale: *The last time anyone plugged something in there, the store lost power for three days before an electrician came out to do something about it.* Eventually the tale of the cursed outlet spread to the one person who *would* do something about it—a newly hired Mustard Seed who had no power to uncouple the outlet or rewire it, and simply placed two strips of painter's tape over the whole thing, marking it with a big blue X.

She could only hope they'd continued to ignore its presence. What was the closest object with a plug?

Quickly as she could, Ruth grabbed a hot glue gun from the shelf, hunching so she might conceal her plan from the cameras above, ripping the packaging away. Another yellow apron was likely on his way to her, right this second. The glue gun free, she dashed to the forbidden outlet at the end of the aisle.

The painter's tape remained in place, curling at the edges, dust and glitter caked onto the exposed sticky end. The same piece of tape.

Now she smirked up at the camera. And waved. Bye-bye, power.

Thrusting the plug into the outlet, she flipped the glue gun to its highest, hottest setting.

Ten seconds later, darkness fell.

COLD CASES, LOST FACES

Season 3, Episode 7

Continued

LINDSEY: Remember to use our code LOSTFACES10 for 10 percent off! Now, Sarah, do we think Tom and Barbara ran away together?

SARAH: That would be odd if he was gay, but I guess he could have been bi. At any rate, the woman's disappearance—her name was Barbara Atkins, and her daughter was Elizabeth Atkins—overshadowed Tom's in the news cycle, at least in the local papers. The whole thing is weird—it was basically front-page news in the local paper, but there was nothing outside the Paducah area. We'd tell you Barbara's husband's name, but strangely, it was never included in any of the articles, and we couldn't find anything in the phone books. People in the neighborhood said the family didn't live there very long.

LINDSEY: That was *so* weird! For those who don't know, usually when women and young girls, especially white girls, go missing, there's a ton of news coverage on it.

SARAH: Maybe it was just because of when it happened. Like, maybe at the time, news didn't spread nationally or even statewide very easily because there weren't two girls making podcast episodes about it.

LINDSEY: I don't know—even in some past cold cases we've looked at, there's been more widespread coverage. *I* think it didn't spread because someone had the right connections with the media and police.

SARAH: Ooh, tell me more. Do you think it was a conspiracy or something?

LINDSEY: Maybe. Or maybe someone with a lot of power knew where they went and was covering for them? Or maybe they were the reason Barbara and Elizabeth went missing and didn't want anyone to come snooping and find out.

SARAH: And in comes us, almost twenty-five years later.

LINDSEY: Well, luckily for them, if that *is* the case, we didn't solve either Tom's or Barbara and Elizabeth's cases. But we did end up with some pretty weird clues—and a theory of our own.

SARAH: We *do* think that Tom's and Barbara's cases are linked somehow, even if they didn't run away together. There were apparently some pretty crazy rumors to that effect in Lovelace, though. So, anyway, here are our clues.

LINDSEY: Exhibit A: Tom's door was left unlocked, implying that he may have been taken against his will. And as we mentioned earlier, there were other signs he didn't intend to leave—the clothes in the washing machine, the half-signed checkbook on the table.

SARAH: Exhibit B: While nobody knows exactly when Tom went missing, some neighbors saw Barbara going into his house a few days before *she* vanished—so we have Barbara entering Tom's house around the time of his disappearance.

LINDSEY: Exhibit C: About an hour before Barbara's husband came home and discovered his wife and daughter missing, a large amount of cash was taken out of their account via ATM.

SARAH: Exhibit D: Barbara's vehicle was tracked down at a used-car lot weeks later, about fifty miles east of Lovelace. A salesperson said they discovered her car on the lot, completely empty—even the glove box—with the keys sitting on top of the dash. They didn't know how long it'd been sitting there when they discovered it. However, they did find records of a few cash sales around the time Barbara and Elizabeth went missing. Unfortunately, none of those records led anywhere, and nobody at the lot remembered seeing Barbara or a woman with a young child.

LINDSEY: Oh, my God. That's so weird! Is there a theory there?

SARAH: I mean, nothing official, but it seems pretty obvious to me. Barbara was running away from something, and she ditched her car on the lot and either stole another or, more likely, quickly bought another in cash using a fake name.

LINDSEY: But no one remembered seeing her.

SARAH: That's true, but as we've discussed on here before, witness testimony is notoriously bad, especially when it's about something mundane that only becomes important later. Like, how many people might have come through that week to buy a car? It probably wasn't that unusual at the time to buy a car outright, in cash. And she could have been in disguise, or made sure Elizabeth wasn't seen by anybody.

LINDSEY: Exhibit E: This one is extra weird—and may not be connected to this case at all. But we'll get into why we think it is after. A few years after Tom and Barbara and Elizabeth went missing, a guy went hunting in the woods near Lovelace and stumbled upon what looked like a hidden neighborhood: a bunch of rudimentary buildings congregated together. They were all entirely empty, too. The police came out and investigated but said it was probably just some hippies who tried to live off-grid, or maybe they were cabins for a camp that fell through. Which I suppose is possible, but doesn't seem likely.

SARAH: Yeah, really weird—how could people build a whole bunch of houses in the middle of the woods without anyone noticing?

LINDSEY: Right? And that supports my theory that someone with power in Lovelace—or maybe a lot of people—know more than they're saying. But here's why I think this connects to Tom and Barbara. This clue was kind of hidden in the newspaper a few days later. Something you could easily miss if you weren't scanning every single page. It was a tiny little article in the middle of a bunch of ads. And I think that's why this didn't become a bigger thing.

SARAH: Oh, my God, Lindsey, enough with the suspense! What was it?

LINDSEY: At the site of the cabins, they found what looked like a burn pit. And within the burn pit, they found fragments of bone.

SARAH: That's insane! Were they human?

LINDSEY: The article just said *Police investigating possible human remains at site of abandoned camp*. I searched and searched, but there was never a follow-up article, and it just never seemed to be mentioned again. So it *could* be animal bones, but something in my gut tells me it's not. I think it's human.

SARAH: So how do you think it's connected to Tom or Barbara?

LINDSEY: I think if they were human, they were more than likely Tom's bones. Lovelace is a pretty small place, and there's not many people who go missing there.

SARAH: Do you think Barbara did it? Like, she killed him, destroyed the evidence, and then ran away with her daughter?

LINDSEY: I don't know. That could be a possibility. But I think it seems unlikely. From everything we could tell, Barbara was a pretty thin, short young woman. Could she have really transported Tom's body by herself and burned it, leaving only fragments of bone behind? And done all of that without leaving any evidence tying her to the crime?

SARAH: Good point. But it's suspicious that she left right after he went missing, right? And she was seen going into his house? And it does appear that Barbara intentionally vanished. She took her car and got cash. She was planning.

LINDSEY: That's true, but it just doesn't seem like it fits. What's her motivation? She might have just been a concerned neighbor trying to check in on him.

SARAH: Yeah, maybe she went inside and found something that scared her or something, and that's why she left.

LINDSEY: But if that was the case, why wouldn't she tell her husband where she was going? Why wouldn't she leave with her whole family?

SARAH: Well—maybe her husband did it. Maybe she found the evidence inside Tom's house, or maybe she even asked her husband if he'd seen Tom recently, and he got really weird and defensive or something, and she just knew he did it.

LINDSEY: It does seem more likely that—if Tom was murdered—a man would have done it. And maybe that would explain why we couldn't find the husband's name anywhere. Maybe he had connections at the paper or with the police so that his name didn't get printed. And that's why Barbara vanished instead of reporting him—maybe she knew the police wouldn't believe her.

SARAH: But what was the husband's motive? By all accounts, Tom was a nice, quiet person who kept to himself.

LINDSEY: Well, I think there's one possible explanation. It's a really sad one, but given the time and place, I don't think we can rule it out. From John's testimony, we know that Tom was gay. And we also know that he went missing shortly after his one and only date with John at his house. So, one unfortunate possibility could be that Barbara's husband was homophobic to the point of violence, and he caught Tom and John together.

SARAH: That, unfortunately, is a very real possibility.

LINDSEY: And that is the cold case of Tom Torrence—and by proxy, Barbara and Elizabeth Atkins. We encourage you to say their names and toast to their lives, wherever they may be. We hope that this episode can open up these cases so more evidence can be found to bring their family and friends closure.

SARAH: If you have any information about this cold case or would like to tell us your thoughts, you can join our Discord server—the invite link is on our website.

LINDSEY: This has been another episode of *Cold Cases, Lost Faces*. I'm your host Lindsey.

SARAH: And I'm Sarah, signing off. We'll end by saying their names one last time.

SARAH AND LINDSEY: Tom Torrence. Barbara Atkins. Elizabeth Atkins.

Chapter 8

Only a few dim fluorescents flickered across the store, perhaps attached to a different breaker than the faulty outlet, everything else cloaked in darkness. It looked closer to midnight than late afternoon. The little red recording lights on each camera had been extinguished. Deep and ominous, the new shadows seemed to hold secrets and monsters inside them, endcaps of fuzzy yarn appearing more like the fur of a grotesque creature.

The Mustard Seeds couldn't see Ruth anymore, couldn't track her on the security feeds, where she imagined her image had been burned on the screens before they fizzled into blackness themselves. She had a fighting chance now. They couldn't see her, but neither could she see *them* coming. She had to move.

The mirror aisle: where she'd shattered one into sharp shards—the perfect weapons. The next Mustard Seed would be headed to floral now, to the outlet that had killed their bird's-eye view. She skirted the exterior wall, charting an indirect path. He'd surely be taking the unswerving path from the manager's office to where she'd last been spotted, a path she could graph in her head. She imagined she could navigate through the store blindfolded. But so could they.

She hung back in the shadows at the end of the aisle. Between her and the mirror aisle lay the large, central pathway. She couldn't be sure where her foe might be hiding, whether he was puzzling at her disappearance by the outlet or waiting just around the endcap to wrap his paws around her. Taking a quick breath, Ruth had no choice but to dart across.

No sooner had she stepped into the wide pathway than another Seed appeared a few yards to her left, like clockwork, her luck sour.

"I have her in sight," he grunted into the headset, trailing Ruth as she dashed into the mirror aisle.

Ruth snatched up the largest glass shard from the floor as the man's massive hand squeezed a fistful of her sweatshirt. Reaching over her shoulder, she slashed until the sharp ends of the mirror hooked onto something, slicing through the resistance of his flesh. He released her with a Creator-approved curse beneath his breath.

Ruth had to crane her neck to meet his eyes. The man towered over her, seeming to stretch to seven feet tall. His body was a tangled skein of coiled muscle, so wide that his shoulders seemed to graze either side of the aisle, the tabletop frames and mirrors rattling and vibrating as he stepped forward. But he couldn't truly be this giant—it was just her terror warping things. Wasn't it? A slender trail of red oozed from the back of his hand. Barely a scratch.

Something about him seemed familiar to Ruth. She didn't recall ever meeting such a hulking ogre of a man before, yet a spark of recognition bloomed deep within her. Then it clicked: it was the birder. She'd seen him in the woods next to her house, sporting a pair of binoculars—several times, in fact. She was sure of it.

He hadn't looked quite so large when Abigail had spied him from a distance across their driveway or behind the glass of their kitchen window, but he'd still creeped her out. *What was he doing back there?* she'd wondered. *Why was he hanging around outside their house in the woods?* There wasn't a trail there that they knew of, and he wasn't one of their neighbors. Ruth had joked—kind of—that he must have been spying on them. Abigail didn't think it was very funny.

Trying to reassure her, peering through the shuttered blinds, Ruth had said, "He's probably just a land surveyor. Or maybe he collects pinecones or something nerdy like that."

"I don't like it," Abigail replied. "It's creepy. It's like he's watching us."

Ruth rolled her eyes. "Why would he be spying on us? We're boring as shit. He'd just fall asleep right there in the woods."

Abigail had not been convinced. The next time he'd appeared, Ruth—the more friendly and pragmatic of the two, *and much stupider*, Ruth thought now—approached the man while the pair had been outside tending their garden. He'd materialized, once again, at the edge of the trees like an omen, just on their side of Hell for Certain, the creek that ran parallel to their driveway.

Ruth went to investigate, a ghostly pinprick still lingering on her skin from Abigail's pleading pinch to stay put.

The man said he was a birdwatcher. He pointed up into the trees across the creek, explaining the need for binoculars. Ruth threw her head back in laughter—of course, just birdwatching, not Ruth-and-Abigail watching. They had some premium birds living in the woods next to them, apparently. If you want to see birds, you go to where they live.

But Abigail had been certain she'd seen his lenses pointed at them: at their house, into their windows. She shut the curtains and blinds on the side of the house that faced the woods and kept them sealed. Abigail had been right. She wasn't paranoid: Ruth was naive. The world was against them, each day seeming to bring some new law against them, some man pointing binoculars at them.

Standing next to him by the creek, Ruth had lightly touched his arm, an endearing gesture, something she did without even realizing it. The thought made bile churn in her stomach now, standing before the same man. Never again would she be so trusting.

The little cut from the mirror shard had merely caught him off guard, like a nick from a razor against stubble. He didn't even seem to notice it. He advanced toward her, hand outstretched, and Ruth swiped the shard at him until she felt the friction of it slide through skin, disappearing inside his flesh, opening a dark, weeping slash across his palm. But the oozing hand curled around her shoulder as if he didn't even feel it. Ruth sliced frantically at his arms, too, at his chest, at any part of him within reach, the reflection inside her weapon doubling each wound. Nothing seemed to faze him.

"I can bear the burden of your sins," he said. "It is difficult to repent, but you only need to accept the love of the Creator."

His hands gripped her shoulders, squeezing so hard she thought her bones might snap, might shatter and crunch inside his meaty grip. He pulled her toward him, his body growing even larger in her eyes, ready to toss her over his shoulder and carry her to the back, a sack of potatoes ready for whatever feast they might be preparing.

Her feet floated away from the concrete floor, dangling in thin air. She kicked, her heels bouncing away from his thighs like a reflex hammer. His warm blood seeped through the sleeve of her old sweatshirt, the little river of blood still pulsing out of his palm, his grip so tight that her fingers started to tingle. So tight that she nearly forgot that she was still holding the mirror shard.

"Our Creator will tread down our foes," he said, his voice distorted with bass, so loud it pierced her eardrums, as if his vocal cords had expanded. None of this seemed possible, but Ruth couldn't explain it away, couldn't make sense of the supernatural foreboding that raised goose bumps across her skin.

"We are conquerors through Him. We prefer to convert, to have you join us, but if you refuse, the Creator will help our cause with His great power. Wouldn't you rather join us in heaven? Wouldn't you rather revel in love and not hate?"

"I'm not the one spreading hate," she growled.

"Do you really think you know better than our Creator?" the man boomed. "What if you are wrong?"

Now at close range, her nostrils filled with the stink of his breath, she aimed for his jugular. The shard caught his cheek beneath the sharp edge, the point skipping across the elastic skin like a rock across water. A second slash caught his neck, grazed it, not deep enough for permanent damage.

Still, he did notice these cuts, and he dropped her. The chunk of mirror slipped from her hand as she landed, hard, on the concrete. Beneath her was the crunch of breaking glass—sharp teeth biting into her flesh. Each one stung, lightning bolts of pain shooting up her arm as she pushed herself up and darted out of the aisle. She turned a corner, running without destination, all thoughts devoted to getting away from the hulking mass of muscles, not yet worrying about the exertion lowering her blood sugar.

Grumbling curses sounded from the broken-mirror aisle, then heavy footsteps. This one wasn't silent like the other. He remained relentless in his holy task, moving slower, taking his time, but still in pursuit nonetheless. He would not abandon whatever mission he'd been assigned.

Where was the rest of the yellow cavalry? Why was there only this one hulking Mustard Seed trying to nab her? It made little sense—shouldn't they send out everyone, all at once?

Ruth took a heaving breath as her adrenaline waned. She uncurled her palm. Little silver slivers jutted from her flesh like sparkling quills. Every cut on her body screamed in agony, the incoming oxygen like little teeth biting into her flesh. But the pain of every ache and scrape put together was overshadowed by the throbbing of a deep gash that bisected her palm.

"Shit," she said under her breath. She needed to deal with that cut, needed to seal the mouth shut. The small cuts and scrapes weren't too bad—she wished she had time to pick out all the little slivers, at least they weren't gushing—but this? This long, jagged slash spanned the entire length of her palm, two diagonal lips that spat blood, starting at the base of her index finger and terminating at the base of her palm right across her lifeline. Too much blood loss, and her blood sugar would tank.

Nothing lining the shelves before her would help sew the ragged lips shut. She'd landed in the *Live Laugh Love the Creator* home décor aisle that rotated seasonally—they'd just changed over from *Live Laugh Love America* season to *Live Laugh Love the Creator with a Pumpkin, but Absolutely NOT a Jack-o-Lantern* season. She could *Gather Here with a Grateful Heart*, but she could not create a bandage with a foam pumpkin. Even the few scraps of ribbon adorning the fall squashes were made of mesh, too holey.

In the adjoining aisle, the man's oversized feet stomped across the river of glass. Plodding, loud. As if he wanted her to hear his approach, to feel the vibration of each step closer, one stomp at a time, never relenting, as if his success was inevitable, as if he'd chase her forever.

He wouldn't need to if Ruth couldn't seal her wound. She tugged the worn sleeve of her sweatshirt over her bloody palm and wadded the cuff inside her fist, squeezing to try to stanch the flow, crossing her arms against her chest like a wounded bird, hoping the elevation would keep the waterfall at bay.

His footsteps continued. *Stomp, crunch. Stomp, crunch.*

"I will not be shaken," he said, the words low and confident. "The Creator is right beside me." He had nearly reached the corner.

For once, luck was with her, appearing at the end of the aisle. Lined up in neat rows beneath foam pumpkins were huge bottles of super glue. Her back against the endcap, she worked to strip the plastic seal off.

No longer on the river of glass, the man's footsteps grew quiet. Fighting to open the seal one-handed, Ruth had stopped listening for them. Just as she peeled the seal away with her teeth and uncorked the spout, the oversized man appeared beside her, wrapping his enormous hand around her arm, blood crusted over his fingers. Forefinger to pinky, his meaty hand spanned the entirety of her upper arm.

"Come with me," he said, "and I can give you the gift of heaven. Aren't you tired of struggling? Join us, and all of your troubles will be gone. You'll do good. You'll save the world and go straight to paradise."

Ruth resisted, planting her feet as though she'd doused them in the glue. Sighing, as if disappointed, the man yanked her forward like she was a knit doll, dragging her back through the décor aisle, revealing a perfect breadcrumb trail of bloody droplets that had led him right to her. Ruth dropped her weight, making herself as heavy and unmovable as possible—something Abigail's mom, Judy, had taught her.

Ruth didn't remember what had spurred the conversation. It seemed like Judy always wandered her way back to the topic of safety, always had some sort of sage advice: *never stop for a broken-down car if you are a woman alone; hold your keys in your palm in the parking lot; make yourself heavy as a rock, limp as a rag doll if someone is trying to kidnap you.*

Judy had always been nervous that way, as if she were being hunted down, as if someone would appear in the middle of the night to break down the door and steal her and Abigail away. Even when Ruth was a child, she remembered the long series of locks that lined the inside of Judy's front and back doors. Each time Ruth visited Abigail, the pair inseparable since kindergarten, Judy would close the door behind her and spend what felt like hours redoing all the locks, sliding chains through some of them, twisting knobs on others, even turning keys through several of them, requiring her to sort through a giant ring she kept on her hip at all times.

After Ruth had moved in, Judy jangled as she moved through the house, keys always safely at her side. Judy had seemed even more guarded than she'd been when Ruth was a child. Maybe it was the difference between living in Judy's home and witnessing her habits all day, every day and not in small bursts. Or maybe she simply hadn't noticed that kind of thing as a child. Had Judy always mummified herself in scarves and sunglasses when she left the house? Had she always kept the shades drawn and taped in place? Had she always paced, bitten her nails to the quick, any time Abigail stepped outside the safe cocoon she'd built for them? If Ruth had listened to Abigail—had heeded the constant warnings Judy had doled out to stay the hell away from the New Creationists—she'd be safe in the cocoon right now.

But Judy was gone—had gotten sick last year and had passed away only a few months ago. Now, both Ruth and Abigail were, effectively, orphans. They only had each other.

So Ruth had to get out of here. Whatever it took.

Chapter 9

Ruth relaxed each and every muscle, every tendon slackening besides those in her two hands, one still squeezing the sopping sweatshirt cuff and the other clutching the bottle of super glue. Her tote bag remained hooked around her elbow, clacking against the concrete along with her shoes. She thought her arm would be pulled from its socket, her ligaments turned to taffy before he'd release her. What was going limp supposed to do, again? Maybe it only worked in crowded spaces—only when your kidnapper was bold enough to try to grab you in the middle of the street. Not in a locked store, you against everyone else. Not when the person snatching you had muscles stitched to their muscles. Had Judy said anything else of use? Ruth couldn't remember now.

Toward the end of the aisle, the Mustard Seed finally did drop her, apparently annoyed or frustrated with her rag-doll weight, an exasperated growl escaping between his clamped teeth.

"Why do you insist on resisting the Creator?" he asked.

"We're trying to help you!"

She scrambled to her feet at the same moment that he wrapped his arms around her torso from behind, hefting her into the air. He continued his meticulous plodding toward the back, toward whatever fate they held for her, grumbling beneath his breath at her ungratefulness.

Ruth thrashed, kicking wildly, aiming for his groin, for some sensitive part among the muscle, but always missed, always hit a rubbery coil or a rock-hard thigh instead. In a repeat of their first dance, she flung her balled, bleeding fist backward, striking his collarbone, but he, again, did not seem to register any of her movements—like she was a tiny, harmless fly, buzzing close to his ears. His arms remained clamped around her waist, so tight she could feel purple bruises forming. Her rib cage bent inward, seeming to poke into her stomach and lungs, leaving her gasping for air.

She kept swatting at his head but succeeded only in knocking the headset from his ear. She kicked more purposefully now, aiming for the pocket that held the receiver. It clattered to the floor. The Holy Hulk did not stop to pick it up. He was out of range of his cohort now. If she was able to scramble out of his grip, he wouldn't be able to call for backup or report her location—at least not before she could dash to a new place in the store.

Something else dropped from his pocket, too—something unrecognizable to Ruth, something odd: a small vial, sealed with dripping wax, filled with a dark, syrupy liquid, hanging from a long chain.

Ruth continued buzzing—nasty, persistent fly that she

was—trying to scratch at his face, his neck, hoping her fingernails might find their way to his eyes, might carve a notch into his cornea or hook beneath his eyelid so she could pull, could peel it away from his face in one tacky, red strip.

A piercing drop of super glue sizzled against her skin. With sudden inspiration, Ruth stilled herself, took a breath, and hardened every muscle into a rock. He continued on as though nothing had changed. Just as he had not registered her constant movement, neither did he seem to realize she had suddenly stopped resisting.

She gripped the bottle of glue firmly in her hand, positioned it above and over her head, the tip pointing behind her, and squeezed hard.

"What the—" the man exclaimed, before his words turned foul and guttural and indistinguishable, syllables wobbling behind the goop. Glue puddled across his cheeks, already clotting among his eyelashes, crusting over the bridge of his nose and filling his mouth. His arms released her, and she thought she was free.

Her feet danced on tiptoe, each follicle threatening to rip itself from her scalp, perhaps even to bring the flesh with it. Her hair had become stuck in the glue, right along his cheeks like a beard. The man, now bumbling around the aisle like an enraged bear, his fingers fused to the skin of his face, one mass of sticky flesh, paid no attention to her. He towered above Ruth, so tall that she could do nothing but attempt to keep her feet on the concrete beneath her, to let him lead the waltz. With each wild turn of their dance, the bond grew stronger, her hair matting into the hardening glue.

The glob retained a tackiness that attracted and collected each speck of matter, searing into his retinas, fusing his eyelashes to his fingertips to Ruth's follicles to every crumb of dust hovering in the air. So much glue had been squeezed onto his face that fat droplets fell away from it, latching onto their shoes. It nearly locked their feet in place on the floor, two sitting ducks forever entwined.

She had no choice but to yank her hair free, to peel the flesh of either her scalp or his face. Ruth wrapped both hands around the hank of hair caught on his chin and tugged as hard as she could. The hulking man led the waltz backward. The opposing forces reached an impasse, finally tearing them apart. A bead of blood bubbled at her lip, her teeth slicing through to hold back her scream as chunks of hair were left behind, taking her scalp with it.

The man's face was a shiny, globby mess, complete with a beard of her own hair, little scraps of scalp hanging loose at the ends. There were weeping coins of exposed flesh on his chin where her hair had torn free. The glue had begun to solidify around his eyes, one nearly glued shut and the other open, his cornea searing red, perpetually staring through the thick, glossy lens wedging the lids open. His hands, too, were stuck against his face. The left was fused to the bottom of his cheek and the other clamped over his nostrils and mouth, air forever out of reach.

Still conscious, purple edging into the unmarred skin on his face, he bumped and wobbled like a sloppy drunk, his body walloping into the shelves. He no longer had a mouth to scream, but he created a cacophony just the same. Ceramic pumpkins and candle holders and mugs toppled to the floor with a clattering smash. The shards skated across the concrete toward her feet, skittering into the fallen headset's earpiece. Ruth plucked it from the floor, the exact same model she'd worn as an employee.

She'd grown to hate the stupid headset when she'd worked there, but now she yearned to feel its sweaty embrace. She wanted to hear every single snippet it could transmit, any sort of hint about what they wanted her for, why they needed her alive. Why that was even a question. Why the fuck any of this was happening.

Ruth slipped the earpiece around her neck, scanning for the receiver. She spotted it between the man's feet, just inches behind him. His exposed skin was now a dark hue beneath a topographical mass of glue, starved of oxygen, and he seemed to be attempting to pry his hands away from his face, his elbows fluttering like wings. He produced soft grunting sounds, only a sliver of vibration making its way through the thick stopper of glue. If he had been able to uncover any air holes, he'd surely be gasping for breath.

Ruth skirted around the man, keeping a wide berth. She didn't want to risk being hit by his wild jerking and twisting, didn't want to chance the man regaining his ultrahuman strength, purpose reinvigorated, ripping his hands free along with the skin of his cheeks. Who knew what he might do in the name of his Creator?

Each of the Mustard Seeds she'd encountered were a strange concoction of desperation and cockiness: cautious enough to lock her in and disappear the blades, but confident enough to wield none themselves—like it was a testament of their faith in the Creator, that they needed only to trust in His eternal, all-powerful love, and using anything but the two hands He had bestowed upon them would negate that trust.

Or maybe they were unprepared because she'd been a timid Good Girl when she'd worked there, never setting a finger out of line, always seeking a pat on the head. Always biting her tongue raw and swallowing her anger over the shitty management and shittier practices until she got home, when it could bubble over to Abigail while they cooked dinner.

The receiver sat behind the glue man, just beyond his twitching feet and flapping arms. Ruth sidled closer, pressing her back against the shelving, the metal lip pinching between the bones of her spine. His elbow swiped backward toward her, forcing her to jerk her head back to avoid the impact, her already scalped head slicing painfully open against the sharp lip of the shelf. She clamped her uninjured hand over her mouth to keep from screaming.

The exposed skin of Glue Man's face was almost entirely purple now. He seemed to be convulsing, his elbows shimmying and his calves straining to keep his knees from buckling. Ruth inched a bit closer. He stepped backward, his huge heel folding on top of the receiver with a crunching of plastic. When he fell forward to his shivering knees, she slipped behind him and plucked the cracked brick from the floor.

Next to the receiver lay the wax-sealed vial, the dark syrup inside still and unsloshing, the glass small and thick enough to have survived the fall intact.

It didn't resemble anything the store would have sold—

maybe all the pieces separately, the vial, the wax, surely, but what rolled thickly inside? What was it? And why was he carrying it around?

Ruth stared for a moment longer, almost mesmerized by the thing. Goose bumps crawled up her spine. It seemed to draw her in, like some power permeated the inky substance inside it. Behind her, Glue Man collapsed to the floor, his torso careening into the shelves, a hailstorm of seasonal décor crashing down with him. The noise startled her back into motion, and she grabbed the thing along with the receiver. It felt warm and right inside her hand.

Chapter 10

The first bottle of glue was long gone—probably a permanent relic glued to the floor—so Ruth grabbed another as she rounded the corner into the next aisle. She made sure she didn't leave another trail of bloody breadcrumbs behind.

Dizziness consumed her, and she moved slowly. Her blood sugar was lowering, fast—she could feel it draining along with the blood and ooze still pumping from her scalp and palm. She needed to stay alert and conscious. Something sugary might hide at the bottom of her tote bag, but first she needed to sit down. Before she fell down.

She'd landed in the aisle of heavy things—cast iron hooks and pans, stone doorknobs and stops, paperweights. On the bottom shelf, she carved out a Ruth-sized divot as quickly as she could without clanging the iron pans together like a siren, careful that no misplaced pans or knobs poked into the center of the aisle, a beacon that would lead them right to her.

Ruth nestled into the hole she'd made, knees to her chest, curled out of sight like a burrowing rodent. If someone came sniffing down the aisle, they'd spot her. But if they merely peered down the aisle from the ends, she'd be invisible. Her raw scalp sent daggers through her skull as she leaned back against the plywood shelf. Closing her eyes against the pain, she exhaled deeply. It would be so easy to fall asleep right now, to just breathe until the pain dissipated into a hazy cloud of nothingness. Maybe this was all a nightmare, and if she fell asleep here, she'd wake up, warm and cozy, in bed next to Abigail. She could feel it happening—her muscles unclenching, her limbs growing heavy, her chin dipping toward her chest.

A muffled sound drifted over from the next aisle, one so faint she might have missed it if not for the silence that had settled in the absence of the fluorescent hum. Perhaps, she thought hazily, Glue Man still screamed behind his sealed mouth. He was surely suffocating beneath the hardening, shiny layer of glue, his meaty palm encased over his mouth and nostrils. She wondered if he would have the resolve, the strength, to use his terrifying muscles to pry his hands away, to peel the skin from his face, to expose the shiny red muscle of his cheeks for one last gasp of air.

Ruth tried to muster some sort of sympathy for him, for a hopelessly suffocating man—he was still a person, after all. A human being of some caliber. He probably was a father and a husband, and would be, perhaps at this very moment, making a widow, leaving his children fatherless. She tried to discover his humanity, to conjure any speck of sympathy within herself, but she couldn't. Maybe she could have a few hours ago. But things had changed.

Now she wanted him to suffer.

To choke.

To slowly, painfully, with awareness, suffocate.

Fuck him.

His wife and kids would be better off without him, just like Abigail had been.

Judy had never given her daughter the full story of why she'd left her husband, why she'd decided Abigail did not need her father's presence in her life. Abigail had been only a few months old when her mother ran away with her; she didn't remember anything at all. She'd never even seen a photograph of her father. Even after Judy passed, they'd found nothing among the dust-laden boxes shoved in nooks and crannies of the house. The best clue had been a photograph of Abigail and her mother standing in front of a house, presumably the one they'd fled, presumably with her father behind the lens. But their bodies obscured the house number, making the search for the address nearly impossible.

Standing together at the funeral, Ruth and Abigail had no one left but each other. Alone in Kill Devil.

"I wish I could find my dad," Abigail said. "He'd probably want to know."

Ruth didn't reply. She hugged Abigail close. Abigail's search for her father made Ruth's skin crawl. The only constant from Judy was her ire toward Abigail's father, and Ruth could only assume her extreme safety measures stemmed from whatever he had done to her, whatever had made her flee with Abigail in secret. She didn't think Judy would want that man to know a single thing about her, let alone find Abigail. She didn't think he was a man worth knowing. But Ruth knew it was not the time to share these feelings. It was the time to indulge fantasies, to find comfort in nice, hopeful thoughts. Reality could set in later.

Ruth squeezed Abigail's shoulders and handed her a tissue. They both needed one: their faces were twin mirrors of reddened eyes, halos of peeling skin around their nostrils, and swollen, tender eyelids.

The large wooden box raised at the front of the room had made everything too real. Nothing else had made the finality stick. Not Judy's short illness, not her death certificate, not even her absence from the house, her massive set of keys silent on the kitchen table. Nothing had wedged itself permanently in Ruth's mind until seeing her still body, caked with makeup and perfume, lying inside a coffin.

Abigail had insisted on publishing her mother's obituary, laboring over each word, paying extra to include the only photograph she had of her mother as a young woman. She'd found it slipped into the middle of an old book when she was in high school, puzzling over her mother's features: sans stress lines, sans darkened undereyes, sans the overwhelming paranoia and doom that seemed to permeate into her face as an adult. In the photo, Judy smiled wide, her teeth in a neat row, her eyes scrunched above her full cheeks.

When Judy found out, she had scoured the rest of the book, making sure there were no other hidden treasures—going so far as to rip some of the pages out, as if some terrible secret might reside inside the thread of the binding or beneath the glued-in endpapers. But she'd let Abigail keep the photograph, and Ruth had watched as she'd carefully removed it from the frame at the top of their mantel to scan it for the submission.

"I'm not sure she'd want her picture in the paper," Ruth had said, treading carefully. She'd always felt that she'd understood Judy's paranoia, having had her own life upended, having her own secret to keep from the outside world.

"I want to," Abigail replied. "I want people to know her. She never let anyone in—I don't want her to be forgotten."

Despite printing her mother's visiting hours for the wake, only a sparse few occupied the sea of seats: A couple of Ruth and Abigail's former teachers, who had known Judy only in passing from parent-teacher conferences. A few neighbors, who had waved to the mummified version of Judy that left the house, nearly every inch of her skin covered by hats, sunglasses, scarfs, long sleeves and pant legs, despite the weather. People who came more for Ruth and Abigail's benefit than because they mourned the loss of Judy. These people took their hands and repeated the refrain: *I'm sorry for your loss.*

The meager crowd shuffled out, saying their goodbyes to Ruth and Abigail. The last in the line was someone only Ruth recognized: a man in a clean black suit with a little golden pin on the lapel.

Ruth had first seen him when she'd attended a service at the newly completed church with Charlie. He'd led her into a sea of plush seats crashing down like a wave of blue velvet. For this service, one of the first, only the initial few rows had held bodies when the silhouette of a man appeared beyond the halo of hot light that lined the stage. He'd seemed to emerge from thin air then, just as he had now. The lights created the illusions of shadows on his face, a harsh black line beneath each blue eye.

Ruth dropped Abigail's hand, stunned by his presence. It was James, the pastor. The man who'd given the terrifying hell-fire-and-brimstone sermon about obeying the Creator, lest he cast you into the fiery pits of hell.

Instead of taking their hands and repeating the same five words as the others, he peered down at Judy, her face gaunt and still, her hands folded over her chest. He leaned over the casket, so close that Ruth thought he might kiss her.

"Did you know her?" Abigail asked.

He unfolded himself, turning toward her and Ruth. "I attend every funeral service in town," he said. "To offer my condolences and invite the bereaved to attend our grief support groups." He handed them a pamphlet, a portrait of a distraught woman holding a tissue to her eyes, before placing his hand on Abigail's shoulder, saying the five required words, and exiting.

There had been no stories about Judy from this crowd—they didn't really know her. That was an intimacy that had been reserved for Abigail and Ruth, the only two who got to witness her eyes, her hair. Her laugh. Her penchant for horror novels. Her unconditional love for Abigail and Ruth alike. When Abigail came out to Judy during high school, she'd merely said, "Men are too much trouble anyway."

Now she was gone. The woman who had packed up her daughter and landed in Kill Devil, by some chance, some thread of decision-making, was gone. Abigail didn't know why she picked this place—and now she'd never know all the factors that twisted their path here. Her mother never revealed that in any of her evasive answers, compiled and collected over the years, never coagulating together into any sort of cohesive story. Ruth had often thought about the little invisible string that threaded through all of these decisions and made it possible for her to meet Abigail, all the way back as children in school.

It felt like fate. After the funeral, they'd pick apart Judy's decision to move to Kill Devil, make a little game out of it, tossing out ideas on why she'd picked this town. Maybe she threw a dart on a map. Maybe she closed her eyes and went wherever fate led. Maybe she put hours and hours of research into the decision, trying to find some perfect blend of population and distance, some complicated math that made sense only to her, looking for a place big enough that she and her daughter could blend in, but small enough that it was just a blip on the map. Maybe she just drove until she ran out of gas.

But it didn't matter, because they'd landed *here*, the place where Ruth had spent her whole life. As shitty as Abigail's dad sounded, if he hadn't done whatever he'd done, then all of those dominoes wouldn't have fallen. Ruth and Abigail wouldn't have met, wouldn't have become friends, wouldn't have fallen in love. Ruth would have an entirely different life, one that had been sanctioned and approved. She'd be married to Charlie, kids in tow, a dreadful cloud of discontent hovering above her at all times. She'd be miserable without knowing why. Maybe she'd have her own epiphany, lonely and stuck. She wouldn't be here, trapped and hunted in a craft store. Or maybe she would be, but she wouldn't have a reason to fight. She wouldn't have a reason to not wave the white flag of surrender and let the Mustard Seeds do whatever they wanted to do to her. Her parents had disowned her. She doubted she would have found anyone else in this town, nor would she have been brave enough to move somewhere else all by herself. She'd more likely have become one of the people in Abigail's true crime podcasts, a nice person who lived alone before disappearing under mysterious circumstances, never to be seen again.

No. If not for Abigail—hell, if not for Abigail's dad, who she'd never been able to find, despite many attempts—Ruth would be utterly alone.

So, fuck Glue Man. She hoped he did suffocate. Maybe his own wife was packing her bags right this second.

Ruth hoped she drove until she ran out of gas, and never looked back.

Chapter 11

Soon, the muffled noises of the man in the next aisle faded.

Had Ruth really been at home, knitting away, just a few hours ago?

Now she sat trapped and bleeding, curled up inside a shelf while religious lunatics hunted her for reasons that remained inscrutable.

Maybe the radio would reveal their secrets. But before she could attempt to unravel their knitted plans, she needed to bandage her wounds. Unclenching her fist, her fingers white at the knuckles and tingling with sleep, she took a breath and peeled the stained, wet cuff from her palm. The ragged gash was a screaming mouth coated in a sloppy red-brown ombre, dried and crackling at the lips. It was angry, curved like a grimace, but not as deep as she had feared. She fished the super glue out of her bag and clenched her teeth, bracing for the sear and sizzle. She squeezed the nozzle over the wound, forming a layer just thick enough to coat it, just enough to shut the mouth up, but not so thick it could catch onto something and peel away in a huge chunk, taking more skin with it.

The back of her head throbbed. Her probing fingers came back with fresh blood, the sight of it sending new woozy pulses through her skull. *Shit.* Too many things were happening at once, and none of would them matter if she didn't get her blood sugar back up. She'd pass out and maybe have a seizure. Maybe worse. It could get very bad very quickly.

Something sweet would do the trick—would buy her a little more time, at least. Maybe there was something at the bottom of her tote bag, miraculously still hooked around her shoulder. Slowly, not wanting to deplete the remainders of her energy, she extracted the contents: her keys, the pamphlet that the missionary had shoved into her hands, and the wire clippers she had stashed. She dug further, her hopes dwindling, eyelids drooping. If she found nothing, her only option would be to somehow slink to the baking section or the front registers to pilfer candy or sprinkles or icing. Those shelves seemed so far away. And she was feeling very cozy, nestled into the Ruth-sized hole. She really could just take a nap here. Fall asleep and never wake up.

A fresh flare of pain shuddered through her skull, radiating down her neck and through her chest. *No.* She couldn't let them win. At least she wouldn't let them take her that easily. She'd fight and scratch and scream until her bones snapped or her muscles tore or her voice gave out. She owed that to Abigail. If she gave up on herself, she was giving up on Abigail, abandoning her.

Abandoning the girl who baked loaves of bread they'd pull apart with their fingers, steam rising from the crust. The girl who always carried candy in case Ruth's blood sugar dropped, who would dump a bag or two into the cart at every grocery run, when Ruth forgot. The girl who pushed Ruth to know herself, to not settle for a life someone else expected her to live.

The girl who had insisted they share a room when Ruth appeared on her doorstep with nowhere else to go, who had pushed their twin beds together. Who had been brave enough to tell Ruth she loved her, the pair lying next to each other, hands and knees grazing.

Ruth had hesitated, her breath caught in a knot in her throat, not knowing what kind of love she meant. Knowing the kind she held in her own heart, but too afraid to say it, lest she lose Abigail, too, if she meant the friendship kind.

"I don't want you to feel weird about it," Abigail said, her hands and knees retreating, the warmth fading from the sheets between them. "I'm sorry. I shouldn't have said it."

"It's okay," Ruth said—still keeping the cards close to her chest. Missing the heat. Wanting to reach out and pull Abigail closer.

"It's okay if you don't feel the same way."

Ruth bit her lip, focused on the sharpness, the pressure of impending bloodshed. When Abigail didn't continue, Ruth pressed: "What do you mean?"

Abigail maintained her silence. The sheets shifted, Ruth feeling Abigail's body curl into itself, her hands shielding her face. Reaching across the cotton sea, Ruth pried one of them away, squeezed it inside her own.

"Tell me," Ruth said, needing her to say it. "It won't be weird. I promise. You're all I have now."

"I'm gay," Abigail replied. She kept her eyes closed. Ruth squeezed her hands again. "I've known for a while, since middle school. And I love you, like—really. As more than a friend."

Something inside Ruth burst, heat and ice radiating through her. She couldn't speak. The moment, the confirmation, was more than she could have asked for. The girl she loved, here in the middle of conservative Kill Devil, here in the land of the New Creationists who had rebuked her, had even convinced her parents to erase their only daughter—that girl loved her back. Still, some piece of her couldn't help but wonder: What if it was a trap?

Abigail's hand slithered out of Ruth's grip, cold with sweat.

"See, I shouldn't have said anything," Abigail said. "I'm so stupid—"

"No," Ruth said, taking a deep breath. "I love you too."

They fell into each other, their bodies sinking into the divot between the conjoined beds, and they'd been inseparable since, still sharing the same bedroom. She couldn't give up on that girl.

Now, Ruth slipped her hand down into the bottom of the tote, her fingers scraping against canvas, the mine depleted. Her heart dropped before they grazed it at last—something crinkly. Ruth yanked it free: A small, Halloween-sized bag of candy. A single-serving red bag of Skittles. Tearing the package open, she ate them, one by one, the ragged, broken skin on her scalp mirroring the up-and-down movement of her jaw, twin mouths working in tandem. As the sugar worked its way into her system, the fog inside her head subsided.

The store seemed too quiet, silence settling into the gloomy darkness shrouding the aisles. Had another Mustard Seed come searching yet? Had she been too delirious to hear them? Had any time even elapsed since Glue Man's muffled screams fell silent?

She tried to perk her ears but heard only a distant fluorescent hum from one of the still-powered lights. Maybe they were regrouping. Maybe they thought Glue Man was still working on capturing her. Maybe she was already dead and trapped in hell, which just happened to resemble the craft store. Maybe she'd finally reach the back door and it would swing open on its hinges, revealing a fiery pit of lava.

But just in case she was still alive, she needed to fight. To fight, she needed to finish sealing up her wounds. The gash on her scalp had become gummy, its red insides starting to congeal. Ruth squeezed a searing line of super glue into the gaping mouth, using her fingers to gently ease its lips shut, so the glue could harden and close it forever.

She fed the tote bag all of the items it had regurgitated, pausing at the pamphlet the missionaries had handed her a lifetime ago. It was crumpled, wrinkles warping the text from where her fist had closed around it, from the force she'd used to shove it inside her tote. She smoothed it out as much as possible, bringing it close to her face to read the small text in the dark aisle. The sun had moved below the trees, no longer pouring into the front windows, the distant fluorescents casting eerie spotlights on the floor.

Don't be a *LOST SHEEP*!

Do you know a LOST SHEEP? Are *YOU* a LOST SHEEP?

LOST SHEEP are those who have strayed from the Love and Truth of their Creator. This may include:

- Liars
- Fornicators
- Gamblers
- Thieves
- Hypocrites
- Idolators
- Atheists
- Homosexuals
- Punk Rockers
- Goths
- Witches
- Feminists

WE CAN HELP PURIFY THEIR SINS!

WE WELCOME ALL TO OUR FLOCK!

While others might shun these lost sheep, the New Creationists believe no one is beyond saving.

"If a man has a hundred sheep, and one of them has gone astray, does he not leave ninety-nine on the mountains and go in search of the one that went astray?" Matthew 18:12

Through the Power and Love of our Creator, nothing is impossible!

LOST SHEEP ARE SAFE IN OUR CARE!

Our Creator has imbued us with his Awesome Power, and we use this Power to bring **LOST SHEEP** back to the flock through ministry, weekly services, volunteer work, and prayer.

For truly **LOST SHEEP**, we provide intensive workshops, courses, and overnight retreats.

We will not stop until every **LOST SHEEP** has returned to the righteous path set forth by our Creator. It is the only way to keep our community Pure!

KNOW A LOST SHEEP?

We can help.

Some **LOST SHEEP** may be hesitant to return to the flock after being away for so long. Some may even be resistant. The temptations of sin are strong. When someone has been living in sin for a long time, they become comfortable with their sin and filth.

Some **LOST SHEEP** have been lost for so long that they don't realize the errors of their ways. They don't know what they are missing by ignoring and turning away from the Creator, who provides Love and Truth through the New Creationist community.

Call our anonymous hotline or report any **LOST SHEEP** to one of our Noble Shepherds during our services. They are stationed around the sanctuary wearing a golden shepherd's crook pin over their hearts. Their mission is to find any **LOST SHEEP** and lead them back to the flock!

HELP KEEP OUR COMMUNITY PURE!

HELP SAVE SOULS FROM THE FIRES OF HELL!

At the bottom of the pamphlet was the church's address and the hotline number. Bile seared the back of her throat. Ruth was certainly a *lost sheep*.

She and Abigail had received pamphlets from the New Creationists before, and they'd even read some of them, marveling at their ignorance and crazy prophecies, at their dumb sales pitches. What could they say to convince Ruth and Abigail, two heathens in love, to repent and join their ranks? They had to laugh.

But this one was different. The words seemed sinister, somehow, and not just because she was trapped in their store, not just because they *needed her alive*. There was something between the lines that she couldn't quite grasp: a hidden code embedded in the text, like a curse or spell, like she merely needed to cross out every other letter to reveal the *real* message. But Ruth couldn't imagine this group believing in that type of thing. Hidden codes? Witchcraft? But wasn't prayer just that—a wish, a spell, an ask made to a more powerful force? Was prayer really all that different from witchy intentions? From stuffing things into a jar and burying it in someone's yard to curse them?

Like that *thing* that had been in Glue Man's pocket. It sat next to her on the shelf, the glass edges glinting, catching light from some unknown source. The dark liquid settled inside, soaking against the wax-sealed cork. It creeped her out. She almost couldn't stand to look at it.

There was one phrase in the pamphlet that she understood: the Noble Shepherds with the "golden shepherd's crook pin over their hearts." Each of the men hunting her bore that pin, the little golden hook on their aprons. So they weren't Mustard Seeds. They were Noble Shepherds, here to herd the black sheep to Salvation under the Creator. But what did they do with *Lost Sheep* who still refused to join the flock? If only she could parse the text beyond the unsettling feeling that had lodged itself deep and heavy in her stomach. A headache bloomed behind Ruth's eyes as she tried to put all the pieces together.

Next to the vial sat the headset. She'd nearly forgotten that she'd taken it in her low-glucose haze. Maybe they'd spill something there, something other than blood, thinking their words private. Ruth slipped the earpiece around her head, the smooth plastic hook nestling in the spot where her ear met her neck. The cord dangled along her side, a little node where the microphone sat about a foot down. She plugged it into the cracked receiver, a too-familiar gesture, hoping it still worked. She hated the way the headset felt, her skin sweating beneath it, the weight of it pulling her head down to her shoulder.

The channel they had always used when she worked here was channel 7, the supposed holy number. Never 6. She hoped that had not changed.

Ruth switched it on, her own breath echoing back to her. Panicked, her fingers automatically found the button that toggled the mic on and off, her muscle memory intact, but the button didn't *click* like it should have. It was jammed, permanently turned *on*. On instinct, Ruth shut the whole thing off, hoping she'd been quiet enough that no one else had heard her breathing.

After a moment, the spike of panic subsiding, she registered that she had not heard any other voices on the other end. Ruth examined the receiver, the brick of plastic with an antenna on top—this was bent at an odd angle, courtesy of Glue Man. Next to the antenna was the little knob that controlled the channel input, the white pimple on its face pointed to channel 5. She breathed a sigh of relief. They hadn't heard her. She turned the little knob to 7, took a deep breath, and powered it back on, her fingers loosely curled around the microphone to intercept any sound.

"—is he?" The voice bounced through the earpiece, terse and taut, as if the speaker was furious. As if he was not accustomed to not getting his way.

She waited, taking only short, silent breaths when necessary, sinking deeper into her hiding spot. Whatever question had been asked, no one seemed to possess an answer—or wanted to give an answer unless they were absolutely sure it was correct.

"Where is she?" the man hissed, cutting through the static. "She can't have just disappeared! She has nowhere to go! She's somewhere in the store. We are men of the Creator; she cannot evade us!" There was a hint of recognition for Ruth in this booming voice. Had she heard it somewhere before?

"Elijah, where are you?" the voice demanded.

The staticky hiss returned. Nobody responded. Elijah must be Glue Man, suffocating alone among the broken ceramics. So they hadn't found him yet. Ruth tried to remember if he'd radioed in her location once he found her—if he had, they'd know where she was last, and her hidey-hole was only a row over. But she couldn't risk moving now. They seemed to have been waiting for Glue Man to respond for quite a while—they must have been extra confident in him.

She held her breath, too vigilant of the live mic broadcasting her every noise. They had to let something slip eventually.

"Elijah, report your location," another voice said, laden with fear. "Do you have her?"

Again, silence. The muffled moans she'd heard from his aisle had stopped minutes ago. Glue Man, or Elijah, was dead.

"Do you think she got Stev—Elijah, too?" asked a third voice, one that squeaked with youth.

"Quiet yourself," said yet another voice, this one distant, as if the young voice continued to depress the microphone button, a newbie who hadn't yet learned radio etiquette or was too stupid to work the three mechanisms of the device.

"Someone find her!" the first voice yelled. "Send everyone out to find her—everyone but Ezra and Silas. You two are in charge of retrieving my daughter. Go now."

"Yes, Gideon," they replied.

"The clock is ticking!" The booming voice—*Gideon*—became grave. "We need to initiate Elizabeth as soon as possible and complete the ritual before midnight."

Wait. What the fuck?

Ritual?

She must have misheard. It seemed too ridiculous. A ritual? For what?

Swallowing her gasp, the shock wedging in her throat like a rock, Ruth honed all of her focus to her right ear, her own face growing as purple as Glue Man's from holding her breath. More static pulsed through the radio, no one daring to reply without a response that Gideon wanted to hear.

Say it again, she thought.

"You all know the consequences if we don't complete the ritual," Gideon screeched, angry and desperate now. Where had she heard his voice before? The tones felt familiar, but Ruth didn't know anyone by that name.

Finally, someone responded. "We've sent out men to every corner, but we don't see her. We're spread too thin. The store's too big. It's too dark."

"Keep looking," Gideon said.

"We couldn't have known she'd be this difficult to wrangle," someone replied. "Ahitophel didn't warn us. We thought she would be docile, one of those who wants to please everyone, despite their sinful ways. One of those who wants to prove that they are nice and worthwhile."

Ruth sucked in air as quietly as she could. They were getting off track. *Go back to this ritual*, she thought. Part of her didn't want to know any further details, wanted to remain buried in ignorance, but another part was desperate to know—*needed* to know what the fuck they wanted to do to her.

"You all know what's at stake," Gideon said, his voice dripping with daggers. "*It* must be kept contained. If we don't maintain the seal, it will be released. If it escapes, it will deliver the world to hell."

She nearly giggled at that, her delirium reaching its peak. It was too cartoonish—or it would be, if it didn't mean her death. What were they trying to contain?

"She's still in the store," another voice said, cutting through the static. "The front is still secure, and we'd know if she'd gotten through the back door."

"How hard can it be to find one person in an empty store?" Gideon said, practically growling at their ineptitude. "Where could she possibly be hiding?"

"She's already killed one of our brothers, possibly two," the young voice replied, overflowing with hesitation and fear.

"Then those were not worthy," a commanding, elder voice said. It boomed through the static. "Those were not devoted to our cause. They were not ardent about absolving the sins of this poor girl and humanity and themselves. If they were True and righteous, the Creator would have Imbued them with the power to overcome her sins, whether through force or persuasion. Their superior sacraments—the Imbuements—would have held."

The silence crept back in, the constant buzzing static worming its way into her ear canal. Ruth continued to hold her breath, anxious that the Noble Shepherds roaming the store would somehow be able to triangulate which shelf she was nestled into by a single staticky exhale—would snake their golden staffs down the aisle and hook them around her neck.

"Are you Right with Him?" the elder voice continued. "Do you place all of your trust in Him?"

Ruth wasn't sure whether he meant the Creator or the group's ringleader. More silence came in reply, a tense collective hesitation.

"If the answer is no, then you *should* have cause for fear." The elder's voice poured through the receiver, clear as the water of Hell for Certain. "But if you truly trust in Him, and in yourself, and in our mission, then you should not fear, for He will instruct you, and He will protect you. So long as you are Pure and True, He will Imbue you with His great power. So, do you trust in Him?"

"Yes" came a multivoiced reply, a chorus.

"Good," the elder said. "Good. Now let us go forth, ye noble shepherds, and retrieve our soiled flock, our wandering black sheep who has strayed from His light. Bring her to our sacred place, and we will instruct. But do not let your devotion overtake your judgment. The sacrifice needs to be alive."

Ruth snapped the radio off, slicing her teeth into her tongue until she tasted coppery blood, trying to halt the scream wriggling its way up her esophagus. Who the fuck were these people? What the fuck had she stumbled into? They still hadn't given her many useful clues about the ritual they needed to perform, but Ruth—the straying, sinning sheep—would not survive it. They needed her alive, apparently, to begin the ritual, but that squirmy little word—*sacrifice*—told her it would not end that way.

Fuck. Her chest constricted. How was she supposed to win here? The only exit was the back door, and they said they were monitoring it. She didn't believe in their bullshit powers, their supposed imbued strength from the Creator or whatever the fuck. But she did believe in the power of suggestion, and these people, these Noble Shepherds hunting her, believed in it. And they were getting more desperate as the clock ticked toward the deadline. She could hear it in their voices, strung through even the tones of the elder who spoke with such confidence and assurance.

They needed her in order to contain *it*, whatever that was.

They needed to complete this ritual in order to cleanse themselves or her or the earth or all of the above of sin. But what was the other piece? The part about releasing something? More sin into the world? No, that would be solved by killing her. They'd said *it* would deliver them to hell.

Whatever *it* was, they fervently believed in it. And believed it was worth containing, at all costs. They were willing to risk their own lives over it—or believed they were invincible so long as they were right with their Creator. *Go ahead and think yourself invincible*, she thought. *Underestimate me.*

If they became truly desperate—any more desperate than they already were—she was sure they'd do everything they could short of killing her on the spot. They needed her alive, but nothing gave her the impression she had to be unharmed. They'd leave just enough consciousness, just enough blood still pulsing through her veins. They'd catch her, perform their ritual, and she'd be gone. The only person who'd notice Ruth was missing was Abigail. And what could Abigail do about it? Go to the tiny police department, which had too few resources to mount any kind of search? Whose officers were all members of the very same church that had disappeared her? That was probably why they picked Ruth to be their *sacrifice*—because almost nobody would even realize she was gone.

Fuck. Ruth smacked her head against the back of the shelf, sending rippling waves of pain through her scalp and down into her neck and shoulders. She toyed with turning the headset on again. Maybe they'd reveal crucial information, or some hole or flaw in their plans. They'd probably just continue to talk around it, their mouths full of bigotry and empty nonsense. Besides, she wasn't sure she was ready to know more about their plans, lest the screams trapped behind her teeth release themselves.

Ruth closed her eyes, just for a moment. She was so tired. Her pulse thudded against the hardened glue on her scalp, on her palm. She had no more little red bags to save her if her blood sugar tanked again, and anything sugary in the store was in the wrong direction. The exit seemed so far away. And even if she managed to get that far—

For a brief moment, she considered killing herself before they got the chance. She'd be dead at the end of all of this anyway, right? Something inside her, something wormy and soft, felt sure of that. So why not beat them to the punch? Why not ruin their ritual and make them losers by default if the end result—for her—would be the same either way?

She lifted her head and dropped it back against the shelf again, heedless of the sound it made, more waves of pain rolling through her.

No. They'd still win if she did that. To them, the world would still have one less sinner. They might even find some new victim to take her place.

She thumped her gashed scalp against the rough shelf once more. And again. And again. She wasn't worried in this moment about being discovered. She needed the pain to consume her and the spiraling, suicidal thoughts. She needed the pain to erase all other thoughts besides those of Abigail. Abigail, who had nobody but her. Abigail, who loved her. Abigail, who needed her as much as she needed Abigail.

Ruth might not be able to craft a plan with all the variables at play, but she would not let them win by taking her own life. She'd save that escape hatch until the very, very end. A final Hail Mary, the rosary beads closing around her neck like a noose.

She knew the store like the back of her hand. There was something she could use in nearly every aisle, something not as obvious as a blade, but just as deadly, just as sharp or bludgeoning or bone-cracking. Surrounding her were pans to smash skulls, hooks to gouge eyes, rolling pins to crack and shatter bone. And this time, she'd kill, if she had to. Fuck 'em. So what if that made her the sinner they thought she was? She could be a sinner if it meant she was a survivor, too.

She would get out. She would fight as hard as hell to do so.

But to get out, she first had to get up.

Chapter 12

Moving her own bones was a herculean effort. The moment Ruth began to stir from her cozy cubby was the same moment that footsteps sounded against the concrete floor. Two men haunted the end of the aisle like ghouls, walking in tandem, their silhouettes appearing in the gap, chatting and strolling as if it were an ordinary Saturday evening perusing the aisles, wondering what color they should make their next scarf.

They barely glanced down the aisle containing her hiding place. Were they blasé about the whole affair, or were they extra confident that their Almighty Creator would lead them to her, like some weird, celestial compass? Carefully, silent as a whisper, she slid a twelve-inch cast iron pan off a hook on the shelf—just in case they truly possessed godly tracking skills. Holding the pan like a shield, Ruth perked her ears, trying to arrange the muffled syllables into words and sentences. But she could only hear the suggestion of words among their hushed tones, nothing more.

Then, louder, the lurking pair made twin squeaking noises

of surprise. They must have discovered Glue Man in the aisle behind her. The earpiece still attached to her head, she clicked the headset back on.

"Elijah is gone," one of them said—the one with the youthful voice. The one who hadn't learned his manners yet.

A sigh hissed through the earpiece, laced with annoyance. "That's a shame," Gideon said. "He must not have been True. I've always had my doubts about him."

"But didn't he do all those missions?" the young man asked in a quavering voice. "He was the one who went and spied on them, right? Getting intel and confirming her sins, learning their schedules and patterns. Looking in their windows with binoculars and—"

"He did, yes," Gideon said, cutting him off. "But did he do that because he believed in our mission, or did he do that for his own glory and praise? His motivation must have been corrupt."

A burst of static bloomed and then extinguished. From her spot in the shelves, Ruth could hear hushed, chiding tones—whoever was with the younger man must have covered his mic, told him to bite his tongue with the leader. Silence hung on the line, and Ruth's eyes jumped up, scanning the aisle, worried that meant they'd found her.

Then the chiding voice came through the headset, the same elder that had spoken with such confidence previously. "What would you like us to do with him, Gideon?" he asked.

Gideon seemed annoyed—like he couldn't be bothered with the task of directing the removal of such an inconvenience, this hulking corpse. Glue Man was no longer useful to him. No longer worthy, not to him, and not to their Creator.

"Bring him back and put him with the other," he finally said. "We'll deal with the bodies after we've completed the ritual. Once we've sealed the demon in, we can dispose of them."

Ruth smacked her hand over her mouth to contain the scream bubbling up from her guts. It sat right behind her clenched teeth, begging for escape, an expanding balloon threatening to give her spot away. The harsh glue along her palm dug into her lips.

A *demon*?

What the *fuck*?

"Thank you for your guidance," the elder man said—so matter-of-fact, so disturbingly nonchalant, like Gideon had told him to add oranges to the grocery list.

Ruth clicked off the headset. She couldn't risk any noise snaking through the live mic. She swallowed her shriek. How could they be so calm when faced with two bodies of their comrades? And a *demon*? Maybe she'd misheard him. Maybe it was an acronym for something. Maybe it was metaphorical, like Satan, a symbol of all the evil and sin in the world. Ruth's childhood church had been fuzzy on whether Satan and his minions, or demons, were real or figurative, but either way, they were supposed to be confined to hell—not something that needed to be *contained*. Whatever demon these Shepherds had mentioned must be like that. Something that sounded scary, but wasn't actually real. *Right?* They couldn't really believe in a demon. There was no way they actually meant a literal, fire-and-brimstone, fallen-angel *demon*.

Ruth's belief in Satan—metaphorical or otherwise—and

his benevolent twin anagram, Santa, waned as she got older and she questioned all the things the church taught would send her to hell. Things she didn't see anything wrong with, or couldn't understand how they were so bad you'd be tortured forever for it, like being gay, for example, or watching horror movies, or getting a tattoo.

Not to mention that the whole thing seemed backward to Ruth—too sharp, even as a child, to beguile; wouldn't Satan praise sinners, welcome them with open arms like their Creator did for believers? Why would he torture them for doing the things he *wanted* them to do? These thoughts only intensified, the spark spreading into a wildfire, as she battled internally with her attraction to women. The church claimed it was sinful, a one-way ticket to hell, but she had never been given a satisfactory answer as to why. But, in the end, her parents sided with the New Creationists, not willing to risk their spot at the pearly gates even for their own daughter. They truly believed she was damned to burn.

It was bullshit. Satan didn't exist. *Demons* didn't exist.

But these were righteous, Noble Shepherds, Imbued with the Awesome Power of the Creator. They probably did, *truly*, *purely*, believe there was an actual, real-life demon to be contained. Their faith informed them that there really was a fallen angel whose skin had turned bright red like a waxy apple and who had sprouted terrible, glistening horns from either side of his forehead. They really believed he was down there, in hell, for certain, reveling in his defiance of their Creator, burning sinners eternally in hellfire and lava. They believed in hell as much as they believed in heaven.

Ruth wanted to scream. She might have laughed if her own life weren't at stake. Over a *demon*. It was all so ludicrous.

Now, the pair of Shepherds appeared again at the end of the aisle. They continued their conversation, too quietly for Ruth to hear, dragging Glue Man's body by his feet. One was a very young kid—maybe seventeen or eighteen if she had to guess—and the other was much older, his face lined with nooks and crannies.

When Glue Man's body came into view, it was so unrecognizable that Ruth wondered for a moment if it was the body of an entirely different person. How was it possible that he looked *smaller*, more in proportion to an average man? When she'd first seen his hulking form in the aisle, hadn't his shoulders appeared to span the entire width, grazing the shelves? Hadn't the muscles of his bulky arms spanned the entire length of her torso when he wrapped them around her?

But now it was as though his body had deflated, as if he had shriveled back down to the size of a normal human man. No longer did coils of muscle balloon beneath his skin, which sagged like loose fabric draped over a skeleton. His hands remained adhered to his face, obscuring his nose and mouth. He'd managed to pry his fingertips loose, the bottom of his eyelids peeled away with them, the glue more powerful than his own skin. The effect gave the impression that his eyes were bulging from his head, one obscured by a marble of glue, both scleras engraved with deep red capillaries.

Ruth almost expected his pupils to move, to shift and lock onto her own, and for his purple mouth to make a muffled, gagged noise to alert the pair to her location. But no part of him moved beyond his flaps of skin slithering across the floor. His skin was purple and blue, a twinge of green tendriling in.

Ruth wondered where his soul had ended up. Was Gideon right? Was Glue Man roasting in hell because he had not been True or Worthy enough? Had his failure meant sin, and sin meant hell? Or was he being welcomed at the Pearly Gates to a reward of everlasting pleasure?

Or was he just a dead slab of meat, ready for dirt?

The pair talked gravely, dragging their friend toward the back of the store. Scraps of their conversation bounded toward her, but Ruth still couldn't catch everything, especially beneath the scraping noise Glue Man's body made against the uneven floors, his skull clacking and bouncing. The words *demon* and *vessel* floated to her ears—the elder's voice. He must be explaining things to the younger one, she thought. Her ears caught a few words that she wished they hadn't: *flesh, sinner.*

Then the pair moved past the edge of the aisle, and their conversation became completely unintelligible. Only Glue Man's upside-down body greeted her in the gap, the peeled eyelids like Halloween makeup. His glassy eyes stared at the ceiling, unmoving even as his head bobbled and bumped across the floor.

She had to know what they were saying. She needed to know what these people actually believed. Maybe there was some loophole she could offer them, some other avenue to achieve their goal without needing her to take part as sacrifice. Still clutching the cast iron pan, she clipped the receiver onto her waistband and unfolded herself from her hiding spot.

Her tongue scratched in her mouth like sandpaper. She

wished she had something to drink—her blood sugar must be spiking after the Skittles. Not ideal, but better than being too low. Every movement of her tongue inside her jaw ricocheted through her skull, but at least she wasn't worried about passing out and leaving herself for dead.

Ruth was constantly battling her blood sugar, especially when funds ran low and she had to ration her insulin—then her blood sugar would hover too high, and she'd drop weight rapidly. She'd become an expert at dosing, at rationing, at knowing the smallest amount she could inject without going into ketoacidosis and having to trek to the ER. High blood sugar wouldn't kill her—at least not *imminently*, not like the lows. She lived by the adage, the phrase drilled into her head by every doctor since diagnosis: better to be high than low. But sometimes she pushed it too far, even if out of necessity.

Now, her mouth gummy and dry, everything felt foggy and blurred at the edges, a general feeling of nausea bubbling inside her. She still wasn't sure how long she'd been in the store, all markers of time hidden inside the enclosed warehouse. She unpeeled herself from the shelves, shouldering her bag, and tiptoed to the end of the aisle, pressing herself flush against the shelf.

The Shepherds were immersed in their conversation, paying attention to nothing but themselves and hauling Glue Man, who continued his staring match with the ceiling. His head bounced over a particularly large crater in the concrete, twisting his neck. His skull landed at just the right angle for his glassy eyes to stare right at her, his hands pulling his lids down to see her better.

"Are we really going to—" the younger one asked, his sentence chopped in half from exertion, a grunt filling in the back end.

Going to what? Ruth wondered. She edged closer to the endcap.

Their voices grew quieter, their footsteps farther and farther away as Glue Man vanished, too, inch by inch, now only his wobbling head in view. She didn't dare to poke her head around the corner. She couldn't take the chance that they'd see her.

There was a part of Ruth, a part she didn't want to acknowledge, a part she actively suppressed, swallowing it like a stone, that already knew what their plans were—what the ritual entailed. A part that had gleaned enough glimpses, enough little puzzle pieces to put it together. But she buried that little nagging voice. She didn't want to believe it was true—that that were *really going to—*

Then Glue Man's head stopped its procession out of view, his apron caught on a broken notch in the concrete. With one sharp yank, the pair pulled his body free, the crazed movement bouncing his skull against the concrete hard enough for it to crack, for a dark, syrupy liquid to spill away. Ruth dropped the pan as she covered her own face with a hand, the falling iron ripping the glue bandage away.

Chapter 13

The oversized pan crashed into the bottom shelf, into other dangling cast iron wares, knocking them from their pegs. Smashing and clattering to the floor in a cacophonous rumble, the heavy objects—oversized hooks and drawer pulls, decorative iron wall hangings, trivets, pans increasing in size from left to right—cracked the thin linoleum squares glued to this part of the concrete floor.

Shit.

No time to peek around the corner, Ruth darted down the aisle, her eyes scanning the shelves for a more lightweight weapon, hesitating at the end, afraid to venture beyond the endcap to the open walkway.

Then she realized where she was.

This was the spot where the brilliant owners had shoved two shelves against a support pillar, leaving a little gap between the beam and the shelves: another Ruth-sized hole.

When she'd worked there, she'd once tried to fetch a box from the top of these aisles. She hadn't been able to find the proper rolling stairs, and had to use a standard tall stepstool instead, a bedazzled thing from an odd new glam kitchen line. When she tried to pinch the edge of the cardboard box between her fingers, she ended up pushing it in the wrong direction, enough to nudge whatever box had been shoved behind it out of place. It fell straight down into the gap with a plop.

The store never truly performed an inventory check; if she walked away, Schrödinger's box would collect dust for all time in that gap. Eventually whatever it contained would sell out, and they'd scour the whole store for the replacement box, finally giving up the hunt to order more. If another Mustard Seed hadn't spotted her, she might have left the box in its dusty grave.

At some point in time, this must have occurred with enough frequency that someone carved out a rectangle from the bottom of the endcap to access this small cavity.

Of course that was the fix. Five minutes of one employee's time, and at no cost to the owners. They couldn't even expense a few pieces of plywood to lay across the top of the aisles, covering the gap. Instead, Ruth had to reach her arms through the ragged hole to wrangle a box that had lodged itself into the tiny space between the shelves.

Now, Ruth crouched down in front of the endcap; it was just as she remembered. Two cheap hinges were screwed on the left side of a makeshift plywood door, and a hook-and-eye closure held it shut on the right. It had not been created to accommodate a human body. But Ruth was small enough to fit. Ironic, she thought, that the owners' tight-fistedness would for once be to her advantage.

Ruth pushed the picture frames lining the bottom shelf gently out of the way and unhooked the loop from the eye. The plywood door opened inward. A metal shelf bisected the doorway, cutting her clearance in half. But she could still wiggle in. She had no other choice.

The noise of footsteps had reached the scene of the crime, crunching and clanging across the wreckage, the aisle now strewn with cast iron and destroyed tiles.

"How is it possible that she could have killed Elijah?" the younger voice asked. "I thought he had been Imbued."

"He had, my child," the elder replied, "but even that is not foolproof if one is not True. To remain Imbued, one must also keep the object of Imbuement on his person at all times. If he loses it, or if the object were to break, then the Imbuement will dissipate."

"The spell won't work?"

The elder's voice scoffed. "It's not a *spell*," he said, spitting fire. As if magic were blasphemous but it was hunky-dory if it were simply relabeled.

"Sorry, Solomon," the kid replied.

"Say your penance."

"*O Lord, wash my soul from every stain, do not let the guilt I mourn—*"

"Remain," Solomon guided.

"*Remain. Here in my flesh the burden lies, and my offenses pain my eyes. But thy love shall—*"

"Inspire my . . ."

"*Inspire my tongue. Salvation shall be my song. And every power shall join to bless the Creator, my strength and righteousness.*"

Ruth had only a minute before they would reach her, having climbed over the cast iron mountains. They didn't seem to care if she heard them coming; perhaps they thought they were *Imbued* with the power of silence or stealth. Or maybe it was simple arrogance.

Pushing the little door inward, she scrambled in. Rough strips of cardboard and scraps of paper littered the sticky floor, this space never cleaned or even accessed unless someone dropped a box. Little pebbles of debris stuck to the gummy blood on her palm, her sleeve sliding away as she wrestled her way inside, the loose fabric of her sweatshirt catching on the rough sides of the opening. After she slipped her arms inside, she twisted her torso through, and finally pulled her legs in after her, contorting them until she stood upright.

Darkness pervaded the tiny space. At any moment, the pair could round the corner and see the door open. Ruth curled back down to rearrange the little frames on the bottom shelf as best she could before closing the door. She couldn't repierce the hook into the eye from the inside, and the plywood door canted inward, as if to scream, *She's in here!*

She could try to hold it closed, but any slight movement would give her away, could make the hinges creak or groan. Ruth stuffed her hand into her tote bag, feeling around for anything useful to pin it shut. Her fingers grazed the small wire clippers, the ones she'd grabbed in haste before realizing they'd be useless against burly Noble Shepherds. Leaning sideways in the narrow gap, she stabbed the sharp ends of the wire cutters into the soft plywood, pinning the door to the frame, two little biting teeth that held.

The space between the shelving units contained no room to turn around and barely enough space to expand her lungs. Now upright, she could only shuffle a few inches side to side, like a crab. Ruth felt like a beetle on display, its legs and arms pinned forever in one spot. Any large movement could rattle the shelves and shift them just enough to make things shiver off the hooks on the other side, frames or mirrors crashing to the floor, revealing her hiding spot, transforming it into a trap.

Fuck. Had she doomed herself? How was she supposed to get out of here? She couldn't see anything outside of the confines of her tomb.

The pair circled the aisles on either side of her. They whispered to each other, a constant murmur. She couldn't make out what, exactly, they were saying, but they made just enough noise that she could triangulate their location.

Ruth pressed her weeping hand against her chest, trying to put pressure on it, and rediscovered the hard little pebbles coating her bloodied palm. She thought they might be bugs, little bits of roaches, perhaps—this wouldn't have surprised her at all. New Creations had never shelled out for pest control. Ownership never dealt with the root of the issue; they merely found the cheapest possible solution, which was a can of roach spray in the cleaning closet. But the pebbles were hard and perfectly round. Sprinkles?

I guess some unlucky fuck dropped a box of sprinkles down here, she thought. Maybe she could even eat them, if worse came to worst. She shuddered at the thought.

The pair of Shepherds circled like vultures, like they could smell the blood trickling from her palm or the stink of her supposed sin but couldn't quite pinpoint the source. Like they were Imbued with geolocation. While she clutched her ruined hand to her chest, her breath shallow, she snatched only small snippets of their conversation.

Something about a *meal.* Something about *mortal sin.* Something about *sacrifice.* Something about all those things put together.

There was something about a *daughter* sprinkled in there too, something that Ruth couldn't fit together with everything else. Maybe the older one—Solomon—was describing his own daughter, safe at home, glad that she would be raised in their ranks, raised *correctly.* Not allowed to become a sinner like Ruth.

She toyed with turning the headset on. Before she could move her hand to her hip, her fingers not needing light to find the knobs, the two Shepherds halted, planting themselves, to Ruth's horror, just beyond the endcap with the little door. Now she really was trapped.

"We haven't seen her, sir," Solomon said into the headpiece. "She should be right here, but we can't seem to locate her. We heard the clatter and dropped Elijah, followed the noise. It *feels* like the right place, but we haven't spotted her. We've been circling these aisles for a while now. She must have slipped away somewhere else—maybe she dropped one of her things nearby."

A pause, a gap in which a reply would have come. Ruth wished she could listen. Was Gideon angry? Was he disappointed? She hoped he was fuming. She hoped he was losing patience, biting his fingernails to the quick, the cuticles sprouting blood. She hoped the fucking demon would come out early and escort him all the way to hell.

"Okay, sir," Solomon replied. "We'll stay posted here while the others comb the store in case she pops up. She feels near."

Fuck. It felt like the shelving was closing in on her, inching closer and closer until it would squish her, pulverize her bones and squeeze her juicy innards out like a tube of paint. She inhaled slowly, biting her lip to keep from screaming.

Maybe they really are Imbued with some sort of tracking ability, Ruth thought. They'd landed right where she was, as if they had some sense, some intuition that she was *there*, even if they couldn't see her. That weird thing, the little vial she'd taken from Glue Man—was that one of these objects Solomon had mentioned? Would it *Imbue* her with some sort of power? Could she use it against them somehow? It was buried deep inside her tote bag now.

No, that's stupid, Ruth thought, shaking the delusion away. *That's not possible.*

If it were, wouldn't the magical vial make her muscles balloon to the point of exaggeration, like Glue Man's seemingly had? To the point of suffocating her, trapped in this tiny corridor? She didn't notice any changes—no tautness against the baggy fabric of her sweatshirt, no swelling of her pectorals. But maybe it took time. Maybe the vial had to be closer, touching her skin.

Ruth didn't want to believe in whatever magic the Shepherds believed they had—but it was yet another thing her gut and her mind disagreed on.

The man and the boy didn't seem to know about the gap

between the shelves, confirming her suspicion that most of the Shepherds—excluding her former boss—weren't actually employees, just Shepherds wearing Mustard Seed clothing. How could they not know the ins and outs of their own store? Surely they weren't stupid enough to believe that she was still fooled by them. So why were they all still wearing the aprons? It seemed more like the uniform of a cult.

A *cult.*

It was the first time she'd actually conjured that word. And it fit.

There had been signs, even from the beginning. Charlie's odd fervor after meetings with the church leadership, the sudden zeal in her once apathetically faithful parents. How had she not noticed the strangeness, the overabundance of righteousness in the sermon she'd heard the one time Charlie had taken her to a service?

"What time is it anyway?" the young man asked, now close enough that every word was clear as a bell. "How fu—how damned are we?"

A rustling sound followed. Ruth pictured the older man digging out an ancient pocket watch. "Patience, Travis. We still have a few hours left until the blood moon crests in the night sky."

"Should we be worried?" Travis asked. "Shouldn't we have caught her by now?"

"We would have, if the others had been True and Right," Solomon replied, parroting the nonsense Gideon had spewed. "Otherwise," he continued, "she wouldn't have been able to best them. If they were True and Right, they would have not only been Imbued from their relics, but from the Creator Himself, and nothing can defeat the Almighty."

A pause followed this pithy speech. Ruth imagined the younger man wrinkling his face in confusion, trying to work out the meaning of all those pious buzzwords.

"I'm kind of scared," Travis said finally. His voice squeaked on the last word. He must be even younger than Ruth had imagined, perhaps just leaving puberty, just having graduated high school. That age when you thought you knew everything, but you really knew absolutely nothing. Ruth couldn't imagine sending out a teenager, a *child*, to hunt another human being.

Her heartstrings pulled taut, some deep scrap of empathy for this kid she didn't know she could still possess for any of the Shepherds. Her stomach roiled, the acid churning up the small packet of Skittles, the little candies jumping like popcorn.

How had he found himself here, inside an empty, locked craft store, hauling the dead bodies of his fellow cult members and hunting a woman? Was he raised in this cult? Had he been brainwashed into joining? Had he found himself in some hopeless predicament, some low place that they took advantage of, the church swooping in to offer food and shelter and promises of love? Wasn't that the best way to lure someone into your cult? To give them what they needed and promise them more?

Or perhaps they'd shown him something wondrous—or at least the illusion of something. That was how they'd captured Charlie—he'd come home from a church meeting one night raving about something they'd shown him. He wouldn't say what, exactly, it was. He'd seemed feverish, fervent in a way she'd never seen him before, pacing frantically around the room.

"I've witnessed the miracles and powers of the Creator," he had said. He held her hands in his, and his skin seemed to buzz with a crazed electricity that lit up his wide eyes. For a moment, she thought she could see little golden arcs between each of his eyelashes.

"I have seen wonders and miracles that you could not imagine," he continued. "I can't wait until we are married so that I can share them with you."

"Was it something at the church?" Ruth asked, confused. "Like a new initiative they're doing or something?"

"I can't say more right now," he said. He released her hands and continued pacing, a fierce burning behind his eyes. "But there are things great and powerful in this world, things we have been blessed to possess from the goodness of the Creator, who has shown us His love and truth."

"What are you talking about?"

"All will be revealed later, my love," he said. "Once we are married, I will happily share with you the wonders I have seen. But we must be joined in holy union, for only the True and faithful may know their power."

Something unsettled bubbled in Ruth's stomach. He'd always been religious and traditional, but he'd never acted like this, had never spouted holy-sounding buzzwords at her or been so zealous that he wore holes in the floor from his energized love for his Creator. What had he seen?

Now, stuck inside her Ruth-sized hole, she wondered—had

he seen these *Imbuements*?

"Don't be scared," Solomon said to Travis. In Ruth's mind, he placed his wrinkled hand on the young boy's shoulder. "Do you have faith?"

"Yes," the boy said, barely audible through the thin layer of plywood that separated them.

"Are you True? Have you remained without sin since your last Cleansing?"

"Yes," Travis replied, a bit louder. A little more confident.

"Then what reason do you have to be scared?" Here, Ruth pictured a gentle smile plastered on the old man's face, his ancient yellow teeth poking through the gap in his cracked lips, a reassurance that the boy would be fine, that everything would work out.

"Well, she killed others," Travis said hesitantly.

"'Be not afraid of them that kill the body; after, they have no more that they can do,'" Solomon quoted. "'Who you shall fear is the Creator, which after He hath killed, hath power to cast into hell.'"

"But the others were Noble Shepherds much longer than me," Travis pressed. "Surely, they were True and Right? At least more so than me. And they're still dead."

The elder chuckled.

"I know how you see us, as Wise Elders," he said, "those of us who have been here long enough to have many children and positions of power and badges of honor. I'm sure to you, we seem infallible and perfect. But we are still only human. All humans are tempted by sin, especially now, when sin is so widely accepted in the world. This is why we have the cleansings; it's important for you to never miss a cleansing, even if you feel that you have not sinned."

"Yes, sir," the younger boy said.

Ruth wanted to burst out of her hiding spot and scream at the boy to flee. To escape along with her, assuring him that he didn't need to be part of this cult to be happy. To be loved and accepted. But she knew that if she wanted to escape, she would not be able to save this kid. She would not have the choice. It was going to be her or him—there would not be time to save him, to dismantle all the fallacies they'd convinced him were truths. She hated that realization. It felt like one innocent bystander being exchanged for another.

"Everywhere we go, whether we're on missionary trips or going to the grocery store—even in the sanctuary of the Church, on days when we invite in the general public, sin is pervasive," the elder continued. "It's emblazoned on T-shirts. It's printed on advertisements, bumper stickers, billboards. When you go to spread the Word, people will open their doors, and their televisions will scream sinful words and images at you. It's nearly impossible to avoid unless you never leave the comfort of others within our ranks. But there's the rub—if we are to follow our Creator's guidance and spread his Word, then we have to go out among the sinners. We have to go out into their world that is full of evil and temptation. And the more you see these sinful things, the more tempting they are—the more the woeful human part of you wants to sin and join in on the fun. That's how the devil works. He tempts you. He makes sin seem like a good time. Sin is easy. Being True is not."

Ruth ground her teeth. She'd heard this exact line of thinking from the New Creationists before, from the pastor in the sermon she'd heard. From her own parents after they'd joined. If you gave in to temptation—and *temptation* was usually just a normal, fun thing to do, or something you couldn't help—you'd go to hell unless you repented. "You let the devil inside you," her mother had said to her after her failed engagement, after she'd been brave enough to come out to her parents, thinking their love for her would be unconditional. "You let him take hold of your heart, and what's worse is that you don't even care. You revel in it. The diabetes should have been our clue. We won't let the devil reside in our home. Go flaunt your sin somewhere else."

Ruth had barely been eighteen when they kicked her out. She knew how it felt to be abandoned as a young, confused kid, and wondered what might have happened to her if the person taking her in had not been Abigail's mother but instead a cult soliciting for new membership. She might have been in the exact same position as this kid, might have found herself wrapped up in something insidious and horrible, something that looked nice on the outside but was writhing with maggots once you unpeeled the thin surface.

She'd arrived on Judy's doorstep with less than a suitcase of clothing. After the litany of locks were undone, Judy only had needed to see Ruth's bloodshot eyes to embrace her into a hug and pull her inside. She'd slept on the couch and awoke the next day to a second mattress in Abigail's room. Judy hadn't asked any questions. She simply opened her arms.

Solomon got to the point. "As a new pledge, your tasks are all within the confines of our community," he said. "You still remember what happened when you lived sinfully. You were hungry. You were in pain. You were lonely and you didn't know why you felt all of these things. You didn't know it was because of the sin—and how could you have known? The sin felt so good in the moment, didn't it? When you joined the commune, you were no longer exposed to all of that sin. You live simply now. You are surrounded by others who strive to be True and Right. You are still eager to please the Creator and bask in all of His beautiful power. So while it may seem like years of service would bless one with wisdom, it also comes with prolonged exposure to sin, and increased temptation."

"Wanting what you can't have," the boy said.

"Precisely. The longer you have a pure heart, the harder you have to work to keep it that way. Elijah and the others who fell must have stained their hearts with sin, and sin is not always visible to others—most often, it rests in the soul, where only the Creator can see its stain."

Ruth wished she could jump out and shake sense into the young boy, tell him he'd been brainwashed to hate instead of love. Tell him that they were feeding him lies to keep him complacent. Making everyone else seem like a villain, making him crawl back to the cult like a wounded animal when the rest of the world rebuked him for the hate he was taught. But she could only keep her mouth clamped shut, her teeth slicing into her tongue.

She had now been trapped in this endcap coffin, in the same upright position, for so long that her toes had started to tingle and numb. The pair outside her little cage were deep in conversation. It seemed like they had forgotten their mission entirely, the elder so caught up in his bullshit and the younger so eager to absorb it that they'd managed to erase the ritual—and the ticking time bomb of the deadline—from their minds entirely.

As quietly as possible, Ruth lifted her foot and shook it, trying to sling blood back into her toes. Once the pins and needles receded, she lowered it again. Her toes touched down first, tingling with the pressure, and then her heel sank.

It landed on something soft.

Something that moved.

Chapter 14

The thing beneath her foot *squealed*, skittering around her ankle. She yanked her foot back, her offending shoe hovering in the air. Other dark shapes darted around her body, a whole family of them, all screeching and running in a panicked scurry.

She'd stepped into a rats' nest.

Had the rats been there the whole time, lurking in the dark? Or had her ears been so attuned to the chatter of the two cultists that she hadn't noticed them crawl into the space with her, hadn't heard the clicking of their claws against the concrete? It explained the stray, oblong sprinkles among the rainbow ones that had coated her bloody hand like a strawberry sundae—rat shit.

A rodent infestation didn't surprise her. She was more surprised there hadn't been one during the span of her employment. The rats were smarter than the owners—they'd figured out that this spot was never cleaned, never disturbed: possibly the one bit of square footage in the store where they could nest without being discovered. They could gorge on sprinkles or fondant or whatever else they could find, so long as they brought it back here.

Her hovering foot shook with exertion, the vibration rippling up through her body. The shelf wobbled, too, not stable enough even to support her weight—another cut corner, the material too cheap to hold the hundreds of cast iron fixtures dangling from it. She couldn't lean on it and risk things falling off the shelf—the cacophony would rouse the cultists from their chatter. They would eventually figure out that it wasn't a holy ghost who'd thrown the pans to the floor. For now, they were mere inches away and none the wiser. She aimed to keep it that way.

Ruth inhaled a deep gasp of air through her teeth. On the other side of the endcap, Solomon droned on and on about being True and the perils of sin—she wasn't paying attention anymore; she had to focus on her slow-motion footwork in the dark.

Every muscle in her body tensed, tendons taut as guitar strings, as she slowly lowered her foot, jerking it back up when it touched down upon something soft and squirmy. She repeated this dance two or three times, her teeth bared in a grimace, the pain in her palm forgotten, until her toe finally grazed bare concrete, her heel still hovering.

At the moment of touchdown, one rat crawled over her foot. Its claws poked through the thin fabric of her sneaker. Its naked tail swiped against her ankle, sending a shiver through her, little goose bumps blooming against her skin, the disgust enough for her to slam her heel down reflexively. She heard the crunch of tiny bones, like dry twigs snapping against mud, felt the broken, furry body twitching beneath her heel, before the squeal—no, the *scream*—the noise so loud she was sure the cultists would hear. For the rest of the rats, it was like an alarm siren, and the imminent threat threw them into a panicked frenzy.

The cluster swarmed between Ruth's ankles, over her feet, hundreds of clawing talons, an entire horde of them in a crazed stampede. They came in furry waves, in *layers*, rats climbing over each other and trampling the ones beneath them like a panic-stricken crowd trying to flee a burning building. Their claws and teeth peeled away the fibers of her shoes, digging down to her skin, trying to burrow to freedom. Before she could even react, as the madness crested, the whole pulsing mass started to crawl *up*. They coated her legs, their little claws scaling the fabric of her jeans like a ladder. They dug in their teeth with each twitch and breath. Her hand clamped over her mouth to hold back her bubbling screams, tacky, drying blood smearing across her lips.

The rats climbed her like a tree, scratching a frenzied, bloody manifesto on her skin. What felt like an unending stream of them ascended in such a frenzy to get away from the perceived danger that they bit and scraped at her, at each other, a rodent fight club on her kneecap. Each movement she made, no matter how slight, resulted in more bites, more frenzy.

Ruth's teeth clamped over her tongue, hard, tasting coppery droplets. She honed in on this taste, memorizing the metallic stickiness, trying to ignore the scurrying and lacerating her legs, trying to stay as still as possible, to not agitate the rats further. She could do nothing but stand still and let them climb.

There was no room in the cramped hole to swat or throw them off, no room to thrash or fling them away from her without tipping over the shelves. What could she do besides wait for them to—*what*? To get to her face? Her head? There was nowhere else they could go. She imagined a writhing wig of wretched rodents all clawing for the top spot, a rat king crown heavy upon her head.

A shudder vibrated down the length of her spine at the thought, the ripples causing a frightened rat to dig its teeth into her thigh. She had no choice but to endure. She could do nothing but stand as still as possible and hope they calmed down eventually, went away on their own, climbing back down the mountain of her body and back into whatever hole they had crawled out of. She bit into the torn flesh of her palm, her teeth catching on the remaining mountain caps of hardened glue. The swarm of rodents clawed at her knees now—newcomers at the bottom of the pile pressed the others upward, like a tidal swell. They bit at each other, lost in their mad panic, anything and anyone a villain. In her mind's desperation to expunge the chunks of flesh carved by angry fangs, the conversation of the two cultists slithered back into her consciousness.

Or maybe the question posed was so insane that it could not be blocked out.

"Is that really part of the ritual?" Travis asked. "Are we really going to . . . *eat* her?"

Ruth's heart stopped in her chest, the pain of the rodents biting and clawing into her flesh fading into nothing.

There almost seemed to be a twinge of excitement in the

boy's question.

"Yes, that's a major part of the ritual," the elder replied, his tone flat and matter-of-fact. Like he was providing instructions for how repair a rotten piece of flooring. "I know how it sounds. It sounds like it should go against our tenets and teachings, and if you take it at a surface level, perhaps it does. But we don't do this for pleasure. We do this for the greater good. We do this in order to save ourselves and others from sin and the fires of hell. We make one sacrifice in order to save millions more."

"What does eating the sinners do?" The young man's tone had cooled a bit, as if he'd realized he was not supposed to be eager, was supposed to see this ritual as his own personal burden to carry and not an exotic meal.

"We eat sinners' flesh in order to purge their sins," Solomon said. "We eat their flesh to prove to the Creator that we will do anything for His grace, even if it means we must take on their sins."

"Purge their sins?" Travis asked.

Ruth's mind was still loading this information, a lag separating their words and their meaning. She didn't want to believe it. It seemed insane. Murdering her to appease a deity was still out of the realm of anything she'd thought possible, but *cannibalism*?

"Yes, my child," the elder continued, still speaking in a monotonous tone. "Eating a sinner's flesh during this ritual allows us to cleanse them and create a pure soul. It's like the act of communion, but reversed. She's a kind of sacrificial lamb, just like Jesus. When we take communion, we are Imbuing ourselves with the Creator and His love. We are joining together with everyone else who participates in this holy sacrament. The ritual we will perform tonight is still a ritual meal, but instead of absorbing Truth and Purity, we are dissolving the girl's sins into our own Pure and True bodies and souls, removing the sinner in the process so that they cannot continue to sin. By consuming their flesh, we absorb their sins, and because we are Pure and True, because we have chosen to take on this burden, we are able to remove the evil altogether."

Ruth's body had grown numb beneath her. She couldn't blink, couldn't breathe, couldn't think. She barely registered the continued frenzy on her body, the rats now clustered on her thighs like a garter made of vibrating barbed wire. Every once in a while, a furry, crazed body would slip off and fall back to the floor, restarting its climb or leaping straight onto her knee, catching its talons against the fabric of her pants.

"The sinner is extremely lucky," the old man continued. "They perform the ultimate sacrifice, and in doing so, they not only save many souls from the fires of hell, but also their own."

"I'm really excited that Gideon allowed me to join this mission," Travis said, the elation slipping back into his voice. Clearer now, unmistakable. "I didn't think he would since I haven't been initiated yet."

The rats had crested her hips now. One wormed its way beneath Ruth's sweatshirt, its teeth and claws even sharper against the thin fabric of her T-shirt. Her front became a bulging, squirming mass. The frenzy intensified as the rats realized they were trapped, their claws like razors slicing across her waist. But still, she must remain silent. She bit down harder on the piece of her own flesh between her teeth, a ragged section of her palm. It tasted salty and bitter.

"He saw your devotion," the elder replied, "to this mission and to our cause. We're always searching for new members, but we must be selective. We need those who are truly devoted, who strive to be Pure, who are willing to put their faith in our missions and rituals. It's unfortunately rare to find someone like that. We're lucky to have found you."

"Yeah, when you guys showed up on my doorstep, I instantly knew it was the place for me," the boy said. "I mean, like, it felt like fate—like it was really His plan to set me on this path. I think I can really do some good with you."

Travis paused for a moment. The rats were on either side of Ruth's sweatshirt now, wading across the sea of loose fabric at her belly.

Then the boy asked, "What does it taste like? The sinner's flesh?"

There was no mistaking it now. Pure exhilaration oozed inside his words. These questions escaped his mouth in a quick clip, the words all strung together like a kid rattling off his wish list of toys to Santa.

He wasn't just an impressionable kid, desperate to please, desperate for belonging—he *wanted* to eat her. It wasn't just some ritual he felt obligated to do.

He wanted to eat her.

"I mean, I just want to know what to expect, you know," the kid said, backpedaling a bit, again remembering that this was supposed to be hard, was supposed to be a burden.

She chewed her own raw flesh to keep from screaming, separating it from a chunk of glue, tasting gummy copper and salt.

"I don't want to mess up," the boy continued, rambling, trying to convince the elder that he wasn't a cannibal, no, he wasn't eager for the chance to eat human flesh, he was just eager to please and it came out wrong. "I don't want to, like, throw it up or something and ruin the whole thing."

"The taste isn't unpleasant," the elder finally said, apparently accepting the explanation—or unfazed by the boy's excitement. "You'll find out soon enough. It's not much different from eating any other kind of meat. It just has a special purpose. You'll do just fine."

Ruth swallowed the chewed piece of skin, the tiny morsel of herself—the only thing she'd eaten in hours. Blood flowed from the wound, and it dribbled down her chin. Her hand remained clamped over her mouth.

There was no denying it now, that inkling of intuition that she'd been trying to quash for the last few hours: these cultists were not only going to kill her, but they were *going to eat her*.

The rats fought on her torso now. One had nearly reached her shoulders, had surpassed the others, free and clear of the melee. Three or so twisted themselves into a knot within the baggy front of the sweatshirt. Their teeth and claws ripped miniature tears in her skin, and she felt each one—every single slice, every single panicked nibble.

How many tiny scrapes could she sustain before too much blood was shed? Each one seemed to drain a little bit of life from her, making her feel faint and weak, death by a thousand little cuts. She hoped her blood sugar wasn't plummeting again; she had nothing to raise it.

The pain of each bite was dulled, ever so slightly, by the news that her body would soon be some demented meal for these fucking bigots. That fact continued repeating inside her head, a red chyron looping across her psyche. *Breaking: Girl to be eaten by bigots who couldn't stand to have her employed at their store. The same people who gave her a wide berth at the grocery, not even wanting to chance their skin grazing, apparently will bring her flesh to their mouths, piece by piece.*

Ruth fumed with each revolution of the ticker. These fucking people who fired her, who spied on her in her home, who thought she was scum, who showed up at her door spouting some demented script—they didn't want to touch her living body, but they would cook and eat her after killing her? Or even . . . *before*?

A rat beneath her sweatshirt became impeded by her arm, which was pressed against her chest. It poked its muzzle against the barrier, trying to squeeze through, until its head became trapped. For a moment it stilled, as if accepting its fate, before attempting to bite its way through. Ruth's arm jerked reflexively, the shelf rattling faintly.

Maybe the rats would give her rabies and it would transfer to the cultists when they ate her. For a single second, she welcomed the bites. She reveled in the idea that the rats would make her sick so she could fuck up these fucking people, if only by proxy. These fucking Noble Shepherds would think they'd won, but they'd all die slow, horrible, painful deaths. Because of her. If she couldn't make it out of here—and, if she was honest with herself, that was a long shot; she was so tired, and her blood sugar was surely tanking, and there were so many of them, both rats and the men—at least she could spite them posthumously. Or, if she could stay quiet until she passed out from low blood sugar, maybe she could just stay hidden in her Ruth-sized space and run out their clock, collecting dust until she started to stink and rot. Or maybe the rats would eat her instead.

Now, one fell off her chest, pushed or slipped after brawling with its brother. Once it reached the ground, it leapt straight back up, its weight settling on Ruth's torso, little talons digging into the knit of the fabric. A lone rat reached her shoulder, settling on the surface like a parrot. It paused, confused that it had reached the top of the mountain, greeted by mere air, nowhere else, apparently, to go. It wobbled on its hind legs, sniffing at the air. At her ear, it squeaked and sniffed, and its little whiskers grazed her earlobe as it turned its head. Then it dropped to all fours and darted up her neck.

Ruth clamped her eyes shut, dug her fingernails into her cheeks. She didn't care if she created a halo of bloody crescents along her cheeks. She didn't want it to burrow into her mouth, to use her eyelids as a rung. It crawled up the side of her face and perched atop her head. Still, she dared not move.

"What happens when we're done?" the boy asked.

"The first part of the ritual cleanses her sins," the elder said. "Once her soul is purified, we can use her blood to renew the seal on the vessel. You know this already, my son. I know you're nervous. Afterward, we honor the sacrifice by—"

"No, I know that part," the boy interrupted. "I mean, won't

people be looking for her? What if they find out what we did, and don't understand or believe us when we say why?"

Solomon chuckled. Actually fucking laughed. "No need to worry about that," he said. "The selection process takes those sorts of things into account. Members are allowed to nominate a person, and Gideon selects the sacrifice based on many factors, including whether there is any family or contacts who may cause trouble afterward. She only has that girl she lives in sin with. That's the only person who would care if she disappeared."

"What about her parents?"

"They are with us, though not part of our inner community. They attend weekly services at the church. They disowned her years ago. She has no grandparents or any other extended family she keeps in contact with."

"No friends?"

"Maybe some people online, but our research did not find anyone local or nearby. Any online communities or acquaintances seemed to not know her personally. I suppose it could be a risk, but we felt that those relationships were tenuous at best."

"Well, what about her girlfriend?"

Here, the elder made some noise of disgust. "The ritual will also free and save the girl she lives with," Solomon replied, balking at the usage of the word *girlfriend* in relation to another woman, "from her sins. Then the girl can atone. She will be alone and vulnerable. Once we're done with the ritual, we can increase our efforts to convince her to be True. Convince her to join us. Maybe she will even be assigned to you."

"Assigned to me?" The boy's voice grew eager again.

"To be your wife," Solomon continued. "After she goes through initiation and cleansing, of course."

Ruth's guts boiled inside her, her stomach acid cooking the little piece of her own flesh. How fucking dare they. How dare they even entertain that idea. Abigail wouldn't be swayed, Ruth knew, Ruth trusted, but fuck them. Just the thought that the very people who would take Ruth away from her, the ones who would leave Abigail all alone—they would have the audacity to then go and try to convert her? Force Abigail to be an incubator for them? Ruth didn't think Abigail would accept their offer. She would probably slam the door in their faces before they even got that far.

At least at first. With Ruth gone, she truly would be all alone. Her mother was the only other person she had been close to. After Judy's passing Abigail had been vulnerable and devastated, but she'd had Ruth to lean on, to help her through. To grieve with her. How long would she wait in this miserable town, searching for Ruth? How long before she gave up, put all of Ruth's things in boxes? How long before her grief took over, leaving a gaping hole? A hole that this cult would offer to fill—first with kindness and then with hatred.

Would Abigail really change everything about herself, all of her beliefs and personality to join this cult? Ruth couldn't imagine that. She didn't want to admit that it was possible for a person grieving their sole connection in the world to be convinced to join a cult posing as a loving community, one that offered assistance, food, friendship, comforting reassurances about the afterlife. One that would not expose their extreme prejudices right away, slowly ensnaring her, slowly turning up the heat until the water in the pot was boiling before she had a chance to escape it.

Something inside Ruth cracked. Her teeth found another ragged, loose piece of skin lining the wound on her palm and snapped down upon it, tearing it away to keep her jaws busy, to keep from screaming at the top of her lungs. The newly exposed nerves screamed for her.

The rage boiling beneath her skin was so hot and furious that she barely felt the rats still clambering up her torso, another one scratching at her scalp now, lifting its body into the blank air to find the next foothold.

"You are both around the same age, more or less," the elder continued, the pair still standing right outside her hiding spot, "and we don't have many young adults. Lots of children, now, but it has been a challenge to keep them in the fold once they become teenagers, especially when we're still working to build up our schooling programs. We can't help what they see when they attend school, the sins they're tempted by. We have a lot of runaways. But it might be better to assign you to one of the younger girls—once they come of age. We don't get many newcomers like you in these days of sin, and we can't risk mingling our bloodlines more than we have to."

"What if her girlfriend refuses to join and tries to find out what we did?"

"Who would believe her? Who would listen to a sinner like her?" the elder replied. The soft chuckle that escaped his lips fanned the flames inside Ruth. "We need a sinner to perform this ritual every blood moon. If she refuses to join, and she tries to make trouble, then she would be first in line."

The cracked thing inside Ruth shattered. The shards spilled across her body, little daggers prodding and poking every inch of her. Her hand still clamped over her mouth, the rage overflowed, covering her torso, her limbs, every inch of her shuddering, unable to contain her anger any longer. The rats panicked again, biting and scratching, holding on for dear life from the impending avalanche. But Ruth didn't feel a single thing.

They'd kill her, and then kill Abigail, too, if she refused to join them. Ruth could not let that happen. She had to get out of here, whatever it took.

Fuck these fuckers and their pious bullshit, she thought.

Why was she working so hard to spare their lives? Why was she only fighting back when they attacked? They were the ones spreading hate, the ones infecting the community. *They* were the ones whose absence would strengthen the town. So fuck them. No more hiding. No more just defending herself. She needed to get the fuck out, whatever it took. If she had to set complicated traps for these motherfuckers or gouge out all of their eyes with knitting needles, she'd fucking do it.

She didn't even feel the clawing, clamoring horde along her torso anymore. A rat might be tearing more of her hair out with its teeth right this second. The one under her sweatshirt might be chewing a tunnel through her midsection. Even her ragged palm submitted no sensations to her, completely numb. All she felt was searing, boiling rage.

She wouldn't hide any longer. She wouldn't try to wait out their fucking deadline. She was going to be like these rats.

She would claw and bite and fight her fucking way out, striking down anything and anyone that got in her way. She had to get out of here, this Ruth-sized hidey-hole, *now*. The pair still stood outside, chatting away as if they weren't murderous cannibals masquerading as righteous. She couldn't crawl back through the little door.

The rats had figured it out first.

The only way out was up.

Chapter 15

Finally, the flood of rats had diminished to a mere trickle. A few still scurried up Ruth's body, restarting their climb or leaping back up if they fell. One remained tangled in her sweatshirt, still wriggling beneath the fabric, winding itself into a knot, a twisted tangle of rat and fabric bulging from her stomach like a tumor. Another had reached her shoulder and stood there on its hind legs, trying to figure out its next move like the ones who'd summited her skull before it. One clawed at her thigh, its third or fourth or millionth attempt. The majority of the rats left tangled themselves in her remaining hair, biting and scratching at each other and at her scalp, searching for somewhere else to go but trapped at the peak.

Beneath her rage it was mere background noise, a painful static.

She would scale the shelves. She had no other choice. Twisting her head from side to side, her vision partially obscured by the dangling tails of the rats on her head, she tried to assess the best way to clamber up. Three sides of the hole were nothing more than thin plywood and pegboard, the backs of the flimsy shelving. The fourth side was the support beam, a giant metal pole that reached all the way to the ceiling. The beam had seen better days despite the store being only about five years old. Already chunks of the metal had fallen away along with the paint, little rusty bite marks along the edges. It was the only way up, though at the expense of the gaping mouth on her palm.

The pair outside continued their constant chattering as she crab-walked the few inches over to the rusty support beam. The pulverized bones of the first rat casualty scratched against the concrete, the bottom of her shoe leaving splotchy footprints of its guts. She no longer cared what the cultists were saying. It was irrelevant. Whatever plans they had were not going to happen. Ever.

The tangle of rats on her head, her warm crown, remained twisted in her hair, and the weight of the mass ripped more strands from her scalp as it slithered to the side with her movements. The rest of the rats panicked. The one hovering on her shoulder scrambled toward her ear, screeching directly inside, scratching and nibbling at her lobe, its little claws gripping for purchase before she shook it off, another one dropping to the ground with it. A rodent at her thigh latched on, and she took a moment to pinch its tail and gently drop it away from her. She plucked away the remaining strays and dropped them, too, to the ground before she tackled the squirming crown, heavy on her head, barely enough room to unfold her arms to reach it.

Her fingers dug through the tangled mass of tiny sharp

teeth and claws on her scalp. The presence of her fingers agitated them more—her fingertips, already bleeding, were sliced and gnawed by a dozen more razorlike incisors. The new slickness inked its way through her enduring strands and pooled on her scalp, seeped its way into the rats' fur, the crown becoming more intricate, more entangled. She had no choice but to rip more hair out—squeezing each warm, wiggling body inside her fist and pulling until there was a harsh, sharp *pluck* along her scalp and she could drop the rat to the side, her torn hair floating down after it. Each time she repeated these steps, the rats squealed and screeched, so sharp and loud she did not know how the cultists didn't hear them. Maybe they simply weren't smart enough to think to investigate what had stirred the rats into a frenzy. When she had finally finished, she wondered whether her head still bore a halo, now one of her own flesh, pale and ringed with rosy droplets of blood.

There was not space enough to dislodge the one rat still tangled in her sweatshirt. It would have to remain, nestled there, its little breaths increasing as the oxygen depleted, the humidity of each one soaking into her T-shirt. This time, the rats on the floor did not start another ascent, but instead scurried toward the endcap—they must have found the exit.

Ruth placed a hesitant hand on the support beam, too afraid to lean her whole weight on it. Red-brown rust flakes coated her fingertips like dandruff. Who knew if it would simply crumble beneath her like a pillar of loose salt. She bit her lip, still playing the quiet game, not wanting to draw attention to herself until it was inevitable.

Now, the young and old cultists paused their conversation,

the sudden silence jarring. An occasional reply—*Yes. No.*—made Ruth think they were relaying updates over the headset. She'd almost forgotten about it, about the one she'd stolen. It still looped around one ear, the cord dangling loose. The rats must have disconnected it. Out of pure habit, she plugged it back into the receiver.

"No signs of her," Solomon said. "I really had the sense that she was here, though. Nobody else has spotted her."

Their footsteps padded away from the little door.

For a moment she thought she'd been saved, that she wouldn't have to figure out how to climb up, that she could wriggle out of the gap and somehow find her way to the back door.

But then the elder said, "We'll circle this area. She has to be nearby. I can feel it."

No more waiting. No more hesitation. It wasn't ever going to get easier. She would only grow more tired; she still had not eaten anything beyond the small packet of Skittles, and she could already feel the effects of her blood sugar tumbling from all the little scratches, all of the tiny scrapes and blood loss, drop by drop, taking their toll together. Ruth took a deep breath and started her ascent, her uninjured hand wrapping around the edge of the large metal beam. She tried to find a spot for her foot, but it slipped back down to the floor, and for a moment her mind flashed back to her last footfall, to that horrid *crack* beneath her heel. But except for the one still tangled at her front, the rats seemed to have made their exit. The static silence descended once again.

The climb would be more difficult than she expected. Every

muscle was pained and exhausted, not willing to heave the weight of her body. But then a spark of remembrance jolted through her mind—that *thing*, that weird little vial. In the tiny space, narrow as a sarcophagus, she managed to squeeze her fingers into the tote bag still slung around her shoulder and dig it out. The heft of it, the smoothness of the glass felt good inside her fingers, some feeling of warmth, some feeling of *power* zinging through her nerves, as if the thing held a dark electricity, lightning in a bottle.

Ruth was still not certain she believed in its powers, that it could Imbue her or gift her strength, or do anything at all, but she draped the delicate chain over her neck. It seared against the bites and scratches there, as though she were a vampire repelled by silver.

Ruth tried again. This time, her foot found purchase. Using her good hand, she clutched the corroded support beam, the missing chunks acting as hand and foot holds. She grimaced whenever flakes of rust would wedge themselves into her still-weeping palm. Her grimaces transformed to winces whenever a sharp, rusty piece of metal tore the wound on her palm open wider, whenever it ripped away a chunk of the mountain range of stiffened glue. But she ascended. Somehow this attempt felt easier and more fluid, each movement propelling her body up.

Her elbows and forearms became leverage against the shelf backs, and she pushed against them as hard as she dared to wedge herself in place. Each foot in turn replaced the adjacent hand in the rusted grooves of the beam, the other limbs pressed against the opposing shelf. Even her exhaustion seemed to dissipate and dissolve, her muscles buttery and rejuvenated. The back of the shelf holding the cast iron seemed to shudder, to sway as she ascended, shifting more and more the higher she climbed. She had to take this tilting into her calculations, her limbs extending more and more to maintain the equilibrium lest she slip and fall all the way back to the floor.

But she did not slip, the muscles in her calves tensing automatically each time her sneaker wanted to lose its grip, pushing pressure into her toes that steadied her ascent. Halfway up, the headset receiver at her hip knocked against the beam's edge, clicking the button that turned it on. The earpiece, still clipped smartly around her ear, buzzed to life with static. She swallowed a gasp, realizing that if the headset was turned on, so, too, was the microphone.

Despite the odd ease of her climb, each limb was vital in maintaining her spot; she didn't trust that removing her hand from the beam to switch it off would not cause a chain reaction of each limb popping out of its precarious place, sending her crashing back down to the floor. For a few moments she ascended silently, not even daring to breathe. No matter; once she reached the summit, they'd finally spot her and she'd have to fight them. She would have to be like her namesake, *ruthless*. Do whatever she needed to get out and get to Abigail. The thought of her reminded Ruth what the cultists wanted to do to both of them, and the rage boiled inside her stomach once again.

No more hiding and reacting. Now was the time to fight.

She pushed upward once more, no longer caring if her breath, if her growls, rang through the microphone, broadcasting her rage to every single Shepherd in the store. She breathed hard, pushing through the pain on her scalp, the pain all over her body from the rats' bites and scratches. The one in her sweatshirt barely stirred, like it had been lulled to sleep. Maybe it was coiled too tightly within the fabric to move. Or maybe it had simply accepted its fate and suffocated, leaned into the comfort of the worn sweatshirt, the warm twist of fabric. But Ruth didn't accept her fate, the destiny these people wanted for her. She'd buck and kick and bite like the rat's siblings if she had to.

Over the headset, she heard the booming voice once more.

"Have you found her yet?" The words dripped with disdain, with vile poison.

"No signs of her," the elder said, his voice echoing through the earpiece, bouncing between two microphones. *He must be very close*, Ruth thought.

Solomon would probably figure out what the reverb meant. He was a bigot, but he wasn't stupid—at least, he wasn't *that* stupid. He'd figure out that she was somewhere nearby, just like he had suspected all along, like he'd somehow *sensed.* All he had to do was wait for her to appear. She couldn't go back down into her hole. She refused to hide. She'd have to see it through, face them sooner or later. The vial dangled and bounced against the front of her sweatshirt. Was it working? Was it making her feel more confident, stronger and bolder?

As she neared the top, the shelves rocked beneath her. With a few more movements upward, her feet pushing against the beam, spots of rust flaking away like snow, she spilled onto the top of the shelf. The wire on her headset snagged on one of the jagged, corroded spots and the whole thing slid away, the clip at her side snapping and the piece of plastic securing the earpiece to her head pinching at her upper ear before the whole apparatus fell into the pit with a clatter, dragging her tote bag along with it.

On top of the shelf, she shimmied forward on her belly, trying to shift the pile of boxes residing there to make room for her body. But all it took was one wrong move, one twitch of the rat still trapped inside her sweatshirt, the little thing trying to escape the sudden weight of her torso, for Ruth to jerk forward, making the shelf shudder and sending a box careening off the edge, where it smashed onto the ground.

Fuck. She almost spoke it aloud. What would it have mattered if she did? She could scream it at the top of her lungs now. It was inevitable that they'd spot her up here, but she'd hoped that she could at least have a moment to think of a plan, maybe steady herself enough to figure out what was in the boxes up here with her.

"Something just fell off the top of a shelf," Travis said, a giddy statement that she knew had been transmitted over the radio.

"No eyes on her," the elder said after a brief pause.

"She has to be up there, right? But how would she have been able to climb up there without us noticing?"

Another pause hovered in the air, like Solomon was piecing it together. A soft chuckle escaped his lips, breaking the silence as if he were thinking, *Oh you silly girl, you thought you were so clever.*

"There's a little space between this shelf and the next," he said. "She must have gone in there to hide. That must be why I could sense her presence so strongly but we could not lay eyes on her. Remember, child, the devil is cunning. He will always find a way to trick you."

The once-docile rat trapped between her torso and the shelf now scratched and bit and tore at her abdomen as if trying to dig its way out. Ruth sucked in her stomach—now suddenly a major feat, as if there were more stiff muscles there—and lifted her body off the surface of the shelf just enough for the rat to wriggle free, praying and hoping it was smart enough to find the way out. It wasn't.

"Bring a ladder over to aisle six," Solomon radioed.

Ruth slid her hand around the rat's wiggling body, its teeth digging into her flesh, too confused and scared to understand when a hand was helping. Beneath her fingers, there was a soft crunch and a renewed thrashing, and she loosened her fingers, just slightly, her grip stronger than she'd imagined. Pulling it free of its knitted tomb, she launched the rat over the boxes in the direction of the cultists' voices.

"Holy shhhhh—*shoot*!" the younger one exclaimed, barely catching himself before uttering an unholy, sinful word.

The commotion from the unexpected flying rat gave Ruth enough time to settle into a more comfortable position among the boxes. She scanned the labels of the surrounding cardboard, hoping for something with blades or even more cast iron to defend herself with, something more dangerous than a rat to launch. But her luck had run out. The boxes held embroidery thread, yarn, tiny trays of plasticky watercolor paint. She could almost laugh at her misfortune.

When she worked at New Creations, an empty place on a shelf was cause for dread. There was no inventory system and no rhyme or reason to where extra stock was stacked—it was just shoved wherever there was a gap on top of the shelves. Hell, if the boxes hadn't been labeled at the factory, she imagined they'd have to rip open each one every single time they needed to restock. She'd been such an idiot, such a perky, ready-to-go-above-and-beyond Mustard Seed at the start of her tenure that it was almost a fun little game to see how fast she could search the boxes atop the shelves to find the paintbrushes or bobbins to restock. But by the end, she'd do what most of the other employees did: ignored those empty spots unless a manager called it out. Sometimes on her shoplifting sprees, she'd pull the whole stock of a single item off the shelf, something in demand like glitter or glue sticks, and hide them behind some obscure, expensive thing that'd been collecting dust since before she even worked there, leaving an empty gap that would be sure to result in a manhunt around the store in short order.

So it didn't surprise her, when she shuffled around to face the other direction, that just across the beam-sized gap was a box with a handwritten label that read *BLADES.* Ruth smiled.

Chapter 16

The gap between the shelves didn't seem vast, but it still spanned inches beyond the ends of Ruth's fingertips. She hooked her forearm around the beam to allow herself to lean a tiny bit farther. Although she stretched herself as far as possible, every tendon taut and every joint straight, she got no closer to the box of blades. Her fingers grasped at air. Beneath her, the shelf shifted, teetering and wobbling like it was not bolted down.

"I've got eyes on her," Solomon reported into the radio. His voice sounded too close, like he was directly beneath her in the aisle. It sounded like Travis was there too, glued to his side, giggling, the balloon of his giddiness leaking air.

She began to rock the shelf, shimmying her hips, hoping it would topple and crush them. She imagined the giant shelving unit collapsing on top of them in slow motion, knocking them to the floor, the weight of the shelf crushing first their feet and then their legs, the pressure squeezing their guts up and out of their mouths like a tube of paint. The grisly image made her grin, made her pump harder. She wrapped her arms around the beam and tried with all her strength to push it over, the muscles in her legs taut and tingling. She felt invincible. Was the shelf really not bolted to the ground, or was Ruth strong enough now to send it swinging free of its tethers? She could not tell. She only hoped she could hang onto the beam long enough to not be crushed herself; as long as she remained on the right side of the domino stack, she'd be okay. As long as this vial hung around her neck, maybe this strength would hold her up forever.

The cast iron knickknacks that still clung to their hooks now shook and clattered away, landing on the pile of their fallen comrades with loud, deafening clangs. On the backswing of each rolling wave of the shelf, more and more heavy metal tumbled to the ground, the aisle sounding like a war zone, cast iron shrapnel exploding around the two cultists.

"Oh my—" the younger said, stopping himself before he uttered a blasphemous *God* to complete the outburst. An angry tone entered his voice and he nearly cursed again before his words morphed into something she didn't quite recognize, something sinister but rehearsed, like an incantation. "*Sin has a thousand treacherous arts she uses to deceive, while the heedless wretch—*"

The elder cut him off. "Not yet!" he screamed. "Not until she's on the altar!" Desperation soaked through his words. "Bring a ladder to aisle six!" Solomon screamed beneath her. "As fast as possible!" From her vantage point, she could already see the other Shepherds, like yellow beacons, scurrying to find the rolling stairs.

There were only so many items on the shelves that could fall away and crack their skulls open. It wasn't enough. The shelf needed to topple. Ruth took a breath, made herself stop and assess the situation, eating into time she didn't have. The only thing preventing the domino effect was a thick metal wire looping around the top of the shelving unit and the metal beam, the wire loose enough to allow the shelf to tilt and then swing back.

"Fuck!" she said, out loud, the first word to escape from her dry mouth in what felt like an eon, and it emerged in a furious scream, a single syllable that she hoped reached each and every ear in the place, worming its way through the plastic earbuds. If she hadn't used the floral wire cutters to secure the plywood door leading into the gap, she could have snipped it and shoved the unit over with ease.

She was a sitting duck. Any second now they'd roll the ladder over and drag her away.

No, she thought. *There has to be a way.*

Ruth looked closer. The wire wasn't welded together. In their everlasting laziness, the Mustard Seeds had merely twisted it around itself. If they weren't going to take the time to properly fix the shelf, why would they properly adhere this wire? An unlucky stroke of luck—the twist sat as far away from her as possible, a mere inch closer to her than the boxes stacked on the other shelf, on the back side of the beam.

Ruth leaned precariously forward, pushing the shelf to its limits, the stairs now located and rolling toward her second by second. The clanging and clattering had ceased—no more cast iron projectiles remained on the shelf. The wire was stiff and rusty, and it cut her fingertips, breaking open and ripping wide the little rodent bites already there, everything becoming stained and slippery with blood. Yet only a twinge of pain blossomed there; her fingers worked deft and quick with each backward twist. Beneath her, the old and young duo argued, the young one wanting to climb up to get her down himself—*I can do it, why are we waiting around when she's right there*—and the elder telling him to *Be patient, we need her alive, after all, and we have her trapped. It's a matter of time. She has nowhere to go.*

A new burst of rage bubbled inside her, the blood spilling from her fingertips seeming to scald against the wire as Ruth worked at untwisting. Let them underestimate her. Again. A whole army of Shepherds assembled in the aisle beneath her, pushing aside the sea of cast iron to line up the stairs with the shelf. *Good,* Ruth thought. She could take them all out in one blow, like bowling pins. *Strike.*

She had seconds. Each time she untwisted a section, the shelf beneath her shifted, angling further, the remaining wares hanging at the edge of their hooks. A couple of Shepherds wheeled the stairs into place at last, the whole thing squeaking like that rats' nest had. As they began to climb up, their footsteps hollow against each stair, Ruth felt the shelf give way beneath her, the weight of it ripping the rest of the wire free.

www.forum.archaeologia.net

Forum Hub > Current Events

Subject: Strange disappearances of antiquities

Diggemup
August 23, 1997 @3:14pm
I'm on site in Damascus and a buddy of mine said that he heard a rumor that there was a lot of black market activity to sell and smuggle antiquities over to the states. He said it was mostly old religious texts and objects. Obviously, this thirdhand information isn't quite reliable . . . anyone heard anything about this?

Carbon-dater
August 23, 1997 @6:45pm
Haven't heard these rumors before, but I'm curious!

Ageofaquarius
August 24, 1997 @2:15pm
I've heard these rumors, too. What I was told was that the items came from all over, Damascus, Persepolis, Palmyra, etc. Supposedly the buyer is getting them back to the states by labeling the boxes as "tile samples" or the like. Apparently this has been going on for a really long time.

Diggemup
August 24, 1997 @5:46pm
That's interesting. I'm not surprised that it's been ongoing. Probably hard to source that kind of thing . . .

Bone2Pick
August 27, 1997 @10:16pm
Oh man, I heard a really crazy rumor about this. At least, it seems like it'd be connected. News from the grapevine over here is that this type of smuggling has been going on for centuries, like since the 1800s . . . and the craziest part is that supposedly whoever is buying all this stuff is looking for an angel.

Diggemup
August 28, 1997 @9:53am
An angel? Like, a statue of an angel or . . . ?

Bone2Pick
August 29, 1997 @11:11pm
No, like, a literal angel . . . Apparently it's some group that thinks there's a real, outta-the-Bible angel stuck in an old jar somewhere, and they'll buy any religious artifact from the region, thinking they'll find some text or clue or something. But that's just the rumor I heard!

Ageofaquarius
August 30, 1997 @8:34am
A real angel??

Diggemup
August 30, 1997 @9:12am
I spoke with some people over here, some locals, and some of them seemed to know what I was talking about, though the language barrier made it a little difficult. One of the guys on my team tried to translate, but he seemed to get confused about what they were saying. He said he wasn't sure if he understood . . . said they were talking about magic or powers or something. I don't know – he said what he thought they said was really odd, so he wasn't sure if he misheard them or if he couldn't quite translate it.

Ageofaquarius
August 30, 1997 @2:40pm
I asked around over here and nobody has heard of anything about an angel or magic . . . just that religious items were being smuggled for a long time.

Bone2Pick
September 1, 1997 @10:55pm
I haven't heard anything about magic, either. Just the weird angel thing. I'll let you know if I hear anything else.

Diggemup
September 2, 1997 @2:30pm
It seems like it might be a local legend or rumor – nothing in the news about the missing items but there seems to be some kind of spooky lore among the locals. I'm headed back in a couple days, unfortunately, so won't be able to dig much more.

Chapter 17

The snapped wire ricocheted into Ruth's arms, slicing through skin, leaving long tracks of dribbling blood. The cascading shelf pulled her feet along with it, and for a moment she worried that they'd be sucked beneath the rubble, leaving her pinned beneath the shelf, the rest of her body in full view of the cultists. Instead, she slammed into the plywood back of the shelf, denting it, the weight of her body sending cracking veins across the expanse. Yet one more Ruth-sized hole. Miraculously, no part of her became crushed beneath the wreckage.

Ruth's body lay still, but the sound of crashing calamity continued. The shattering of glass replaced the clang of iron, followed by the hollow gunshots of exploding plastic, as the shelves beyond toppled like a set of dominoes. The shrieks of the squished Shepherds sounded amid the collapse, a discordant harmony lasting mere seconds after the last shelf had crumpled—the height of the final domino not enough to reach across the wide aisle encircling the store. The top of the last shelf nearly kissed the still-upright row beyond it. Inches prevented the rest from starting a true domino effect, all the shelves lining the edges of the store falling in tandem, one after the other.

Cracks continued to snake through the plywood amid the tremors, the shelf groaning as it settled. Debris spilled away on all sides, glittering glass glinting underneath the sparse light and orphaned storage lids scattered like a dropped deck of cards. A cloud of dust hovered, suspended, clogging Ruth's throat, settling along her eyelashes.

In the foggy daze that followed the fall, she barely registered the metal prongs poking the wrong way through the shelves, a skewer just inches from her eyes, so close she had to cross them to see it clearly. She heard no more screams or commotion on the wrong side of the collapse. Once the rubble settled, no sound sprang from survivors, no prolonged panicked or pained yelps, but it was hard to hear much of anything beneath the new, constant ringing that emanated from inside her own head.

Her ribs suddenly hurt like hell, everything fuzzy and swaying around her. She needed to move. That was the only thought in her head. She knew she needed to move, to get somewhere else, though she couldn't quite remember why, and she tried to get her body to follow this command, but it was as though she was trapped in molasses. Everything moved in slow motion, including her own limbs.

Wobbly, she started to lift her body from its cozy dent in the plywood. Bolts of pain zipped through every nerve, nearly blinding her with each new position. Her ankle had twisted beneath her in the fall and throbbed when she tried to put weight on it, the liquid sloshing through the swollen tissue like a water balloon. She grimaced and forced herself to move, to crawl. Even in her dazed state, she knew she was moving too slowly—she had to get away because of *something*, because . . . they were going to catch her. Surely whoever was left had heard the crash and was running toward it. She clambered over the wreckage, her bleeding body accumulating dirt and dust and leaving bloody droplets behind.

Horrifying images swam up to meet her as she stumbled across the wreckage. Beneath the shattered plywood of the shelves, the cracked skull of the elder cultist floated atop the ocean of debris, his face cratered, indented from a pan, his eye socket concave mush. His jaw was simply gone; his head ended beneath the top row of his teeth. His molars were on full display beneath the shredded, stringy meat that had been his cheeks. Like Glue Man, his lifeless eyes stared back at her, almost in blank disbelief, almost as if questioning how someone not True, someone so very False, could have done this to him, could have done this to someone so Pure and Right.

Ahead, an arm stood, propped upright in the wreckage, its hand hanging from a limp wrist like a zombie escaping a grave. A lonesome leg hung above it, like a hairy white flag of defeat, skewered onto a thick metal post. The toes splayed and flexed as though the pole had trapped the tendons in place, stretching them taut before they spilled out where the calf had ripped from its knee. The mess of minced muscle and chipped bone resembled ground beef. Another limb poked through the dusty rubble of cast iron and hooks and flesh and plywood, a thin cylinder of jointed skin Ruth couldn't distinguish. The snapped bone had ruptured its fleshy prison, a bloodstained beacon of white poking through. Ruth might have vomited if there had been anything in her stomach to expel.

At the edge of this mess lay the young kid, facedown. Under the cover of the wreckage, Ruth couldn't tell whether he was breathing, whether he was dead or merely maimed. He'd been the only one aware enough—or nimble enough—to try to outrun the collapse. But only his torso was free, his legs hidden or crushed beneath the rubble. Ruth hoped the bones in his legs had turned to gravel. Ruth hoped his ribs had fractured and poked holes through his lungs, that the shrapnel from those bones had disconnected the valves of his heart. Gone was any sympathy or empathy for a misguided young man.

His giddy laughter had been extinguished. She hoped, if he was still alive, that he would live just long enough to suffer.

She clambered over the last of the destruction, the settling dust filling corners of her eyes. Pain reverberated through her body with each step, spilling through in waves, her muscles no longer strong and supple. She hobbled across the open path and back into the darkened safety of another aisle, this one still standing. Once more she nestled into the merchandise on the bottom shelf, hiding as much as she could, trying to catch her breath and assess what damage had been done.

Her ankle was already swelling and throbbing, a balloon of skin spilling over her shoe. Her wrist pulsed with new pain, as if it was completely shattered, just a skin bag full of loose rocks. She must have hit her head because her fingers came back coated with hot gore when she gingerly touched her skull. Her bloodied hand floated before her, doubled and bobbing. She couldn't keep her eyes focused.

She almost laughed. Was it low blood sugar or a concussion? What a fun game! It didn't really matter, she supposed, because she couldn't solve either of those things right now.

A cold darkness spread across the front of her sweatshirt, a small splotch that stained the fabric. Between her fingers she lifted the little vial, no longer warm or lightning-filled. In the fall, it had cracked, leaking the gore it contained. Now it was just garbage.

As best as she could, she bandaged and fixed herself up, ripping strips away from blank cotton T-shirts on the shelf next to her, wrapping them around her wounds until she resembled a tie-dyed mummy. She used splintery boards of pine on a nearby display, stiff enough to create splints, for each engorged limb.

She could barely walk or move without muscle-freezing bolts of pain. She'd made it to the back row of the store, now closer than ever to the way out. Yet miles stood between her and the exit. For one single second, she thought again about giving up, about just leaning her head back and letting her exhaustion spread though her in a dark, warm cloud. Maybe they wouldn't find her in time. Maybe she'd wake up to a silent and empty store, all of them taken away by the demon they believed in. That thought seemed nice and cozy to Ruth.

She leaned her head back and closed her eyes.

But in the darkness behind her eyelids, that motherfucker's excited giggle surfaced, the noise looping in the space between her ears. And then *she* giggled. She tried to rein it in, but it bubbled and burst out of her.

Fuck you, she thought. *You're dead now or will be soon. Your so-called Creator didn't save you. Guess you didn't believe hard enough, huh? Weren't "True" enough?*

"And fuck your ritual," she said aloud, her voice cracked and hoarse. "I hope the fucking demon is real, and it eats you."

She'd kill all of them on her way out if she really had to—if they made her—and they would. Fuck them and their fucking bigotry.

Abigail was right. She was always right, and Ruth had been too stubborn to listen. They needed to get out of here—out of this fucking town, out of Kill Devil. They should have already left. Thinking of Abigail sent a new pang through Ruth, one that cut deeper than her throbbing ankle or bleeding head. How could she have become so complacent, thinking nothing bad would happen to them in a town full of high-and-mighty bigots? How could she have been so fucking stupid? Precisely what Abigail had worried about had happened—and not only that, but something magnitudes worse than what either of them could have imagined. When Ruth thought of the dangers of being queer in Kill Devil, she'd thought of simple things. Manageable things. Being yelled at in the streets, kicked out of businesses or restaurants. Maybe so far as their house being vandalized, their tires slashed. Maybe, at the very worst, being kicked out of their home by their landlord. But being the chosen sinner for a cannibalistic ritual to contain a demon? Never in her wildest imagination would she have even put all those words together in the same sentence.

If only she'd listened.

How long had she been gone? How long had she been fighting through this goddamned store? Abigail would be worried, especially when Ruth wasn't picking up her phone. How could she have been so stupid as to leave it in her car? Not that she imagined she could call anyone, anyway. She remembered the poor cell service when she'd worked here, and if they'd thought ahead far enough to remove all the obvious weapons and sharp objects, they'd probably installed some sort of cell blocker—unless they were cocky enough to rely on the inherent bad signal, too lazy to make it a sure thing.

Poor Abigail. Ruth wondered what she might be thinking right now. She could picture her face carved full of lines, her eyebrows raised and huddled together, her lips quivering around the teeth clamped behind them. Was she pacing, peering out the door, constantly calling Ruth's abandoned cell and waiting for her car to reappear?

Oh, shit, Ruth thought suddenly. What if Abigail was so worried that she'd wanted to *do* something about it? What if she drove here herself? What would happen if Abigail came up and started banging on the doors? Or would she leave after seeing the empty parking lot, the metal gate lowered? Would she simply think Ruth had also arrived to a closed store and driven the hour it took to get to the nearest Walmart that sold yarn?

Or would she think that Ruth had abandoned her? That Ruth had made up the yarn excuse, made up the whole rush-job commission as a pretext to leave and never return? What other reason would Abigail have for why Ruth wasn't answering her calls?

And what if Ruth made it out of here just for Abigail to be

gone? To have packed all her things and vanished with no trace or note, a tragic mix-up like Romeo and Juliet?

Anxiety wormed its way through Ruth's pain. She took another breath. And another. She couldn't spiral like that. She had no way to know what Abigail was doing right now. It would not help to sit here in the dark, still hunted, and speculate about the worst possible scenario. If she got out and found Abigail had disappeared, she'd simply spend the rest of her life searching for her.

Chapter 18

Ruth's head pounded. She could feel each pulse of blood move through her body, exiting through one of her various scrapes, snips, or slices. The T-shirt strips had already become stained by dark, blooming splotches as more and more blood soaked into the fibers, each little flower draining her glucose levels.

Even though she was sitting still, the shelves around her seemed to twirl, the little bottles of puffy fabric paint dancing and swirling together. If she moved just a few feet to her right, the back door would be in her direct line of sight. Reaching it seemed impossible.

But she'd gotten this far. After she'd hid, more of the little yellow-aproned fuckers came out from the back and scurried to the rubble, picking through it, throwing aside chunks of dusty particle board and an ungodly number of miniature cast iron pans, each one clanging like a thunderclap against the concrete as they tossed it aside.

She could see most of what they were doing from her dark aisle—the frantic archaeological dig, the shifting mountain of debris. They sifted through until they found a body—an arm so caked in dust that the blood was black, thick, and sticky like tar. Like a hive of ants, the living Shepherds clustered together to uncover this body before tossing it carelessly to the floor. Leaving no part of the insane wreckage untouched, they repeated this cycle over and over. In her grogginess, Ruth couldn't figure out what they were doing, exactly. Why would they abandon the bodies of their friends? Sometimes they wouldn't even pull the whole body out, only touching it again if it was in the way.

They were frantic, screaming, not even attempting to be quiet. Their voices intermingled, merged in a cacophonous shriek, everyone speaking over each other, the sound like glass in Ruth's ringing ears. If she'd had any scraps of fabric left, she might have shoved them in there.

Every last body they found was dead. That was the one thing she had been able to discern from their chaotic chorus.

Another one over here!

And a few moments later, *This one's dead too!*

Then she put the fuzzy pieces together. They must have been looking for *her*. They must think she had been devoured by the rubble, too—and, by proxy, that she must be dead. And wouldn't that just ruin their little fucking plans? She almost laughed at the thought. If only she could have done something to trick them into thinking she was dead already—if only she'd had time to switch clothes with one of those idiots.

Now, the exit stood mere feet away, the steel door shining like a metal beacon. She was finally to the end, to the back door that would lead to the fresh, woody air beyond this crummy warehouse. She'd nearly done it—she'd navigated the maze, defeated the monsters, and now stood just beyond the exit. But more creatures might lurk on the other side of it, swarming. She needed something to arm herself with. In baskets on an endcap, plastic toys overflowed inside their boxes—squirt guns made of thick plastic. *Shoots up to 60 feet!* the boxes boasted beneath their orange clearance stickers.

Perfect. The paint aisle sat right before the door. She'd fill it with something from there and she'd have a long-distance blinder. She'd aim for the eyes.

In the paint aisle, the little plastic jars spun before her, all blending together into a fuzzy shade of brown. Her hands fluttered against her chest, her knees knocking into each other. Her blood sugar had dipped dangerously low, but she was *so close.* She just had to get through that door. She could almost smell the dry, earthy scent of the woods that surrounded the store. She was so very close. So close to Abigail.

Abigail. Abigail. Abigail.

She'd figure out how to get her blood sugar up once she was among the trees. Her house sat a mile or two away, a straight shot through the woods. She doubted she could make it that far without passing out, even if she took breaks. Maybe she could try to flag someone down on the street if she backtracked the way she came. There was not time to traverse the store, to retrieve fondant from the baking section or candy bars from the counters.

She grabbed a vial of clear paint thinner from the shelf and filled the gun.

Ruth breathed deep, steadying herself as much as possible,

and moved toward the door, her finger on the neon trigger.

Her relief, her smugness, her joy was short-lived. The façade crumbled almost immediately back into utter, exhausted defeat.

Fuck.

No.

FUCK.

It couldn't be real. She must be imagining this. It must be her low blood sugar causing her to hallucinate. She couldn't have made it this far, all the way to the back door, the one and only exit, just to have yet another roadblock.

On the metal door, right above the smooth steel handle, sat a keypad.

Locked unless you knew the code. She tried the handle anyway, hoping against hope that it really was an illusion, a hypoglycemic hallucination, but it didn't budge, as though it were cemented in place. At the top corner of the number pad shone a tiny red light, a little pimple Ruth wished she could pop, could slice and slash and gut, watch the pus squirt out.

For the millionth time, defeat etched itself into her bones, seeped through her veins like ice. Her twisted ankle and fractured wrist throbbed anew. Tears pooled at the corners of her eyes, blurring the numbers on the keypad. How could it end like this? She'd fought so hard to get back to *Abigail, Abigail, Abigail* just for it to have been futile from the start, the long line of carnage ending here, in front of a locked door.

Ruth tried to think of what the number might be. She was sure that they'd be the type to use the same number for *everything*, and unlikely to change that number at any point. She'd probably passed it several times already. It was probably printed plainly for all to see, across a banner in the break room that she sat beneath for months. But her mind was blank. The little black numbers on the keys were barely legible to her, everything swirling in her dizziness.

Think, Ruth.

In the entirety of her time working there, the months her ex-fiancé spent constructing the building and the church, all of her years of stealing combined, she had never encountered any sort of number or code or series of digits that seemed important to the New Creationists. There had been physical keys for everything. She'd studied the shelves, the customer-facing part of the store. Not cryptic numerology.

Fuck.

Her brain was so foggy now. She couldn't even begin to think of a plan. Her knees became rubber under the weight of her torso. The fog had even eclipsed the pain pulsing across her body. She wanted so much to sleep, to just drift off and let what was going to happen to her happen. But then she thought of that kid's voice, the one so very eager to gnaw the flesh from her bones and take her girlfriend's hand in forced marriage. Fuck that.

Her blood sugar had dropped even lower, dangerous now—she felt jittery and dizzy, her limbs not wanting to cooperate with the signals she sent them. After a lifetime spent managing her diabetes, she'd had to learn to trust and know the cues her body sent her, had to be in tune with what her symptoms were telling her. And her body was telling her now it was at the end of its limits.

She slumped against the door, trying to keep herself upright.

She refused to die here. Fuck them. She just needed to keep thinking of Abigail, to keep that chorus going, louder than the ringing stuck inside her head: *Abigail, Abigail, Abigail. Do it for Abigail. Keep fighting for Abigail.*

She needed sugar. Even if she managed to get through the door, then what? Her home was a couple miles through a darkened patch of trees. Her car was gone. There was nothing for miles by way of the road; nothing else had been developed besides the pavement leading directly to the church and craft store. If her luck still held, a stray driver might be in the wrong place at the right time—but there was no reason they'd traverse that path unless they were lost. If she encountered a car, the driver was more likely to be another cult member. She'd pass out before she even got close to any of these options, unconscious inside the forest.

She had no choice but to backtrack and snatch sprinkles or candy from inside the store if she wanted any chance of getting back to Abigail. Maybe, by some miracle, she'd discover or remember the code to the keypad on the way. She'd fought too hard to lose now. To lose to her body.

She refused to give in to hopelessness, no matter how dire or impossible it seemed.

She left the shining door, hugging the far wall to the baking section, cursing herself for not carrying candy or food with her at all times, for not heeding Abigail's warning yet again. How many times had Abigail chided her about leaving the house empty-handed like that? How many times had they needed to open a candy bar or box of sugary cereal in the middle of the grocery store to avoid a seizure, sheepishly handing over the empty wrapper to the cashier to scan? If she made it out of here, she'd do better. She'd actually listen to Abigail's wisdom. She hadn't thought something as small as a piece of candy or a honey packet would be the difference between life and death today.

But Abigail knew. This was precisely, exactly what she'd worried would happen, why she so fervently shuttered their curtains and bit her nails to the bloody quick. And Ruth had just shrugged it off, like always. Never wanting to listen. Something in her being not wanting to believe it true that there were people in her own community who wished her dead, wanting to remain complacent, to have everything stay still, stay the way it was forever. Just her and Abigail in their little snow globe, scraping by, maybe, but getting by nonetheless. Nothing better, but nothing worse.

Abigail knew they deserved more. *Abigail* deserved more.

Just a little farther. She peered around corners into the perpendicular aisles, but the Noble Shepherds were still rummaging through the rubble, paying her no heed. Even the short distance from the back of the store to the front felt like a marathon, and she was losing steam quickly.

Blackness edged into the corners of her vision, inky tendrils worming their way to each other, trying to meet in the center.

Fuck.

Ruth couldn't stop it from happening. She pocketed the squirt gun and lowered herself before she fell, lest she knock another hole in her skull. Eventually the darkness filled her vision, her last thoughts of Abigail.

Chapter 19

The inky black tendrils receded from Ruth's vision, but a cloudy haze still enveloped her, a cozy state of confusion. Eventually the haze, too, receded, and the nerves in her body awakened, each one erupting anew with throbbing pain. Her back was against something hard and cold, like a slab at the morgue. Where the fuck was she?

She cracked her eyelids, her senses returning to her, her brain feeling less fuzzy. Against her gums sat the taste of honey. She swiveled her head to the side, greeted by a gummy pile, a blurry mix of yellow and ivory. She blinked, and the image resolved itself, revealing the staring, glazed eyeballs of Glue Man, his body crushing a knitting needle deeper into the eye socket of the man lying beneath him. It was a stack of the Shepherds she'd killed.

If she had more strength, she might have screamed. Or vomited.

At the back of the room, a rustling resounded, cellophane crinkling. A man stood facing away from her, moving as though he was packing a bag. Ruth could only guess at what the man might be stuffing in there. The word *utensils* came to her foggy mind, alongside *picnic*. Beyond the table, shelves overflowed with tiny trinkets: little jars hosting indistinguishable liquids or grains, carved stones, small five-pointed objects that resembled tiny idols. Something about the jars seemed familiar, something about the shape or the vining details lining the exterior. The synapses of Ruth's brain fired in recognition but could not conjure specific details.

Zipping up the bag, the man twisted toward her, his face sending a stone careening through her guts.

"Hey, I thought we lost you there for a sec," his familiar voice said, the words curling out of a toothy smile. It took a second for her eyes to adjust to the face, a corona of light peeking out around it like a halo. Like a storybook savior, Prince Charming come to save the day.

Her ex-fiancé, Charlie.

She tried to sit up, but there was something at the back of her skull—his hand, she realized—that clenched, holding her still.

"Let's get you out of here," he said, hoisting her up into his arms, heading for a door at the far end of the room. Now slung over his shoulder, Ruth understood where she was—in the space beyond that weird locked door. Through the open doorway, she could just spot the edge of the break room around the corner.

In Charlie's arms, her body bounced. The vision through the doorway rose away from her like a beacon as they descended a set of dimly lit stairs, the sharp, crisp rectangle growing smaller and smaller. At the bottom of the stairs, Charlie paused, fiddling with keys. He unlocked a door, turning to lock it once more after they'd crossed the threshold.

For a moment, Ruth caught a glimpse of a large, open room with floors made of stone and walls constructed from concrete slabs, a door on every wall. Bare lightbulbs hugged the walls, connected by metal tubing, glowing every few feet.

Charlie carried her through one of the doors, gently dropping her on top of a cot. He helped her into a sitting position.

"Here, eat this," he said, handing her something sticky from the unzipped bag. "Slowly."

"What happened?" she mumbled, still woozy. The room around her resembled a fallout shelter, full of brown cots, canvas emergency packs placed at the foot of each. Charlie smiled at her, gentle and soft, pushing her hand up toward her mouth. She took a bite and chewed. A Cosmic brownie.

"You passed out," he said. "You let your blood sugar get too low. You're safe now. I still keep emergency Glucagon on hand, you know, just in case someone ever needs it. I have ever since I met you. And it looks like you've been thinking of me, too."

"Huh?" she replied, the sound edging out between the mush in her mouth.

He chuckled, tugging on her sleeve. "The sweatshirt? I can't believe you still have that thing. Nearly ruined, now, though. You'll be okay in a little bit. Just eat this and once you're feeling a bit better, we can get going."

Get going? Going where? she wondered.

She mumbled a noise of confusion, trying to ask what he meant, but he pushed her hand holding the food up to her mouth again, urging her to continue eating it. The icing coated her teeth in a sticky film.

Pieces of the past few hours started to reenter her memory, shreds that she couldn't make sense of at first. How did Charlie fit in? He wasn't adorned with a yellow apron, and Ruth couldn't spot the little golden hook anywhere on his clothing. Was he a part of everything? Or had he saved her?

She couldn't be sure yet. She was still weak, so much weaker than him; she always had been. The only time she'd ever felt stronger than he could ever be was when she broke it off with him instead of pretending to be someone she wasn't. That had been her greatest act of courage, of strength.

Ruth hadn't meant for things to end with Charlie. She was ready to be his perfect wife, to mother babies for him. She had loved him, hadn't she? She'd thought so, until Abigail asked that question, that one single question that had churned inside Ruth, burning a hole in her chest: *Is this really what you want?*

Those simple six words seared a hole in Ruth, the singed edges expanding, eating up more and more of her. She tried to ignore the flames spreading across her picture-perfect future, boils and bubbles sprouting at the corners. She didn't want to be bisexual; she wanted to be *normal.* Everyone in Kill Devil was a conservative, buttoned-up heterosexual who clutched pearls and sneered down their nose at anyone who dared to nudge the status quo. She was already engaged to a man—what was the point of addressing these feelings? Before Abigail's bombshell question, she could rinse herself in the bullshit excuses of her rigid faith and repeat.

But those fucking six words kept bouncing around inside her skull. The more she probed, the less she could deny or excuse.

Even after she had accepted her sexuality, she wrestled with whether to tell Charlie. It didn't affect her feelings for him. She still was attracted to him, but she was also attracted to women—even though she didn't have any plans to act upon that attraction. But in the end, she hadn't wanted to keep secrets from him. And she thought if he truly loved her, he would stay with her—accept her no matter what.

Charlie had been attending more and more meetings with the New Creationists, exchanging hushed words in private rooms, more and more evenings spent disappearing behind the thick wooden doors of the sanctuary. When he reemerged, his tongue seemed to be tainted, coated with new words and ideas—newly conjured monsters to battle, new villains made of people who had never bothered him before: *Did you hear? They want men to go into bathrooms with little girls, they want to teach pornography to children. I'm scared for the future, but I've seen the way forward with the New Creationists.*

His voice was always laced with gentle sadness. Once it had been imbued with fervent excitement, this time the words springing out all stitched together, something about having seen *wonders* or *powers*, something mystical, something *beyond belief.*

He'd never shown indignant violence. Still, it scared her. Could she hide that part of herself forever? What if they tied the knot, forever bound to each other in the eyes of the holy being above, and the truth squirmed its way out years down the line? Would he still be gentle and kind by then, after years of deception?

The decision sat in her chest like a boulder for weeks, the pressure squeezing her lungs, each breath like a silent gasp. The dress she'd picked hung in her childhood closet beneath a thick plastic sheet. She couldn't take it. She couldn't keep that secret inside her for the rest of their lives.

She told him the next morning, sitting on the edge of his bed at his parents' house.

"We can get you help," he said, taking her hands inside his. The same warm embrace she'd always known. "The church has programs. They can cure you."

"I'm not broken," Ruth said.

"Of course you're not," he replied. His thumb rubbed a constant circle on her skin. "You're just—*confused*. You only need to pray on it, open yourself to the Creator's love. Put your trust in Him so that He may show you the light."

The acid in Ruth's stomach boiled, bubbling up into her throat.

"Are you feeling okay? You're suddenly pale. Do you need your insulin? Or is it low?"

"It's not that," Ruth said. His thumb continued its orbit, a circle forming on the back of her hand.

"What brought this up?" he asked after a long pause. "Why do you think you're gay?"

"I don't *think* I'm bisexual. I am."

"I'm just trying to help." His hands slid away from hers and settled in his lap. "Did you see something sinful, like in a movie?"

"No," she said, sighing, releasing a cloud of exasperation.

"It is clearly stated to be a sin—there are many passages to guide you. '*The Creator abandoned them to their shameful desires, and as a result of this sin, they suffered the penalty they deserved.*'"

Ruth wasn't sure how she thought he might respond, but she hadn't expected him to quote passages at her. They'd both grown up in churches but were never the fervent type that had memorized verses like a school play.

"I know there are passages like that, but do they ever say *why* it's wrong? It's just loving another person. I don't understand why that's so bad."

"It's unnatural," he replied. "It's very clear. Relationships are supposed to be with a man and a woman. Anything else is an abomination."

"It's an abomination to love someone?"

"*Do you not know that wrongdoers will not inherit the kingdom of the Creator? Do not be deceived: Neither the sexually immoral nor the idolators nor—*"

"Charlie, stop," Ruth interrupted. The boiling welt of tears pooled beneath her eyes.

"I don't want you to go to hell," he said, placing his warm hand on her shivering arm. "I want to save your soul. I just want what's best for you."

Ruth had no response. How could she convince him that she wasn't a sinner? That it wasn't a phase, that she wasn't a crumbling statue in need of repair? She wasn't sure how she thought he'd react. Some part of her expected, perhaps, that his love for her would override the church's teachings—that he might listen to the girl he'd known for most of his life, the person he'd said he would love unconditionally, the one he'd trusted enough to plan for marriage.

"Ruth, I still love you," he said. "I think I always will. But I can't support this path of sin. I can't marry you if you won't repent."

The dam broke, a flood racing over Ruth's cheeks. Slipping the ring off her finger, she held it out to Charlie.

"I'll keep your secret," he said. The ring sat in his open palm, the creases at his brow suggesting it was made of fire, that it was eroding a perfectly round hole into his skin, straight through his flesh. "I won't tell anyone, don't worry. If you ever change your mind, I'll be here to support your journey back to the flock. Back to the loving arms of the Creator. It's never too late to repent."

Something deep inside her had edged around the pain, had been relieved that everything was over, that she'd held true to herself. The next morning, she awoke to a crazed storm, the *scandal of the year*, everyone in their small town wanting a piece of the gossip, all at her expense. She'd heard a million rumors about it, all about how he left her because of something she did—ranging from cheating on him, variations from kissing to full-on sex, to stealing from his family, getting drunk every night, and more. But never once did she hear anything about her being attracted to women—he'd refused to provide a reason to anyone who asked.

Charlie must be helping her, right? He'd never outed her in all these years, and he'd had plenty of chances. Maybe he had been with the cult, but once he saw who they were hunting, he decided to defect. If he wasn't helping, wouldn't he have taken her to the ritual altar? She didn't hear or see anyone else around them. He had said he'd always love her, back when they broke up. And he'd been texting her to meet up recently, but she'd ghosted him. What if he was trying to warn her about all of this? But, yet again, she'd been too stubborn.

"I'm glad I found you," he said. "I don't know what I would have done if I'd lost you. It's so good to see you again."

The fog receding, Ruth regained more and more of herself, but her limbs still felt as though they were filled with concrete, everything still groggy and heavy.

"Yeah," she said. She tried to sit up more. Something stiff poked into her thigh. No one else was around, at least not in sight. "Charlie, we have to go before—"

"It's okay," he said. "You're safe now. Please eat—you need to get your blood sugar back up."

He unwrapped another brownie and brought it to her mouth, pushing the smashed dessert between her teeth as though they were celebrating newlyweds.

"I'm so happy I could help you," he said. "You're so lucky."

Ruth chewed, the sweetness cloying, coating her incisors. Her tongue had become a slimy slug oozing inside her jaw. That word—*lucky*—settled into her brain. It felt out of place, like a jigsaw piece that didn't quite fit.

"I know you must be really scared," he said. "But you shouldn't be. I'll be with you the whole time."

"I should have replied to you all those times you reached out," she said. "Maybe I wouldn't be here if I had."

Even now, he giggled. Like no time had passed. The same

laugh that would escape his lips when Ruth gave an off-the-cuff snarky quip all those years ago. The one that came after their first kiss. He *had* to be helping. She knew that laugh too well. It was an intimate laugh. He only used that laugh when he was alone with her.

He brushed her hair behind her ear, his fingers soft as fleece. "I'm glad you're okay," he said. "I'm glad I found you in time. You look like you're in pain."

Ruth nearly choked on her bite of brownie, a laugh fighting in the opposite direction through her throat. She could only imagine what she looked like: a deep, dark stain smeared across her chest, gelatinous globs of gore pasted across her face, gouges carved from every part of her body, a halo of missing hair.

"I've felt better," she replied.

Charlie settled onto the cot next to her, their two bodies sliding into each other, the canvas pooling their weight in the center. He wrapped his arm around her shoulders, tenderly, applying the exact right amount of pressure. For a moment, it was like nothing had changed. They were, once again, two stupid, naive teenagers in love. Ruth even felt the heft of a band around her finger, the gemstone resting its head against her pinky just as she rested her head against Charlie's shoulder now.

"It's going to be okay," he assured her, and Ruth melted into his frame, his body warm and tender. The heavy weight of exhaustion shuttered her eyes. She sighed, released the tension from her bones, pretending, for a moment, that the pain of the last day, the pain of the last five years, had never happened.

"Hey, don't fall asleep on me," he said, rocking her shoulders, cupping her chin in his hand. A silky grin spread across his face. "We need to get going."

"You're right," she replied, her head once more filled with thoughts of *Abigail*. "You have the keys, right? Should we go back up through the store or—"

"We need to go deeper into the tunnels to get to the ritual," he replied, standing up.

Everything inside Ruth came to a shuddering halt, all of the processes of her body coiling and tensing. "What?"

"It's almost time. They'll be waiting for us." He knelt before her and took her hands in his, the second time in their lives he'd performed this gesture. "Are you ready?"

Ruth took her hands back. "Why are you doing this?"

"What do you mean?"

"You're still going to take me to the ritual? You're going to let them kill me? *Eat me?*"

"Don't make it sound so crude," he replied. "Sacrifices are lucky! Your soul will be purified, and you'll go straight to heaven with a clean slate. The Creator will welcome you, thanking you for your duty, and you'll be revered here on earth. It's more than I could have hoped for you."

The tingly nerves in her arms and toes pinged and awakened. Adrenaline circulated in her veins now. The thing poking the back of her leg was the squirt gun, the weapon she'd filled with paint thinner. But Charlie wore glasses; even at close range, the target would be obscured.

"Charlie, please—"

"It's okay, I'll be with you the whole time. I'm giving you

everlasting salvation, and you're saving the world from evil. What could be better?"

Charlie ran his other hand across her face, and her muscles clenched and shrank in revulsion. He stared at her now, intensely, his face getting closer and closer to hers until he was hovering over her, his nose nearly grazing hers, his hot, rank breath crowding into her nostrils.

"Everyone else is waiting for us," he said.

She couldn't stand to look at him anymore, couldn't hide the emotional bile crawling inside her. When she rolled her head away, she spotted one of the emergency packs, the flap opened, revealing its contents. Inside sat a small lighter. Before she could grab it, Charlie clenched her chin and pivoted her face back to his.

"Ruth, I promise," he said. "You're safe with me. What is a moment of pain compared to an eternity of paradise?"

Now his fingers felt rough, like 60 grit sandpaper, and his nails dug into her cheeks. She reached out for the lighter, trying to find it with spidery fingers. Her fingers grazed the edge of the plastic cylinder. She focused all of her energy into stretching her arm out to wrap around the handle. Charlie didn't seem to notice or care about what her arm was doing.

"I know you're scared," he said. "But sometimes doing the right thing is terrifying. That doesn't mean it's not worth it."

Finally, her fingers wrapped around the lighter. She stuffed it beneath her legs, praying to someone, but not their Creator, that Charlie had not noticed.

Chapter 20

Ruth's hands shook trying to line up the tip of the squirt gun and the top of the lighter, but the pair constantly vibrated out of sync. She held the gun in the hand connected to her swollen, engorged wrist, the purple flesh still cocooned inside the makeshift splint. Curling her fingers around the plastic seemed to inflate the balloon there even more, and she worried the whole thing might burst when she pulled the little plastic trigger.

"Ruth, what are you doing?" Charlie asked, sad puppy eyes pointed at her toy weapon, turning to face her before she had a chance to try out her miniature flamethrower.

She tried to flick the lighter, but her hands were still shaky with adrenaline and shock. She flicked the little metal wheel, sparks spurting as it struck the flint, but no fire bloomed. Before she could manage to get it to work, Charlie plucked the gun and the lighter out of her hands, as easy as snatching a toy from a toddler. He shook his head, as if to say *How stupid to think you could win against us.*

"What is this?" he asked. "A squirt gun?"

Defeat settled into her bones. She tried to shake it away, repeated her refrain of *Abigail, Abigail, Abigail,* but the chorus broke in half when Charlie lifted the barrel to his nose and sniffed, his eyebrows wrinkling. He sniffed once more, and then pieced together what she was trying to do.

"I know this is all scary for you," he said, still holding the gun. "I know it probably seems extreme. But I promise you, you'll go straight to heaven, straight up to paradise. Don't you want to do something good for the world? Don't you want to save Abigail?"

Ruth nearly snarled when he uttered those three syllables.

"You're keeping her shackled to this sinful life," he continued, his voice soft and gentle, as though Ruth were a child who'd thrown a tantrum over her own bad decision. "With one choice you could free her from sin and ensure that her every memory of you leads to salvation and joy. If you really loved her, you would do anything you could to save her. It's your fault she's living in sin, and it'll be your fault she won't go to heaven. But if you come with me, you can save yourself and Abigail."

"Charlie, you can't really believe in all this," she said. "You can't really believe there's a *demon* in a jar!"

"I know there is," he replied, his voice pierced with the same steady calm. "The Creator has shown me so; He has shown me objects of unimaginable powers. You even used one yourself, didn't you? You felt its powers—that vial is still around your neck, broken. How can you not believe there are things greater than this world? How can you not believe in the power of the

Creator after experiencing it firsthand?"

Ruth bit her lip. The thing had felt warm, heavy and powerful and *right* around her neck. She'd been able to climb up the girder with a strange ease, hadn't she? It had even eroded her pain, hadn't it? From the moment the chain grazed her neck until it broke in the collapse, hadn't it been helping her?

She wasn't sure. She didn't want to believe in such things. Was it the vial or was it adrenaline? But she understood now how the New Creationists might collect their Noble Shepherds. Understood what Charlie had been so delirious about that night, the night he'd paced and gushed about wonders unseen.

"I chose you because I love you," he continued, frustration edging through his dulcet tone.

Everything in Ruth froze. He hadn't been texting her to warn her—he'd been trying to snatch her himself. It'd all been Charlie. He was the reason they were hunting her. Was he the reason she'd been fired? A new rage sparked in her stomach, a hellfire that expanded, eating up her insides.

"I wasn't lying when I said I always would," he continued. "I want you to be saved. Do you think I've enjoyed seeing you lead yourself on a path of sin? A path that'll go straight to hell? I want you to greet me when I arrive at the Creator's door."

Ruth was a trapped animal. He held the paint-thinner gun still, the doorway behind him. Her muscles tensed, gearing up to run.

He sighed, a deep sound of disappointment. He flicked the lighter, testing it. An inch-tall flame sprouted and disappeared as he removed his finger. So simple, just a quick snap of his thumb.

"I didn't want to have to hurt you," he said, raising the gun. "I should have brought you straight to the ritual and revived you there, but I wanted to talk to you first, wanted to explain. I hoped the Ruth I used to know was still in there. I wanted you to understand. But I was foolish to think you would abandon your sins so easily. It seems I have no choice."

This was it. Ruth had met her fate. She wouldn't escape. She wouldn't get back to Abigail. This was her end. Charlie would perform their ritual. They'd consume her until there was nothing left, until even her memory was gone, the one person who cared about her, who really knew her, also consumed, either joining her in death or joining *them*.

Rage boiled inside her, but she had no recourse. She could barely keep herself upright, and he had the only weapon.

The lighter flicked to life again in his strong, uninjured hand.

"Leaving you was the best decision I ever made, Charlie," she said. Ruth could do nothing but prepare for the blow. She lifted her arms as high as they would go, trying to shield her face.

With another deep, cutting sigh, Charlie pulled the trigger, the paint thinner squirting through the flame. Fireballs flew through the air, a dazzling display of light, melting the acrylic fibers of the sweatshirt and the T-shirt bandages onto the skin of her arm. The meteors pelted her like a spray of buckshot, little beads of flame searing against her forehead, her elbows, her pant legs, singeing the remaining hairs still attached to her scalp. Any moment, she expected her body to be engulfed, for all the little pebbles of flame to catch, to grow and connect and consume her whole.

Fuck, she thought. *This is the end.* She could almost feel her blood sugar lower with each strike, her knees shaking and her vision blurring, trying to fade into black. Any adrenaline that was pumping through her remaining blood wouldn't be enough to raise it, not enough to help her fight back this time. This would be the final blow that would render her incapacitated. And there was nothing she could do about it.

Ruth parted her lips, ready to surrender, to plead for him to stop, to abandon *Abigail, Abigail, Abigail* when the firestorm ceased. She lowered her worn arms, her eyes growing wide. Whatever outcome she could have imagined, whatever paths this scene might have taken, she never could have guessed what would actually happen, what was happening right before her eyes. It was almost comical in its absurdity—Ruth donned a smirk, a growing grin she couldn't stop from spreading across her burned freckles.

The flame jumped from the lighter, catching on the stream of paint thinner, reversing course. It crawled backward, up the stream, back toward the nozzle. Charlie kept pulling the trigger over and over, pump following pump, creating a constant flow of liquid. Before he could stop himself, before he realized what was happening, the flame had reached the nozzle.

Was it luck? Powers from beyond?

Or had his Creator abandoned him in his time of need?

The flame ducked into the gun, and it exploded between them, becoming a fireball in his hand.

The ignited paint thinner in the tank rained hellfire upon

Charlie, his shirt catching like a candle wick. He stumbled back in shock, his eyes growing larger as the flames spread. Smacking his chest, he tripped over his feet, an interpretive dance that sent him careening over the cot, the canvas fibers lapping up the flames as Ruth stumbled away.

The cot acted as kindling, like it was made from woven strands of the driest fibers of wood. In mere seconds, the flames had engulfed it, had reached all the way to the foot of the metal frame, where the intense heat had already started to catch the pack ablaze. Charlie rolled away from the cot, his mouth open as if to scream, but no sound came out.

Ruth didn't stay to learn his fate, whether he'd put himself out somehow or whether the fire would reach something flammable in the emergency duffel and seal his doom. She dodged out of the door, the scent of burning hair filling the air as she stepped into the concrete tunnel.

Chapter 21

Ruth ran, letting her ankle throb and scream beneath her, only adrenaline and the splint keeping it from snapping. She'd entered a large open space that seemed like a common area, an in-between space to congregate. Directly across from the room she'd just escaped was a twin room full of cots and emergency packs. The rows of brown canvas cots showed through the slice of the open door, each one identical and neat. Pristine and unused.

The only way out was the darkened doorway at the far end of the concrete room, revealing stairs leading down, deeper into whatever the fuck this place was, carved from the Kentucky clay and limestone. Buried beneath Kill Devil. The metal line of electricity followed the stairs down, wires strung through steel pipe along the left side, a hazy bulb every three feet. The light dissipated into blackness, into a void that obscured the bottom. She had no way to know where this path led, whether it would deliver her unto her salvation or her doom. But Charlie had locked the door that led back up to the store, and there was nowhere else to go. She had no choice but to descend into the mouth of this monster.

Ruth hobbled forward, Charlie's screams echoing in her ears. The pain of her ankle, of her engorged wrist, of every cell of her body melted into adrenaline. The brownies Charlie had given her had reinvigorated her. But would it last the rest of the night?

After two flights of stairs, steep and straight and interrupted by a small landing halfway down, she reached a forked path. One doorway was so dark it looked painted-on, like an old cartoon ploy to trick a coyote. Above it, a junction box sat, loose wires poking beneath. Ruth stuck her hand into the darkness, letting it swallow her arm almost to her shoulder before her fingers grazed dusty rock. A dead end.

She continued through the other doorway, the mouth containing another set of stairs, another path delivering her even deeper into the earth. The lights continued at their regular interval, one sickly bulb every thirty-six inches, the halo of each one not reaching the next, the expanse of their lighted kingdoms refusing to encroach on the borders of their neighbors. In the dark recesses, Ruth conjured heaps of skulls like those lining the catacombs of France, each one pushing out of the Kentucky substrate, their jaws agape and grinning.

How deep did this go? What *was* this? Some sort of demented basement? Had they built all of this in the few months that the church and store were under construction? *How?* She could do nothing but push further, descending one step at a time into the heart of this cult.

The bottom of the second flight of stairs spilled into an open room. Concrete slabs lined the walls, the snaking lights at the edges leaving a darkened center, the reverse of the church's spotlit sanctuary stage. Circling around the walls, just under the ceiling, were painted the words:

Not all the blood of beasts on altars slain could give the guilty conscience peace or wash away the stain. But our Creator takes all sin away with a Sacrifice of nobler name and richer blood.

A weight settled in Ruth's stomach, sizzing against the acid there, like a molten ball dropped into a vat of water. Beneath the words was painted some sort of family tree, gilded circles surrounding stern, noble faces, little tendrils curling to their kin.

She tiptoed to the painted display. The left side had faded to near illegibility, but the right was so fresh the paint glistened, glossy as though still wet. As if she could swipe a finger through the face of Gideon, could smudge his eyes and nose and horrible mouth—all of which had some inkling of familiarity, but Ruth couldn't place why. Underneath Gideon's clenched, severe face, a single tendril snaked down to an empty circle bearing the name Elizabeth, with a birth year matching Ruth's own. On the faded side of the genealogy, she could scarcely make out a date beneath one faded patriarch: *1785*. His name had nearly been erased by time, the paint flaking away, but Ruth could spy an *F* and two twin *L*s at the end. Whatever the fuck this place was, it was too ancient to have been built recently.

The room had four mouths, four gaping paths an equal distance apart, each one hosting a small glowing uvula too far back for Ruth to determine what they held. From her left came the noise of voices, of fear and desperation and panic and anger, all rising and jumbling together into a cumulative tumultuous roar vibrating through the limestone corridor. Still, a few phrases squeaked through: *where are—so long—here by now.*

Her feet dragged her in the opposite direction, carrying her automatically into one of the darkened mouths. The hallway beyond stretched deep and far, the strung-together bulbs ending at another rocky dead end. She ducked into an open doorway at her right.

Behind her, vibrating through the murky hallway, the voices sounded more clearly. They must have stopped in the genealogy room.

"What's taking Ahitophel so long with her? He should have brought her down by now."

Ahitophel? Ruth wondered. That must be Charlie, some code name. His Mustard Seed name that had sprouted from their Creator's care. The others must be using them, too.

"He said he needed to revive her," another voice said.

"It's getting late," the first said. "Run up and see what's happening. I wouldn't think it of Ahitophel to have fallen from the Creator's grace, but—maybe he's been tempted."

One pair of footsteps dissipated up the way she'd come. The other pair seemed to still, as if perking their ears, knowing deep down that Ruth had gotten away, once again, had defeated them even after nearly dying from hypoglycemia. They did not even pace inside the stone chamber. No further noise reached her, no scuffing of anxious soles or secret curses too quiet to drift up to their Creator through all the layers of dirt and rock and clay. It made her uneasy, as if, once again, they were *sensing* her.

Ruth nestled into a corner of the room, parallel with the door, afraid that her footsteps would give her away. Only when her body relaxed, when each muscle uncoiled from its skein, did the room itself seem to come into focus. Every wall was covered with shelves filled with glass display boxes, each one seeming to jut out of thin air the moment her eyes scanned it. Each box emanated a haze of light, just bright enough to showcase the objects inside. One held a leather-bound diary propped up at an angle, its yellow pages fluttering away from one another. Another contained a patinaed pocket watch, held aloft on an acrylic pike. Yet another enclosed a worn baseball cap, its stitching forever frozen in the process of unraveling. The items seemed random: a signed check, a pocketknife, a half-empty bottle of blood-red fingernail polish, an empty bourbon bottle with the bottled-in-bond strip ripped halfway off. Some cases even held bones aloft. Ruth feared they were human.

Each glass display bore a small golden placard, centered at the front. She dared not move from her nesting spot, but even at that distance she could discern that engraved on each one was a name and a date. The closest placard, on the case that held the mounted signed check, read *Tom Torrence, January 21, 2000*. The oldest date she could spot was from the 1960s, but some of the objects, like the diary, looked ancient. There must have been hundreds of objects in the room, each enclosed in its own pristine case.

Above the shelves, wrapping around the wall, were painted the words: *The Creator demands soul, life, all. We sacrifice them through His blood.*

The display stilled Ruth's heart. Somehow she knew what this was. Something deep inside her had placed all the pieces together without even needing to read each placard. She knew because there was an empty display case at the end of the row. She didn't want to look closer, afraid she would see *her* name on the golden placard. And beyond that, a barren shelf, space for dozens more.

These were totems. Keepsakes. Fucked-up souvenirs.

They had kept something from each one of their sacrifices, their victims.

What would they keep of her?

Would they keep something on her person? The destroyed sweatshirt, folded neatly? The crushed and emptied Skittles wrapper? A lock of her hair? Her skull? Or would they raid her home for their token? With Abigail out of the way, would they take the perfect representation of Ruth from the bedroom they shared? From the living room? Take one of the vials of insulin from the fridge?

Tears crystallized in the corners of her eyes, hot and sharp and threatening. Hopelessness overwhelmed her once more, a dark, engulfing shroud. Outside the room footsteps pounded up the stairs, backtracking to the apex of whatever this complex was. She was so tired. Exhaustion seeped into every pore, every tendon, every bone. She could no longer even hold her head aloft on her neck, and she let the bulbous weight fall backward into the wall.

Next to her ear rang the hollow vibration of rattling ceramic. A small ornate jar, tucked behind a display case. Ruth traced the designs painted along the sides. She rolled it between her palms. It looked just like the money jar that sat on her mantel. The curving design was nearly the same—hand-painted vines bearing ripe, round fruit, thorns protruding among the leaves. On the lid were the familiar characters Ruth assumed were some foreign language.

She and Abigail had discovered the jar in Judy's closet after she passed. They'd found it in the deepest corner, past the hanging blouses and dresses, hidden by boxes of every single thing that had ever borne Abigail's name, Judy so sentimental as to keep every last preschool crayon drawing, every spelling test. Ruth and Abigail had almost missed it—the jar shoved so deep in the closet that it had actually started to eat away the drywall. Only when they grabbed the final box from the darkened space did it tip over and roll toward them: a sealed, ceramic jar with painted vines twirling around it. Inside were actual vines, anemic thorns and desiccated leaves, a scattering of dirt at the bottom.

What the hell? There was no label anywhere on the jar, no little hang tag to identify its innards as a poisonous cutting of exotic roses or earth from the homeland or whatever. But the jar was nice. And it was Judy's. So they went out back to the compost pile and emptied it, holding it upside down at arm's length so the mysterious dust and plant matter did not freckle their faces, their nostrils and eyelashes.

Then they cleaned the jar in the kitchen sink and set it on the mantel, where they stuffed its mouth with dollar bills, fishing them out far too often.

And now there was somehow an identical jar in Ruth's

hands, deep underground, in a room filled with the tokens of dead people. Murdered people. The same lid, the same curling, paint-stroked vines. How had an identical jar found its way into Abigail's mom's closet? How did she have the same thing as this cult?

Ruth swallowed, not wanting to put all the pieces together. Not wanting to make the leap that Judy had somehow been involved in all of this. She wished she could make herself believe it to be a coincidence, that Judy—the mother of the love of her life, the woman who had given her shelter when she had nowhere else to go, who didn't sneer or shriek when she came out—had bought the thing at an estate sale, had found it on the side of the road. That these jars were mass-produced and it was simply common practice to fill them with powdery pebbles.

She didn't want to accept any other explanation, didn't want to believe that Judy might have been a member of this cult. And maybe, too, Abigail.

Suddenly the jar felt heavy in her hands, the painted thorns transforming, poking into her fingertips, the spots where it met her skin too hot, the whole thing just *wrong*. She raised it, ready to throw it into their fucked-up museum, ready to smash everything to pieces.

Outside, anger and panic stewed, the directives vibrating down the hall to the doorway next to her, freezing her before the act of destruction. "She must be down here somewhere," a voice said. "Ahitophel locked the door behind him."

"Could she have escaped through another exit?" someone else asked.

"I don't think so," yet another said. "We would have seen her if she went the other way. She has to be down here somewhere."

Ruth clutched the jar to her chest, making herself as small as possible, squishing her body out of reach of the dim lightbulbs. The congregated boots stomped away from each other, the echoes spreading like a starburst. She was trapped, utterly this time, crouched in the corner parallel to the door. There were no nooks or crannies in which to hide. She readied the jar in her hands to launch, the last Hail Mary, the last bead on the rosary. If it smashed into her discoverer's face, maybe she could slip past him. She felt the heft of the jar and pictured it shattering upon impact with a skull, the broken shards slicing their way into an iris, across a tongue. Worming beneath boots, causing a tumble backward into their shrine, each glass case colliding, too, with a bloodied face.

But when one of the Shepherds did enter the room, he stood in the center, scanning. He wore a black cape with a hood that engulfed the top half of his face in shadow. On his exposed chin sprouted gritty stubble. He turned in place, the hood moving up and down as though he were searching the floor and ceiling for clues in addition to the space between them. Ruth still clutched the jar, ready to throw it. But when the dark space where his eyes should be hovered over her, seemed even to meet hers, he continued on. As if she weren't there. Then he left without grabbing her, without raising a ruckus of alarm. Was he helping her for some reason? Had he not seen her inside the dark corner?

Or was it the jar? Did it, like the vial, have some sort of

strange power?

Once the slap of his footsteps dissipated down the hallway, she placed the jar in its spot and slipped out of the room, heading back the way she came, the only direction she could go. Sweat coated her hands, rivulets following the contours of the cuts and scrapes embedded there. With each footstep closer to that large open room, her heart increased its beating, blood shooting through her veins like a roller coaster, circling back after what felt like mere moments. She hovered at the doorway, trying to hear voices over that maddening pulse inside her. But the only sound was the staticky hum of the lights in the open void of stone.

One lone sentinel remained there, stationary, his back to her. In his black robes, he stood like the Grim Reaper missing his scythe, ready to snatch her away to bring her to her imminent death, to coil his fingers around her wrist and drag her to their altar. He'd take her there and they'd slice her up and eat her and sit back, satisfied with bellies full of *her*, satisfied that they'd appeased their Creator, that they'd held back a supposed demon that none of them had ever seen. For all they knew, their vessel contained only stale air, held only dust or the desiccated, dried-out husks of tiny insects that had slithered inside. An empty vessel they used to justify hatred, to justify kidnapping and murder and cannibalism.

If she hadn't abandoned the jar, she might have smashed it over his head. She wanted to feel the weight of it burst against his skull, the dust exploding, coating the floors along with the shards. She wanted to poke each broken piece of ceramic into his skin, to slice and prod. To do to them what they wanted to do to her. The thought filled her with a terrifying glee, a grinning little devil of happiness she didn't know could possess her at the thought of bloodshed, at the thought of inflicting such pain on another person.

Only her refrain of *Abigail, Abigail, Abigail* kept her moving.

Biting her lip, just at the precipice of drawing blood, she edged the wall with silent footsteps, heading toward the mouth that gaped directly opposite the staircase she'd descended. The man kept his back to her, his attention fixed on another open doorway. She approached another set of stairs, identical to the others, long and narrow and pockmarked with sickly lightbulbs, but this time leading up. She hoped they led out, too.

The lights too dim to see the end, she darted up. At the same time, footsteps reverberated down the stone steps toward her. Her chest seized, her racing heart stopping as suddenly as if it had smashed against a brick wall.

Five steps ahead was another landing. The line of electricity turned a corner here, spilled light into a space to the left. Drawing the last bit of energy into her legs, Ruth pumped up the final steps and rushed into the hallway. Before her stood a row of rooms, each one just large enough to house a worn, stiff cot—no blankets or pillows. A leather-bound book with toilet-paper-thin pages sat in the center of each one. A bucket sat in each corner. Each heavy door, slung open, boasted a slot the width of a tray.

The last door in the line was closed. A soft wail emanated from the slot set into the steel, a thin, pitiful noise of despair. The sound raised pinpricks of goose bumps along Ruth's arms, the hairs along the back of her neck erect and charged with static. She hesitated. It felt like a trap, like they'd locked someone in there to distract her, to keep her in one place while they scurried around their stone lair trying to grab her. But they believed her a sinner, someone who might commune with the devil or craft curses beneath the grim light of a full moon. Would such a person be lured by such a trap, by the desire to help another human being?

What if it was another one of their victims? What if they had trapped someone else, a backup sacrifice, waiting in a holding cell until the very last second?

"Shit," she whispered under her breath. She couldn't just leave them, couldn't be complicit in the murder of someone else.

"Hello?" she whispered into the hole. "Are you okay?"

The whimpering beyond slowed, replaced by rustling movement toward the slot.

"Help me," a voice said. The words carried a sickly scent, a cavity smell of rotting rosebuds and carcass.

"How can I get you out?" Ruth examined the door. It was constructed with steel, not even a gap large enough for her fingernail between it and the frame. No doorknob. Only a keyhole and the rectangular gap. There wasn't any way to get it open without a key. The patter of footsteps down the stairs had already passed the landing. How much longer until they checked this spot? How long until a horde of robed men flooded into this cramped corridor?

"Are there keys somewhere?" Ruth asked.

The foul breath came again, this time with unintelligible syllables. Ruth crouched, her ear closer to the slot.

"I'll come back," she said. "I'll go get help and tell them you're locked up down here. I promise."

Before she could turn to leave, an arm surged out of the hole, and fingers wrapped around her wrist, fingernails digging in, threatening bloodshed. The limb's muscles had shriveled and withered, the dried skin clinging to all the nooks and crannies of it, dehydrated like human jerky. The fingers that clasped onto her were still permeated with strength, though the cuticles receded from the nail beds and the knuckles floated like giant beads on a thin string.

"This is how you'll help me," the voice croaked. "You'll stay right here while they come, while I scream for them. They'll let me out if I am the one to deliver their sacrifice. That will prove I have become Right and made amends with the Creator."

The stink soared out of the hole as the man behind the door hollered, his grip tightening while she tried to pull free. His desiccated fingertips drew blood now, deep red pearls materializing and slipping down his yellowed nails.

Ruth's pity evaporated back into rage. Even in the throes of starvation, his dedication ran deep, had penetrated his bones and slipped through his veins, pumping poison across the valves of his heart. His fellow cultists were the ones with the keys, after all. Ruth couldn't open this door, but they could. But she doubted this follower would use his freedom to leave.

So she bit. She clasped this jerkylike piece of flesh between her teeth and clamped down, feeling the warm rush of blood fill the spaces between her incisors, coat her tongue, spill down her chin. With a yelp, the man released his grip, the fingers receding from her arm, but her teeth didn't. She kept them sunk in. Maybe the pain would break the spell they had over him. Or maybe it wouldn't. She didn't care. She just needed someone else to feel the prick of torment.

James,

I don't like what you're becoming. I don't recognize you anymore. You're getting too deep with those people.

You're not the man I married. I don't know who you are now.

I'll never understand how you let them worm their way into your mind. How you started a loving husband and father and transformed into a hateful monster who fears anything he doesn't immediately understand.

By the time you read this, I'll be gone. I'm taking Elizabeth. I'm leaving for her sake. I've seen enough to know that I don't want her involved with any of it. Even if it means I have to raise her alone. That's better than the alternative.

I will raise her to love.

I'm also taking that jar—the sealed jar of dirt and thorns you brought into our house, saying it would provide protection and concealment for our household. Some kind of mystical totem that everyone in that <u>cult</u> has. I didn't like the excitement in your voice when you brought it home, as if its existence meant everything to you. Like you'd really made something of yourself because you had been given this jar. You said it would hide us so that no one could discover us, as though we were mice being hunted.

So I'm taking it to use your sorcery against you. I don't know if it's even real, but I know that you believe it is. So I'm taking it, just in case, and I'll do everything in my power to make sure you never find us.

Goodbye and
good riddance,

Barbara

Province of
Clay County Kentucky

AN ACT,

Made and Passed by the Great and General Court
of Assembly of Clay County in the Commonwealth of Kentucky,
Held the 17th Day of October, 1823.

AN ACT TO INDICT *Francis Hill* AND OTHERS FOR WITCHCRAFT AND EVIL DOING.

FORASMUCH as in the Year of our Lord One Thousand Eight Hundred and Nineteen, Several Persons within this Province were Infected with a horrible Witchcraft or Possession of Evils; And a Special Court held in Clay County, in the same Year One Thousand Eight Hundred and Nineteen, Francis Hill *of Fall Rocks,* Antony Killian, *and his Wife,* Joelle Killian, *and* Anneke Willard, *all of Garrard aforesaid:* Jane Ryeland, Marie Ketterer *and* Emma Murray *all of Sibert:* Katharine Jacob, Bernadette How, Isaac Watts, *and his Wife,* Amabilis Watts, *all of Hubbardsville:* Christopher Halloran, Sarah Nazar, *and* Lewis Craig; *were severally Indicted, Convicted, and Attained of Witchcraft and Evil Doing, and some of them put to Death, Others lying still under the like Sentence of the said Court, and liable to have the same Executed upon them. Others having been Accused and Fled the Province.*

The Influence and Energy of the Evil Spirits so great at that time acting in and upon the whole who were Principal Accusers and Witnesses, proceeding so far as to cause a Prosecution to be had of Persons of known and good Reputation. The land in which these Persons performed said Witchcraft and Evil Doing, residing near the Creek of Hell for Certain, has been Attained by the Authority of Clay County, in the Commonwealth of Kentucky.

And some of the Principal Accusers and Witnesses in those dark and severe Prosecutions have since discovered themselves to be Persons of Profligate and Vicious Conversation.

Upon the humble Petition and Suit of several of the said Persons, and of the Children of others of them whose Parents were Executed.

Be it Declared and Enacted by His Excellency, the Governor, Council and Representatives, in General Court Assembled and by the Authority of the same, That the several Convictions, Judgements, and Attainders against the said *Francis Hill, Antony Killian, Joelle Killian, Anneke Willard, Jane Ryeland, Marie Ketterer, Emma Murray, Katharine Jacob, Bernadette How, Isaac Watts, Amabilis Watts, Christopher Halloran, Sarah Nazar,* and *Lewis Craig,* and every of them, Be and hereby are held.

Any Law, Usage, or Custom to the contrary notwithstanding.

CLAY COUNTY: Printed by *K. Good,* Printer to His Excellency the GOVERNOUR and COUNCIL. 1823.

Chapter 22

The brassy taste of blood still lingering on her tongue, Ruth darted down a long hallway to the next set of stairs, her muscles weakening with each agonizing step, the pain crescendoed to its peak. Her brain couldn't pick one area of her body to focus on, which pangs and slices and scrapes and balloons of flesh to feel, as she worked her way down the long tunnel, feeling her blood sugar lowering with every stair.

Just before the stairs, a series of doorways sprouted on either side of the hall, these rooms filled with rows and rows of clear jars, packed with food, with beans and tomatoes and peaches and peppers. A sink came into view through one of them, a whole kitchen appearing and disappearing through the doorway. Hearing no footsteps or commotion, she snatched a jar of sugary preserves before she climbed the next mountain.

The last staircase was long and narrow, ascending out of the earth at such a steep degree that Ruth almost toppled backward. By the time she neared the top, her breath ran ragged, and she paused every few steps to lick jam from her fingers. At the peak of this mountain stood a closed door.

"Please don't be locked," Ruth whispered.

She stamped her ear against the rough wood, pushing all of her energy into listening, every part of her numb except her eardrum. The only thing that entered her ear were scraps of wood, little daggery splinters rustling against her lobe. She twisted the doorknob, as slow as possible, until the softest *click* reverberated through the metal latch.

Unlocked. The relief made her knees weak.

Just as slowly, she pushed open the door. It spilled into a wide, gaping room lined with tables and chairs. A chalkboard on wheels sat in the corner, ghostly white remnants of numbers and letters stained into its face. At the far end was another doorway, bracketed with glass cabinets hosting stacks of dishes. The whole room was cast in a sharp, orange glow. The left side of each tabletop, each chair leg, spotlit; the right side silhouetted.

Outside, a bonfire bloomed, so great that its width spanned the length of two windows in the long room. Mesmerized, Ruth tiptoed to one of the panes, raised just enough for the heat to sizzle at her cheeks, to dry and crust the blood on her lips. Whatever this room was, it led out—she'd made it through the tunnels, aboveground at last. Her breath caught in the back of her throat, right against her tonsils, as her eyes adjusted to the scene.

The orange glow of the fire stretched back far enough to light the trees beyond, three or four rows deep before a wall of darkness. The exit must have spat her out somewhere in the woods beyond the craft store. Beneath the shelter of trees were small wooden cabins, like a summer camp, all encircling the bonfire. Most seemed to be a uniform build, the same pitched roof with symmetrical windows standing guard beside each central door, like distorted faces, the fire casting little orange eyes into each pane. A few larger structures stood behind the bonfire, their details obscured by the oversized flames.

In a circle around the great fire were women and children. They all wore plain—but modern—clothing, the women and girls clad in simple cotton dresses and the boys in polos or button-ups tucked into belted khakis. The women seemed starved, the loose dresses billowing around their skeletons. Ruth spied Charlie's wife among them, sitting with perfect posture, petting the head of a young blond boy at her feet. Something rolled over in Ruth's stomach, the sticky jam clawing against the walls of her stomach. That could have been her.

The youngest seemed to Ruth to be no older than seven or eight years old, fidgeting in place, sitting with their legs crossed on the ground, exhaustion etched into the corners of their eyes, yawns hovering on their lips. Each one held some sort of teddy bear or limp doll, their stuffed heads lolling at their waists, their yarn hair dragging in the dirt. The oldest looked to be in their teens, some rapt with attention and others staring into the dirt, tossing scraps of twigs or rocks into the fire. Whether their boredom was born from standard teenage petulance or rebellion, Ruth couldn't tell.

"I see those yawns," one of the women said. She alone stood; the rest of the women sat in straight-backed wooden chairs among the children, some with their hands in their laps and others rubbing shoulders or smacking heads to attention.

"This is the first blood moon for many of you younger ones. I know you aren't accustomed to staying awake so late, but you must listen well—the Creator sees your inattention just as I do, and tonight is a very important night. Tonight the men—your fathers and elders—have a task to complete. It is not a fun task, and it will be difficult, but they are doing it because they love you, and because they are keeping the world safe, and we must do our part to support them in turn."

A woman at the back of the congregation scolded an older child and pointed into the darkness behind her. The kid grimaced, kicking up dirt as he followed the direction of her finger, vanishing into the shadows.

"As you know, we collect holy items," the woman said, her tone sweet, as though she were reciting a whimsical fairy tale. "We keep them safe and protected, and they help us with our mission to spread the word and love of our Creator. Because we're so Pure and faithful, the Creator gives these items powers. Some of these relics keep us safe from the sinful outside world, and some help us when we go out to try to save the sinners."

By the light of the fire, Ruth could see the little eyes alight with wonder. Little mouths popped open, unable to contain their little gasps.

"Boys—when you're older, if you stay Pure and True, you'll get to see them and learn more about how they work—and maybe, if you're really good, you'll get to go on a mission and use them!"

"That's not fair," a little girl replied, the words seeming to bubble out of her mouth before she could stop them. "Why do only the boys get to use powers?"

"I know it might seem that way, Sarah," the woman said, "but girls have a different calling. The boys are called to spread the word of the Creator and to protect us from sin. It might seem fun to have these holy items, but they are not toys. They are only to be used for very important missions, like the ones your daddies are performing tonight. It's hard work."

The girl's face wrinkled into a sulk, her arms crossed over her chest. Her eyes stared deep into the flames, a miniature fire burning in each iris. Ruth hoped the little blaze of rebellion remained kindled inside her.

"Don't be so sullen," the woman continued. "We girls have much easier duties. While the boys have to save the world, we need merely to do a little cooking and cleaning, and raising babies, after you complete your marriage rites with your assigned husband, of course. When you're a little bigger, you'll join the older girls in their lessons on how a wife can satisfy her husband. Each person has a role, and each role is important."

Sarah still didn't seem content with her lot. The flames in her eyes sparked.

The woman moved on. "A long time ago, we came into possession of a very special jar, an ancient jar, sealed with wax. To look at it, you wouldn't think it was anything out of the ordinary, just an old, dirty ceramic container. But our forefathers searched and searched for this little jar. It took them centuries to find it. Originally, they thought it contained an angel. But later, they examined the inscription and discovered that it actually held a demon. If we don't contain it, it will escape and deliver everyone to the deep fires of hell. You can feel the heat of the fire before you; some of you may be thinking it's too big and too hot. I can see that some of you are pulling at your collars. Some of you have scooted back as far as you can get to avoid the heat. Imagine the heat of this fire times ten, times one hundred! The fires of hell are even hotter than that."

The older kids scoffed, some even rolling their eyes while mothers reassured their younger siblings.

"It's okay," the woman continued. "It sounds scary, but it's a good thing that the jar ended up with us, because we have the Creator on our side to guide us. Who better to be the keeper of such an item, than we who worship and serve? Who else will take the same amount of care to make sure the demon stays inside its cage?

"It is the burden we carry. The burden your fathers and elders carry. Someday you boys, too, will carry the burden of it, will make sure to keep everyone safe from the evil thing inside. That is what your daddies are doing right now. Every once in a while, we have to remake the seal, just like we have to plant seeds in the garden every year or mend our clothes when they tear. Sometimes things wear out and you have to make them new again.

"To do this, we need a sacrifice."

"What's a sacrifice?" one of the children asked. Ruth cringed at his eager, innocent face.

"A sacrifice is when you give up something really, really important to you," the woman explained. "In this case, it's when someone gives up their life. That might sound scary, but they get to go right to heaven. So the sacrifice is lucky!"

"Can I be the sacrifice?" a squeaky voice asked. It was a little girl, her hair long and curled.

Ruth gasped, a pang crushing her chest.

"Well, a long time ago, you might have been able to be," the woman replied, chuckling at her eagerness. Bile rose up in Ruth's throat. She should be moving, she should be making her escape, but her feet wouldn't budge beneath her. "The only way to seal the demon inside is with blood from a sin-free person, so at first, someone from our community would volunteer. But soon we realized how important it was to keep every single one of us in the world. Unfortunately, believers like us are few in number, and we need every last one fighting for good, for the Creator and His word. So, instead, we learned how to purify sinners. Now, whenever we need to re-seal the jar, we go out and find a sinner. And your daddies and elders purify their sins, making their souls clean, so they can be the perfect sacrifice. And how lucky they are! They get to go straight up to heaven with a clean slate.

"Sacrifice is a very important part of being True and Pure," the woman continued. "That's why tonight, each of you has brought something you hold very dear. In order to truly understand the gift our sacrifice is giving us, you will all make your own sacrifice tonight—a very small offering when considering that our real sacrifice is giving up her life to save us. Everyone, line up with your betrothed."

It took everything in Ruth not to scream, instead gritting her teeth against the anger and indignation and shock. The heat of the flame burning her eyes, she watched, mesmerized and shell-shocked, as the children formed a line, tentative and slow. Each girl stood paired with each boy, some similar in age, some not. At the front of the line, the tiniest girl reached up, her hand engulfed by a towering boy, a teenager who had to be nearing adulthood. One by one, they approached the fire and tossed in their precious items, the flames licking and devouring their dolls, their bears, the fibers black and crispy in mere seconds. Some of the older ones tossed in pocketknives or hand-stitched embroidery, hours of work gone in an instant. The fire burst with each offering, the heat seeming to cauterize the bite marks that lined Ruth's cheeks. Tears bubbled out of tiny eyes, wails echoed against the canopy of branches above. The teenagers awkwardly consoled their counterparts, patting their backs or absorbing salty tears on their shoulders.

When Sarah reached the front of the line, she shed no tears, and Ruth stifled a mad cheer. The little girl hurled her doll to the flames, watching the thing disintegrate into char with rebellious glee etched on her face.

When the final child had tossed their precious gem to the heat, the woman spoke again. "I know that was very hard," she said. "I know that it hurts a lot right now to lose those things—to not have your doll to cuddle or to see something you worked a really long time on be destroyed in moments. But in the coming days, you can use that pain to reflect upon the sacrifice you made and how much stronger you are, and how much closer you feel to the Creator. After all, we are in this world to store up treasures in heaven, not treasures on earth. I hope you also understand the gratitude we should all feel toward our sacrifice, who has not lost a doll but has lost her life on this earth.

"Now, let's bow our heads and pray together that your fathers and elders will be successful, that the Creator will be with them."

Every head bowed in unison, each chin grazing each chest, each scalp facing the heat of the flames. Somehow every hand found another, creating a complicated highway of connected arms.

Ruth had to leave. *Now.*

She inched the door open as silently as she could manage and skirted the building, stepping sideways, each step cautious and quiet beneath their prayer. Turning backward into a corner of darkness, into a pocket untouched by the fire, her back collided with something—something warm, something with give. Something that startled her enough to force a small scream of surprise from her lips.

"Who are you?" a young boy said. He was dressed in modest clothes, a linen shirt tucked inside khaki shorts, a brown leather belt around his waist. Mud coated his arms, stretching all the way up to his rolled-up sleeves. More muck spread across his chest in a spray, like blood spatter from a sliced neck. He held a trowel, a small pile of weeds at his feet, their roots sticking out of clumps of dirt like worms.

"Shh, it's okay," she assured him. The heads around the fire remained bowed, their spoken prayer too loud to have heard her outburst.

"Are you okay?" he asked, his eyes growing wide. "It looks like you're bleeding."

"Uh," she said. She must look insane to this little boy—her clothes shredded and bloodied, her skin covered in bites and scrapes, half of her hair torn from her skull. "I'm hurt but I'll be okay."

"We have bandages and stuff inside," he said. "They're almost done, I think. I can go get my mom—"

"No, no, don't bother your mom," Ruth said carefully. "I mean, it's late. But maybe you should go back to the fire? It's really dark over here. Kinda spooky."

"I got punished," he said, "for doing a sin, playing with my toys during prayer."

"Oh, uh." Ruth wasn't sure how to respond. He was just a kid. "Do you know which way the creek is?"

The boy seemed to puzzle on this, as if he didn't know what a creek was, like he'd never encountered the idea of running water in his short life.

"The creek?" Ruth pressed. "Like, uh, a small river? A place where there's running water? I'm just a little lost. I'm trying to find my way back home."

The boy's mouth wiggled like a worm on a hook. "Wait a minute, what's your name?" he asked.

"Uh," Ruth hesitated. "Susy."

"Oh, wait, I know who you are!" He was suddenly giddy, jumping up and down, his little feet stomping the weeds back into the earth. "You're *her*! You're the one Daddy said would save everyone! By dying!"

Before Ruth's muggy brain could process the child's glee, he was screaming for his mother, raising hell at the top of his little lungs, a piercing shriek Ruth never would have imagined could come from something so tiny.

"You motherfucker," she whispered.

The women and children turned in unison, their prayer

paused. The fire crackled, cast their faces in shadow. All eyes found the source of the screaming, and then just as quickly found Ruth, found the missing sacrifice, the linchpin of their whole operation, somehow all the way out here. So close to escape.

The women stood in unison and moved toward her, each one bearing an identical snarl. At the front of the pack, way too close and way too fast, was a harried woman with a familiar face that almost stopped Ruth from running, almost caused her whole body to malfunction and freeze like a broken computer. It was *her*—the woman who had commissioned the blanket. The whole reason Ruth had gone to New Creations in the first place. She'd taken Ruth's card from a swap meet where Ruth was trying—and failing—to sell some hand-knit items.

The woman had rubbed scarves and potholders between her fingers and asked if Ruth took commissions. Her friend was pregnant, and she wanted to get her a custom baby blanket, she'd said. Ruth handed over her card like a desperate idiot and had been texting this woman all week; had been culpable in her own demise all this time.

Ruth's heart sank, wedging between her cracked ribs, as she realized it had all been a setup from the start. That was how they knew she'd go to the store when they needed her to, stepping so easily and willingly into their trap. This woman had lured her; Glue Man had been spying on her, pretending to be a birdwatcher; and Charlie had nominated her. And now she knew how those missionaries had seemed to appear out of nowhere right before she left home this morning: they'd walked from this weird commune in the woods. They'd led her like a sheep to slaughter, all of them, and she'd just gone along with it because she didn't want to believe anything bad could happen to her. She hadn't wanted to listen to Abigail's warnings and worries. She had wanted to believe that they could hide in plain sight forever.

The woman snatched at Ruth, her fingernails scratching her sleeve, catching on like talons, but the melted, thin fabric ripped instead, freeing Ruth to rush away and into the trees.

Behind her, beneath the crunching of brush and her own heaving breath, she heard feet rushing toward her, the sound soon eclipsed by the pounding of her own heartbeat.

Chapter 23

Ruth ran, adrenaline masking the pain shooting through her ankle, slowing down when the trees started to thin a bit, many tacked with *NO TRESPASSING—PRIVATE PROPERTY* signs. Something cut at her ankles, one thin slice and one sharp bite, and she tumbled forward, her body crashing to the wet earth.

Every muscle tensed, awaiting the sharp fingernails of the malnourished women that would claw into her skin like the rats, to pin her to the ground until the men could retrieve her. But only the chill from the air, from the damp earth, sank its teeth into her. Behind her, beyond the tripwire she'd careened over, the women stood in a snarling, sniveling line, baring their teeth like angry dogs on a chain.

It was as though they couldn't move any farther, like the wire she'd tripped over was an electric fence. Like the signs tacked to the trees were a warning to the women to stay inside instead of the other way around. Maybe they had strict rules not to leave—at least not without a male escort. Ruth realized she'd never seen Charlie's wife without Charlie also being there, by her side. The missionary woman who showed up at their doorstep all those hours ago, what felt more like decades, like eons or millennia or centuries ago, had been accompanied by a man. Even the woman who had commissioned the blanket, who had set all of this in motion, who now stood just inside the wire border with drool-soaked, glistening teeth, with brittle nails slicing crescents into her palms, had been with her husband that day at the fair. He'd called her over after she'd taken Ruth's card.

The line of women stared her down. Their eyes shot bullets across the invisible barrier. Yet they would not edge forward to snatch her. One by one they receded back into the trees. Ruth could only assume they would inform their husbands of her location. She wondered if they'd receive any punishment for obeying their directive to stay put instead of placing one foot out of line to capture the sacrifice.

Ruth pried herself from the ground and kept moving, kept running as though they were still chasing her. She was out of breath, heaving and gulping in air, when she finally reached the edge of the forest. She now stood at the side of the road constructed solely for the church and the craft store, at the edge of the dead end, the asphalt stopping abruptly before the trees, the spot where she'd turned onto the little access road that led to the craft store's parking lot. She paused for a moment, waiting to see if it was safe to exit. Waiting for prowling Shepherds to lurch into view. But everything remained quiet and still, the night perfectly dark. She didn't hear anything moving in the woods behind her, not even deer or birds.

Maybe she should just hover here until morning. Try to stick it out by hiding in the woods, just run out their timer. She began to retreat farther into the dark trees, preparing to sit down and make herself as invisible as possible, when a thought screamed through her head: *What if they stopped trying to catch you because they have Abigail?*

What if they'd gone to the house and abducted her or somehow coerced her to go with them? What if she'd come out to the craft store herself to investigate and had been snatched up, the perfect backup sacrifice just walking into the cult's open arms? Ruth hoped that wasn't the case. But she couldn't let herself sit here in the dark, *hoping* Abigail was okay.

She had to move. It wasn't likely, but maybe a car would stop for her, some lost motorist using the access road as a turnaround. She took another cautious glance in each direction before stepping out onto the road. No sidewalk available.

She probably should have stayed within the first row of trees, she realized too late, somewhere she could quickly step back into the darkness if she needed to. But she was tired and groggy, and even though the harsh asphalt made her ankle throb with each step, she had been imagining a Good Samaritan with a car and not a wormy Mustard Seed with evil intent. She was thinking more about getting back to Abigail than her own self-preservation, too many variables jumbled together. Plus, if a car did pass on the road, would she have time to run out to it? Could she exit the trees and wave them down before they drove past her, their headlights pointing far down the road?

She headed away from the dead end and reached the spot

where the pavement curved left into the trees, the only direction available, though there were inklings that more would be developed soon, heavy machinery parked atop gravel beyond the end of the asphalt, as if the New Creationists would stretch their tendrils out forever, both above and below the earth. She followed the turn, her feet taking her toward the main road.

Ruth limped along. She felt like she'd been walking forever, though it couldn't have been more than a quarter mile. No vehicles appeared on the asphalt in the oppressive dark. Clouds obscured the stars and the moon, no bonfire to light the way. Not even a streetlamp. If a car appeared, she might just become roadkill.

But then headlights emerged abruptly, like two eyelids opening, as if the driver had been parked on the road in the dark, waiting for something to pass. The glare blotted out everything, leaving a blank slate of white where Ruth's vision should have been.

Then more lights careened through the darkness, red and blue and flashing ones this time, a siren erupting in unison with them. Two police officers exited the car.

Fuck.

Ruth knew how she looked—swollen and bruised and absolutely coated in blood. She slowly put both of her hands in the air.

Chapter 24

"I know this looks bad," Ruth said, her arms still in the air, heavy as lead. She couldn't imagine what they must be thinking of her: a woman walking alone in the dark, on a road leading to only two places, both of which should be closed, covered in blood-soaked bandages, more patches of red than bare skin, chunks of her hair missing. "I swear—I just escaped. Someone was trying to murder me."

"Come with us and we'll figure it out," the first officer said. Silhouetted by the headlights, he held his hand at his waistband, but Ruth couldn't tell what he hesitated to grab. She struggled to keep her arms above her head, her muscles like jelly trying to hoist a pallet of bricks.

"I'm sorry to do this, but we have to cuff you," the second said, his shadowy figure stepping toward her. "Just in case you're not telling us the whole truth. For our safety."

"Uh, yeah," Ruth said, lowering her heavy arms. "I think one of my wrists is broken."

The officer did not reply. He worked behind her, and she

felt the makeshift splint, the twin pieces of craft pine tied tight with strips of T-shirt, come loose and slide away from her wrist. The pain bloomed back into her nerves, so sharp and blinding that she nearly screamed when he pinned her wrists behind her back and locked them in place with the cuffs, the broken one throbbing, trapped and twisted at a harsh angle. The metal pinched into the swelling so tightly that she could feel her pulse squeeze past.

Limping, she let them push her down the asphalt to the car, tipping her into the back and slamming the door. What else could she do? Fight them? Start screaming at the top of her lungs? None of that would change her fate. She'd be spending the night behind the bars of the holding cell at the sheriff's office, most likely. Once they eventually uncovered the scene in the craft store, she'd be charged with murder, multiple counts, and then she'd spend the rest of her life in prison. That seemed to be the most likely outcome. There was no way the police would believe her that the New Creationists were actually a cult and had trapped her in there and she'd been chosen for a cannibalistic ritual. What could she tell them to make them believe her? She'd disarmed all the security cameras. The last thing they had footage of was her planting a knitting needle into someone's eyeball and then skewering someone else with a metal yard sign. She was fucked.

But there was at least a *chance* here. A chance that somehow they'd believe her, somehow she could convince them. That somehow she'd be able to get free. She could tell them about the tunnels, could lead them to the cult's weird museum of their victims, if they didn't destroy the evidence before she got the opportunity. At least this way she wasn't going to become someone's dinner.

"Can you call my—uh—roommate?" Ruth asked, trying to adjust in the backseat. No matter how she arranged her body, her wrist sent out constant pangs, sharp warning signs of imminent bursting. "Abigail? I have her number memorized. I'm sure she's worried about me."

"We'll sort everything out when we get there," one of the officers said.

Get where? The thought skittered across Ruth's brain but dissipated beneath the agony pulsing from her wrist like Morse code.

"Also, I'm diabetic," she continued. "I'll need food and my insulin, if my blood sugar isn't super low."

"There's a nurse at the station."

"How long will it take to get there?" Ruth pestered. From her spot in the back, she could only see a small glimpse of the road. There were no landmarks in sight, only a sliver of asphalt and trunks of trees illuminated by the headlights. "I understand what I look like, and why you'd feel the need to cuff me, but there are some dangerous people over by the church and the craft store. I'm worried they're going to hurt someone else."

"We've got it under control, ma'am," one of the officers said. "We've already requested for other officers to investigate the scene."

Ruth settled in, closing her eyes. The blood on her chin flaked and itched.

The view from the side window remained dark. Shouldn't

they have reached the main road by now? Shouldn't the streets be lined with buildings and not trees? The silence stretched, reaching its sharp claws through the glass, petting her shoulder. Where was backup? The other car should have already screeched past them, red and blue flashing in the rearview. Kill Devil's police force was small, but it wasn't a two-man operation.

She craned her neck around the officers' shoulders, trying to get a view of the asphalt ahead of them.

"Are you sure you called for backup?" she asked.

The pair in front remained silent.

"I'm really afraid they're going to murder someone," she persisted.

The car screeched to a halt, the momentum sending Ruth, who had not been buckled in, flying face first into the hard metal barrier between the rows of seats.

Now crumpled in an awkward heap of tangled and bruised limbs on the floor of the vehicle, Ruth, unable to push herself upright, felt the car turning around, making a three-point turn to go back in the direction she'd come from.

"The only one here getting murdered tonight is you," one of them said.

Chapter 25

What the fuck.

Ruth should have stayed in the darkness of the trees. Why did she think the police, of all people, would help her, would take her to any sort of safety? They had been *waiting* for her. She realized this now, crumpled in a heap of torment on the floor. The sudden headlights hadn't appeared because they'd turned a corner or because they'd been parked on the side of the road monitoring traffic, trying to catch a speeder under the cover of darkness. There was only one reason they would have been on that stretch of road.

They were part of it. They had to be. They had probably been on alert even before she escaped, waiting there at the only exit, ready to intercept her just in case.

She was so stupid. Why had she thought it would be a good idea to walk out into the open? As she lay crushed on the floor of the police cruiser, her arms pinned and twisted beneath her, the pain ebbing away to numbness, her heart sank. This was it. She'd lost.

The pair chuckled in the front seat, patting themselves on the back for their Oscar-worthy performances. *What an idiot. She really thought we didn't know what was going on. She really thought she'd just be taken down to the sheriff's office, taken to a jail cell or interrogation room, safe and sound behind bars.*

She was still so naive even after what she'd already escaped. They'd been part of it the whole time. They probably had blocked the road, too, to make sure nobody would drive down there, trying to shop for yarn and instead stumbling upon the whole bloody scene. Nobody was coming to help her.

"I was getting bored," one of them said. "After we pushed her car in the river, I thought we'd just be sitting here in the dark all night."

"It's a good thing we were here to clean up their mess," the other replied. "Guess they didn't have it under control. She almost got away."

And now they were bringing her back. She'd fought and scraped and clawed her way through that shit show just to sheepishly allow herself to be put in the back of a car that was delivering her right to them.

Even though this road had not existed just a few short years ago, the pavement still glistening and new, on the floor Ruth could feel every bump, every lurch from the shocks, each one sending stabbing pain through her body. She slammed against the door as they made the single right turn onto the side road that led to the store. After a brief drive, they turned left.

Of course. They were taking her to the church, not the store. Of course whatever fucking cannibal shit they wanted to do to her would happen inside the church—or below it. There was an entrance to the tunnels in the store and their commune, so of course there'd be a way down from the church. It must have sat beneath her as she sank into the plush seat during that first sermon she'd attended. But none of that mattered. She no longer cared about the intricacies of the church and the craft store, whatever anthill of insanity the cult had constructed above and beneath the ground. She'd lost. She'd never see Abigail again, and it was her own fucking fault for not listening to her, for becoming complacent, for believing nothing could possibly happen to her just because she was not heterosexual. That nothing truly bad could happen just because of who she loved.

But it had happened. Just like Abigail had warned. Ruth had been such an idiot. She'd fallen for their traps. All of them so far. The commissioner, the police. Charlie.

The car stopped, and the chuckling officers killed the engine. They looked behind them and gasped for a moment, their laughter cut short. They couldn't see her crumpled on the floor, must have wondered how she could possibly have vanished into thin air. Stretching in their seats, they looked down at her, her body contorted like a smashed pretzel, and resumed their laughter.

The pair opened the door and their hysterics continued, loud, hearty guffaws at her predicament. Grabbing her legs, they dragged her out of the car. She wondered if she could use their moment of hilarity to her advantage, if she could wiggle out of their grip, kick them with her uninjured foot, and run while they were distracted. But exhaustion filled every muscle, worming its way through every ache and pain. When they tried to stand her upright, she nearly fell, smashing her face into the car door frame. Her ankle felt like it was constructed from pins and needles.

They'd parked at the side of the church, directly in front of a set of small double doors, likely an administrative entrance if Ruth had to guess. The one time she'd been inside, she'd gone through the main entrance, wide enough to accommodate the masses that attended each week. The parking lot was an open ocean of pavement, extending in a crown around the church. Only one side of the building was not buffeted by the concrete sea, separated from the woods by only a small piece of land. Even if she tried to run away, she'd have to cross this sea, paddling on a bum ankle, and they could catch up to her easily or simply shoot her, graze her working leg and make her fall face first on the pavement, no way, with her wrists cuffed, to stop her teeth from scattering across the black asphalt upon impact.

Their hands squeezed like vises as they pushed her toward the doors, clamping onto her, tight as hell even though she was a skinny, injured girl with her hands cuffed and her foot numb. They were taking no more chances—at least this pair wasn't.

The buzzer vibrated into the church, and the officers said something cryptic into the intercom, the syllables jumbling together into nonsense by the time they reached Ruth's ears. Some type of code word, perhaps. Why bother with one? Nobody else was around. Who else could have been knocking at the door besides the officers delivering their bounty? Who else even knew to come here, knew that something was happening?

Her heart stopped. *Abigail.*

What if Abigail came here trying to find her? What if she went to the craft store and saw Ruth's car gone and nobody around—what would she do? Would she call someone? Try the police? Or would she go across the parking lot to the church to ask the pastor if he'd seen anything?

Ruth's head hurt. She didn't have any answers. She hoped that Abigail had stayed away. That she had just left. Ruth's gut roiled, knowing Abigail wouldn't do that. Abigail was the type to scour the earth for her.

Whatever the cops said was the right answer. The door buzzed open and they ushered her inside.

Chapter 26

Through the doors, the hallways were lined with thin, stiff carpeting, dark blue fibers that could withstand heavy foot traffic. On the clean, white walls hung an occasional crucifix alongside framed photos, bright teeth behind the curled smiles of the pastor and other families in the church, stock photos of praying children on their knees, and flyers advertising events taped to the wall, printed on gold and crimson sheets. Closed doors stood at attention, portals to offices or classrooms, each one bearing a small, official plaque announcing its purpose. It was almost boring in its normalcy. This was where some big cannibal ritual would take place?

The officers pushed her forward, her fumbling feet raking lines through the carpet. A waiting cloaked figure intercepted her, gripping her arm in a vise, his hand the only visible part of his skin, while the officers removed her handcuffs. His face was shrouded in shadow, soon eclipsed entirely after he slipped a dark bag over her head.

"Don't mess this up again," one of the officers said. "We've done our part. We have to go back to block the road. Let us know when you've finished up."

"We can handle it from here," the cloaked man said. "Thank you for your service. We will settle the matter of compensation another day."

Grunting, the cloaked man dragged Ruth, pulling her forward, expecting her injured body to cooperate instead of snagging on the rough carpet. She could already feel the spidery bruise forming beneath the fingers clamped around her arm, the ones that squeezed and contracted as he pivoted her around corners and turns. Beyond the pain radiating there, Ruth felt like she was floating inside a void. Her ears caught nothing besides the patter of their own breathing and their shoes against the carpet. The bag concealed any sights or smells.

"We're going to go down a set of stairs," the man said. "Be careful."

Ruth almost laughed at the irony, but she supposed the last thing they'd want was for her to fall, for her skull to smash open on the floor, cracking the life out of her moments before they could perform the ritual. If his hand weren't cinched so tight it seemed that their skin had fused, she might have tried to fling herself down the stairs.

The air grew cold, icy tendrils raising goose bumps against her skin. The ritual room must be located down the throat of the one doorway she hadn't entered in that central stone room. How much faster her demise would have been if she'd gone left instead of right, toward their shrine to their victims.

Clambering down the stairs was slow work. Her injured ankle rolled beneath her every other step, her body buoyed each time by the cloaked figure's muscular grip, threatening to dislocate her shoulder. The pair finally reached level ground and proceeded in a straight line for what felt like an eon. Here, even their breath seemed to extinguish around them. The man tensed as if holding it in, as if the air around them were sacred and he was not worthy to breathe it in. Ruth's caught in her throat. A knot formed at the top of her esophagus, like a ball bearing creating a tight seal. The man's fingers curled tighter around her arm, his pace increasing, now guiding her with his other hand pinching her shoulder.

He must be anxious to get started. But Ruth felt something in the air, some reverence, some odd electricity that she couldn't discern.

After a few more stairs down, the cultist swerved her to the left before finally lifting the bag from her head. Before her was the ritual room.

This was closer to what Ruth had imagined, though no less jarring now that she was seeing it for real. It was like they'd been transported to some medieval torture chamber. Shelves stretched floor to ceiling, lined with all sorts of old, dusty artifacts, ceramic pots and small statues and chests and tablets and so many other things crammed together that Ruth could not tell one from the other. And bones. Skulls. Saint relics, chunks of holy people plundered from their graves? Or more trinkets from past victims? She wasn't sure. In the center sat a large stone table, ropes sprouting from iron rings affixed to each sharp corner. Half a dozen figures hovered around it, all wearing cloaks, clones of each other. Candles on iron stands lit the room, casting shadows under each hood. A small table stood off to the side, hidden in the converging dark. But something on it reflected the flames of candlelight—something metal and sharp.

"We're finally ready to start," Gideon said—the same commanding voice she'd heard through the headset—his tone twingeing with annoyance around the word *finally*. Although she could only see the lower half of his face, Ruth finally understood who he was—where she'd heard his voice before. It was James, the church's pastor, the same man who had delivered that insane sermon when she'd visited with Charlie, the words forming a ball of stomach acid inside her even now.

Four hands snatched her arms, pinching her wrists between their strong fingers, holding her in place. The Shepherds snipped away most of her bulky clothing, leaving her nearly naked, each angry, red scratch and dark, purple blotch along her skin revealed.

"The time has come for us to once again perform our divine duties," Gideon said. The cloaked figures surrounded the table, the *altar* that stood empty between them, Gideon standing at the center. Ruth expected them to force her down onto the table, to tie her limbs to the ropes, but apparently the time for that hadn't yet come. "We take on these duties in order to prevent the release of pure evil into the world. We hold these duties sacred, and they are a testament to our reverence and piety. We have little time now to waste, so let us begin in earnest. We start with an initiation."

A body emerged from behind the wall of cloaks. The young kid, the one who had been so eager to eat her flesh, now stood in front of the group. He was the only one not draped in a dark cloak, still adorned with the same clothing he'd been wearing previously, his yellow apron coated in dust and blood, his arm in a sling, bandages with dark halos wrapped around his arms, his knee, his head. Somehow he had been spared the same fate as the elder who had taught him so much, had been pulled from the wreckage alive.

The leader continued. "We welcome this newcomer to our ranks, a young man who promises to be True and Pure, to spread our word and father children, who has already proven himself to be more Worthy than most. He has already survived his first trial from the Creator. Now we will say the rites of initiation."

The young man shifted his weight between his feet, his free hand rubbing the nails on his injured one, eager anticipation shining in his eyes.

"Young Travis, we call upon thee to claim thy spot within the Creator's inner circle. To do so, you must reject the devil and all of his sinful ways. Do you promise to be True?"

"I do," the young man said, the words gummy, as if spoken with a swollen tongue.

The hands along Ruth's arms squeezed harder as she squirmed feebly.

"Sin, like a venomous disease, infects our vital blood. The only balm is sovereign grace and the one above, our Creator. Do you promise to spread His word, so that others may follow the path of righteousness?"

"I do," he repeated.

"Shall this vile race of flesh and blood contend with their Creator? Shall these mortal worms presume to be more holy, wise, or just than we?"

The whole thing felt pithy and grand. Like Bible verses.

Like bullshit, Ruth thought.

"Ahitophel, for the act of nominating our chosen sacrifice, we ask you to do the honor of the initiation. You have brought about our salvation, and now we gift you the sacred task of joining young Travis into our bond."

From the side table, one cloaked member hovered over the items there, a sudden flurry of movement after so much standing still. He brought the items forward, one settled in each fist: a golden chalice with an ornate design, encrusted jewels and script. The other was a matching jeweled dagger with a blade the length of a forearm. From beneath the cloak, the lower half of the man's face came into view. Red streaks of burnt flesh curled above the gauze bandages. So Charlie had survived—but not intact. *Good*, she thought—she hoped he'd be disfigured for the rest of his days.

"We bestow our souls with wounds to feel, we drink the poisonous gall," Gideon intoned, nodding.

With what felt like glee, Charlie rounded the table and, without hesitation, sliced through the skin at Ruth's thigh, collecting her blood in the chalice. Even amid the roiling sea of other pains, this slice somehow hurt worse, the sudden, exposed nerves zipping screams up through her throat and out of her mouth. Once the chalice had filled enough, he brought the golden cup to the mouth of the young kid, who smiled as it reached his lips, who *gulped* it down. Who didn't seem to want to stop drinking it. When Charlie pulled the cup away, the boy's lips were stained with a red so dark it was nearly black, and he released his wormy little tongue to lap up the excess before any of it could drip down his chin.

"With this blood," Gideon said, "we rush with fury down to hell, but heaven prevents the fall. And now, the flesh—"

With that, Charlie sliced once more, the blade so sharp that Ruth's nerves only registered the cut once the metal had passed all the way through. He chopped away a coin-sized piece of flesh from her other thigh. A punched-out moan rose from Ruth's belly.

"Receive and eat the living food," the leader continued as Charlie placed the chunk from her thigh onto the tongue of the young man. "This body, slain for sin, shall nourish and replenish."

At the conclusion of this speech, the cloaks began to move, a fluttering of fabric. A new cloak, shiny black velvet, was placed over the shoulders of the young man, who grinned in pleasure, savoring the tiny morsel of Ruth between his teeth. The old guard surrounding him clapped.

"We now grant you your new name, a badge of honor from the Creator. You shall now be dubbed Nabal."

The room erupted in applause, pale hands bursting from the folds of velvet. The blood pouring from Ruth's thigh tanked her blood sugar, her legs heavy and loose as sand beneath her. The sound of the clapping distorted in her ears, the quick, blurred movements multiplying the hands into thousands of flapping birds. Birds with sharp talons and beaks that circled around her.

"Now we must make haste to perform our sacred duty," Gideon said, taking the dagger from Charlie's hand and setting it back on the small table. "Once more, the blood moon is upon us, the time when the devil is at his strongest, when his power comes to fruition to lay waste to the earth and release the purveyors of sin. When the blood moon crests in the night sky, we must perform our duties lest the evil, his minion, be released from the vessel, of which we have taken ownership. We must once again perform the necessary steps outlined in the ancient texts to keep the demon contained."

One of the cloaked figures held a small, plain jar aloft. The ceramic vessel was tiny—the size of an apple. That was the thing they believed contained a demon? And not a metaphorical one—they truly believed that minuscule thing contained a real-life demon who would deliver the faithful to hell if released? If she still had the strength, Ruth might have laughed.

"Upon the arrival of each blood moon, we must perform these sacred steps. We must reseal the vessel with Pure and Clean blood, free of sin attached to the sacrifice's soul. When the faithful abounded, volunteers would offer themselves for this purpose, and we thank those who came before us and saved us. In our modern world, so few Pure people remain among so many sinners. We, the True and Pure, cannot spare a single member."

The sound of his droning voice bored into Ruth's ear like a parasite. The fleshy nooses around her limbs squeezed tight, her bloodless fingers tingling and cold.

"Instead," the leader continued, "we choose to remove a sinner from the world. We take their sins upon ourselves to purify their soul, creating Pure blood by which to seal the vessel. The sinner is lucky, and we should revere their sacrifice.

They may die with a clean slate to be ushered directly into the gates of heaven, made Pure by our own faith. Once we have absorbed their sins, we, the True and Pure, need only to complete our rites to be forgiven and return to Purity."

Gideon lifted a carafe from the table, some ancient-looking thing with a stopper. With weaselly fingers, he pried off the cork and upended the pitcher into a larger vessel, pouring an amber liquid into something resembling an ornate punch bowl—filled with something thick and just as dark. It sloshed and splashed inside the bowl.

"In the name of our Creator, we join the ancient with the new. Shall the blessing cascade and infect the virgin oil, which we anoint now," he said.

The oil now joined, all of it sacred, the bowl was moved to the table before Ruth.

"Now we anoint thee, for thy Creator, your sinner's blood spilt," Gideon recited. Another cloaked member stepped forward with an ornate cup, plunging it into the punch bowl of oil.

"The Creator delivers all who trust Him from their guilt; with this oil anointing, a clean soul on Him is built," Gideon continued.

Her arms still pinned by fleshy clamps, Ruth could not flee from the waterfall of cascading oil. The stuff plopped onto the crown of her skull, burning the raw tissue of her rodent diadem, and dripped down her head, thick and slimy. It glided like molasses over her shoulders, pooling into the nook of skin at her collar.

The Shepherd scooped another cupful and overturned it

above her skull. He repeated this motion over and over again, one cup after another, his cloak unclasping, opening to reveal two dark pinpricks across his chest, crusty blood dried into the fibers of his shirt. Through the thick glaze soaking her eyelashes, the corners of his mouth seemed to twist up, curling into a slight grin. Her ex-manager—still alive and well.

Soon the oil curtained her vision, a thick, dark lens—like blood, she thought, like they'd simply split open the top of her skull. But it had a flowery, cloying scent that clung to the hairs of her nostrils. Ruth sealed her lips shut tight, but the oil blocked her nostrils, and she had to breathe, sputtering and spitting out the rancid-tasting oil between quick gasps. Her old manager continued ladling her with the stuff, basting her like a Thanksgiving turkey, until Gideon yelled for him to halt, chastised that he must not drain the bowl entirely.

Every speck of her was covered. Ruth had resigned herself to her fate since the moment she entered the ritual room. Now, she needed only to twist her arms, letting the drape of oil slide between her skin and the hands of her oppressors. Then she flailed, a slickened pig slipping through their fingers. Flinging oil across the room with every step, she rushed toward the exit.

Behind her: chaos, a domino collapse of cloaked limbs and torsos in the pool of oil on the floor, the sound of a ring of wobbling ceramic against metal.

Gideon growled. "Secure the vessel!" he yelled. "All is lost if it breaks!"

"But what about the girl?" someone asked.

"The vessel is more important," Gideon replied.

In the slippery chaos, Ruth lunged for the door.

"Let her go," he said. "She'll return to us, once she sees what we have."

Chapter 27

The hallway was dark and empty, the lights flickering in tandem, the faulty power trickling down the connected wires. Ruth backtracked, trying to remember the twists and turns her body had made, trying to reverse engineer the way out. She turned right and vaulted up a set of stairs.

Almost immediately, her feet slipped from beneath her, her chin smashing against stone, her knees and elbows slamming down too. Her oil-coated extremities required more precision, and the ascent was difficult. There was no handrail to hoist and assist—only the ancient stone stairs, steep and uneven, carved from Kentucky limestone. She crawled up, stabilizing each hand and knee before making another movement, leaving a slimy trail behind her like a slug.

Nobody appeared behind her, slow as she moved. Gideon had told them to let her go.

Why? He'd said they *had* something—what was it? What could they possibly have that would make her voluntarily return to be butchered?

Dread cut through her pumping adrenaline after a second short set of stairs spat her out—not onto the ground floor of the church, like she'd hoped, but into another dungeon-like room. As her eyes adjusted to the dimmer light, the bulbs spaced few and far between, for a moment she thought she was hallucinating, her mind conjuring skulls leering out of the walls, bones set into the floor like paving stones. But the nightmare images didn't dissolve—not entirely—when she blinked, when she wiped the oil out of her eyes. Before her were rows upon rows of sarcophaguses and urns, stretching back into the dark. Some tombs had full skeletons laid out on them, while others had only skulls or ribs or femurs, and others still were closed. One pedestal held a desiccated, mummified body, the skin taut and jerkylike beneath blue velvet robes. A little plaque on the base read *ELDER HILL*. She moved cautiously here, inching around the edges of the room as if any noise would wake the dead. This area was vast. The limited light did not stretch to its edges, did not even come close to lighting the entirety of this space, of this underground graveyard. Once again Ruth wondered how these tunnels could have possibly lain curled beneath the forest floor all this time without anyone knowing. The New Creationists had shown up just a few years ago—but apparently their roots ran deep in the Kill Devil soil. It was a homecoming.

She was so tired. All of her previous injuries plus the twin wounds on her thighs were building up into a crescendo of pain. Her adrenaline could only surmount so much. But she had to keep pushing. She had no choice, even if her blood sugar was falling once again. What else could she do? She had nothing at all to use. No more tote bag full of possibilities. No weapon with which to fight back. She didn't even have the sweatshirt anymore, which could have possibly been used to strangle someone or even just pressed against her wounds to stem the blood.

Each movement forward through this underground graveyard threatened to send her careening back to the ground. She stepped slowly, cautiously, each foot planted steadily. The oil, now sickly cold, slid down her skin, little snakelike rivulets slithering through her hair, between her eyelashes; a chilly serpentine down her bare shoulders and neck and spine. When she inhaled, she sucked in droplets of it, her nose clogged and congested, forever smelling the sickly scent of rotting, too-ripe flowers.

Swallowing the ball of dread at the back of her throat, Ruth pushed down the long hallway of the catacombs and, on hands and knees, climbed the steep stairs at the other end that led almost straight up. Each stone step was a feat that left her out of breath, each one a victory against the oozing oil slithering down to her clawing palms and wrecked kneecaps. After what felt like a millennium, she crawled out of the door at the top of the staircase, the door that had been, mercifully, left unlocked.

Now she was back in the sea of blue, scratchy carpet, another hallway leading to Sunday school classrooms and supply closets and conference rooms. Ruth's feet left little oily footprints against the carpet fibers, exchanging the oil for a film of dirt and lint, little squiggly strings of blue that poked out of her soles like Morgellons. Her feet had turned a deep, crusty blue-black by the time she stumbled upon a supply closet. Inside was a vacuum, a duster, and precisely zero paper towels. Hung on the closet rod was a spray bottle with a dirty rag draped over it. She tried to wipe away as much of the putrid oil as possible, but the rag seemed to repel it, the oil sitting on the surface of its rough fibers instead of sinking in. It was coated and useless before she had even finished wiping her face.

Farther down the hall, she found an open door with a small plaque reading *KITCHEN*. On the counter sat a half-eaten cake with the words *CONGRATULATIONS TRAVIS!* still legible, and she shoveled handfuls of it into her mouth, the icing stiff and the cake stale, the perfume of the oil coating each bite. Above a handwash sink sat a roll of paper towels, and she swiped away as much stray oil as she could and discarded the stained paper onto the floor. She gulped water directly from the tiny tap.

In another room, labeled *SUPPLIES*, a stack of boxes towered in a corner, one already toppled, vomiting white cotton T-shirts. Digging through the box, Ruth uncovered one three sizes too large, slipping it over her head like a makeshift nightgown, the front emblazoned with curling yarn, open pairs of scissors, needles, and hooks, all of these items joining together to form the words: *CREATING WITH THE CREATOR!*

Ruth could only laugh.

Outside, the hallways seemed to multiply, to branch on endlessly, and Ruth followed them at her feet's whim, turning only when she reached an impasse. Eventually, her wandering brought her to one final dead end, a set of double doors.

She pushed the doors open gently, just in case there was some catch to them, as if they'd scream or fall off the hinges, clanging to the floor. Maybe the doors opened a portal to hell. She couldn't take any more chances; surely her luck had run out.

Behind the twin doors lay the church's vast, stadium-like sanctuary. Before her stood rows and rows and rows of seats, curving upward to another set of doors at the far end. She spilled onto the giant stage, crowned with a pulpit, oversized projection screens behind it. A set of small, tiered stands stood at the far end of the stage, for the choir, next to an electric piano. Above, there was a balcony full of more and more seats, the bottoms plush and soft. The walls were lined with stained glass, eerily illuminated by moonlight.

Ruth wasn't sure if it was just the ambiance of being here at night, alone in the dark, or if it was something else, but it seemed to her that the glass depicted extra-gory scenes from the Bible. Had they been here the whole time? Had they been there when she'd sat through that awful sermon? She had been so enraptured by everything, so overloaded with lights and music and hellfire that the windows hadn't stuck in her memory. Thick, creamy boils ran the length of Job's skin. Bodies burned in anguish in Sodom. Had they really made a stained-glass depiction of John the Baptist's severed head, the plate running over with blood? The specific scene of Jesus being stabbed in the side, blood gushing down his exposed body?

The surreal setting made her stop in her tracks. The insane windows made her forget why she was in this strange place or where she was trying to go. For a moment, even the pain and exhaustion had left her, and she felt nothing but confusion and disgust and anger at this place, this den of horrors where so many of her neighbors chose to go every single week—sometimes multiple times a week. A place they brought their *children.*

This was nothing like the church her parents forced her to attend in her youth. She remembered a dozen rows of hard, wooden benches with a single aisle running down the center. She didn't remember any particular imagery in the windows—they must have been simple colors or otherwise nondescript, just crosses, maybe a chalice or harp or something innocuous. Not horror scenes. She would have remembered windows like these. They would have inspired endless nightmares.

Even if that church had eventually turned on her when she realized her true self, it had at least felt like a *warm* place, with yellow oak everywhere and pleasant songs. People had been nice to her—until they weren't. She couldn't imagine the same feelings of warmth kindling in this place, this wide-open stadium with screens and giant speakers and horrific imagery set in glass. Even the memories of that first sermon with the New Creationists felt cold, infected with hatred.

She remained stunned by the sanctuary, frozen on center stage like a player who'd forgotten her lines, until she spied movement in the corner of her eye. Across the vast sea of seats and down the long, central aisle, the doors at the far end of the auditorium were opening. She exited stage left and ducked down behind a row of seats that curved, hoping whoever it was wouldn't see her as they passed.

Nestling down in a squatting position proved to be painful, like it was squeezing every bruise, every sprain; pushing blood out of every cut like she was a tube of oil paint. But she feared that if she lay down, she'd be a goner. She'd just fall asleep and be found the next morning when a family came to worship, her bare arms and legs coated in an oily film of grime. At least she'd ruin their ritual—and their Sunday service, to boot.

Maybe that's for the best, she thought, the floor beckoning her weary bones, but she didn't want to risk it. Their ritual was for naught; there was no fucking demon inside the vessel. Nothing would happen when the blood moon reached its peak. Even if she did survive the night, if the Shepherds found her before the public did, they'd kill her anyway just to get rid of her, to shut her up. To dispose of the evidence. Maybe if they felt especially kind, they'd hand her over to the authorities and she'd be locked up for the rest of her miserable life.

Three people entered the sanctuary and walked down the central pathway. Their silhouettes appeared through the gaps between the seats as they moved into and then out of her line of sight. She didn't dare lift her head to get a clear view, though she doubted they could have seen her in the darkness anyway. She wasn't going to risk it.

Their voices carried through the cavernous room, but Ruth couldn't quite make out what they were saying. Their tone indicated that this particular group didn't yet know that she'd escaped. They didn't sound desperate. Their sentences were lilting and much slower than the clipped speed of worry. They weren't turning on the overheads or shining a flashlight over the rows and rows of seats to find the loose sacrifice, the wandering lamb. They seemed calm and collected. Like everything was going to plan.

Did that mean the plan had changed?

What had Gideon meant, that she'd return? He said they *had* something.

What could they possibly have that would make her willingly head back into the teeth of the beast?

As the trio moved farther down the aisle, she could discern a few words here and there—*True, Pure, welcome you.* But one of the voices was higher, softer. A female voice, Ruth realized. Something about it seemed familiar, and when she finally connected the dots, a rock settled into Ruth's stomach.

Abigail.

The voice didn't speak much, but it sounded exactly like her. Like Abigail.

They'd taken Abigail. She was the *something.*

Ruth hesitated before she did something impulsive, something stupid. *It couldn't be her.* Ruth must be so exhausted that she was hearing things. But she couldn't forget what Gideon had said—what else could possibly make her go back, other than Abigail?

Ruth perked her ears, trying to hone in on the voice, trying to discern whether it was actually her girlfriend or someone else, whether she was just delirious and imagining things.

Every time the voice spoke, though soft, it continued to ring familiar. Ruth couldn't let go of the idea that the voice belonged to Abigail. She had to know.

She quietly unfolded her aching joints, biting her tongue to keep from crying out at the pain. She crawled to the edge of the row, as close as she dared while still shrouded in shadow. The group were too far down the aisle for Ruth to see anything but their shadowy frames.

The shortest silhouette seemed to be the right height for Abigail, but it was hard to gauge at this distance. Though the voice was a dead ringer for her girlfriend, the figure wasn't protesting. She wasn't trying to run away. She seemed to be willingly going along with the other two, arms hanging limp at her sides. The two men weren't forcing her down the aisle, their grips firm on her protesting limbs. Surely if it were Abigail, she wouldn't be chattering along with them, as if they were simply showing her a new apartment. The Abigail she knew was a fighter, though she used cunning more than brawn.

Something wasn't right. Ruth couldn't fight past the feeling in her gut that the figure was Abigail. She couldn't make the stone that had settled in her stomach disappear. Instead, it lodged there, tacky with oil and icing.

The trio finally reached the set of double doors by the stage, the doors Ruth had come through, and disappeared behind them, leaving her alone in the darkness.

Chapter 28

Ruth was alone now. They hadn't spotted her, didn't appear to even know—or care—that she was missing. She'd gotten this far, and freedom was so close. Just beyond the back of the sanctuary was the exit. All she had to do was make it down the aisle, through the mall-like courtyard, and out the front doors. Just as in the craft store, she didn't see any emergency exits or signage. *But I guess when you have the local police and the Creator on your side, you can get away with not following code.*

She was so close to freedom, but that nagging feeling wouldn't go away, the stone still stuck in her belly. Should she investigate, try to go back and see if that really was Abigail? Was it a lookalike, a ruse, designed to lure Ruth back to them? But if that *was* Abigail, why was she going along with them? Had they drugged her? Had they used one of their mystical objects to put a spell on her? What if Abigail was their backup sacrifice?

It didn't make sense. But the *voice.*

Ruth had to go back. She'd rather be wrong, die trying to

save Abigail, than earn her own freedom just to lose her.

She struggled to stand up, her legs numb and stiff beneath her, and slowly backtracked to the double doors at the back of the stage. The adrenaline had worn off, leaving her a rag doll of exhaustion, her bare skin raised with goose bumps. Her blood sugar rode the tide of the stale cake. She could only assume that the trio were making their way to down the ritual room.

Following the path of her oily footprints, she arrived at the mouth leading down into the cool tunnels. The door stood slightly ajar, wan light flickering behind it. She moved as quickly as she could without toppling down the stairs, the slime from her ascent still coating each step. They might be carving Abigail to pieces by now.

She reached the hallway outside the room, held her breath, and peered inside. Ruth's heart sank, crashing down onto the rock that had settled in her stomach, knocking it out of place, plummeting into the acid there like a cannonball.

It *was* Abigail. Her face was framed perfectly in the tiny gap of the open door's hinge. She didn't look scared. She wasn't fighting back or trying to escape. While Ruth watched, her own mouth slowly opening, Abigail smiled, even laughed, with the surrounding crowd of cloaked figures.

"What the fuck?" Ruth whispered.

That was all it took. Before she could formulate a plan, the cultists discovered her, pushing open the door before she'd even finished her stray thought, their hands squeezing her arms as she uttered the final syllable.

"I told you she would return," Gideon said, "and just in time."

It happened before Ruth could even think to struggle. Eight pairs of hands held her against the stone table, tying tight knots around her wrists and ankles. The leader, standing next to Abigail, standing too close to her, began the ritual in earnest. Ruth was so stunned, trying to make sense of Abigail's presence, her laid-back attitude, that she almost didn't catch what Gideon said. The words only registered inside her head when he wrapped his arms around Abigail's shoulder, pulling her toward him in a familiar hug.

"While women are not usually present for this sacrifice—it is our duty as men to protect women from such horrible sights, our duty as men to shoulder the so-called dirty work—I will make an exception for my daughter."

Daughter. Had he really said that?

This was the man Abigail's mother refused to tell her about. The man her mother had left, packing as much as she could fit into her car and driving away, an infant Abigail in tow, leaving no trace behind her. Judy refused to give Abigail a name or description of her father, refused to provide any information that would lead her back to him.

This was the reason Abigail's mom had wanted to get out of Kill Devil—right around the time the New Creationists showed up.

"You know, my mom wanted to leave," Abigail had said, breaking the silence on the drive back from the funeral. "A few years back."

"She did? Why?"

"I don't know," Abigail replied. Outside a film of gray spread across the sky. "It was like something inside her snapped. One morning, she's reading the newspaper and drinking coffee, turns the page, and then suddenly she's in the car, driving over an hour to get to a hardware store to buy more locks, door contacts, whatever. Her coffee left to get cold on the counter."

"She's always been like that, hasn't she?" Ruth asked. "I remember her having a million locks when we were kids, too."

"Yeah, but it got worse, ever since that morning," Abigail replied. "She started throwing things in boxes and kept saying, 'We gotta get out of here, as soon as we can.' Like she was wanted for murder or something."

"Maybe that's why she had all the locks." But the joke didn't land.

"I refused," Abigail said. "I was an adult by then, and she couldn't make me go. That was probably our worst argument, and she still wouldn't tell me why she wanted so desperately to leave."

"Why did you want to stay?" Ruth asked. "I mean, why stay in Kill Devil?"

"Because of you," she replied. "I didn't want to leave you here."

Ruth's hands had squeezed against the steering wheel.

"Even though I was still engaged?"

"I could tell there was something going on with Charlie," Abigail said. "He was acting different than when we were in high school. I don't know how to describe it—I just got a weird feeling in my gut every time we hung out. I was worried about you."

A silence permeated the cold air. Comfortable, yearning.

"Even then, I loved you," Abigail said. "I would have supported whatever you wanted to do, but I couldn't just leave you."

"I'm glad you didn't."

"I'm glad too," Abigail. "And I'm glad Mom stayed. I couldn't imagine not being together at the end. She stayed for me."

Even then, even when faced with the evil once again at her doorstep, Abigail's mom had kept everything hidden—and now Ruth understood why.

After Judy's death, Abigail started looking for her dad in earnest. And now she'd finally found him. Abigail's search was over, and even though her father had kidnapped her girlfriend, had laid her out on the ritual table to kill and devour her, Abigail, apparently, was fine with that. It was a price she was willing to pay—in Ruth's blood. This blood was thicker, this blood that gave both Abigail and Gideon—*James*—the same blue-gray eyes, the same curved nose and eyebrows.

"Abigail, help me, please," Ruth whimpered. "They're tricking you—they are lying, they're using witchcraft or hypnosis or some fucking spell to make you trust them. Listen to me—the money jar we use—remember the weird stuff inside? That was one of their spells. I don't know how it works. But they're doing the same thing to you now—"

Ruth craned her neck, trying to meet Abigail's eye. But Abigail wouldn't look at her, her shining blue eyes fixed on her father's face, drinking in every word. It was as if Ruth was already dead, already a ghost—as though she screamed into a void, as though they'd used some spell or artifact to mute her words.

"Abigail, please, it's me," Ruth said. "I love you. *Please.*"

Gideon now lifted the dagger, ready to plunge it into her flesh.

"Let us begin," he said.

The entire room recited the rites in unison: "*Sin has a thousand treacherous arts she uses to deceive, while the heedless wretch believes she makes thy fetters strong. On a tree divinely fair grew the forbidden food; our mother took the poison there and tainted all her blood.*"

The blade of the dagger dazzled in the candlelight, hovering above her chest. On the table, Ruth tried once more to catch Abigail's eye, but she was avoiding her gaze, cutting her eyes away every time they came too close to meeting. Like she was pretending Ruth was not there, right in front of her, beaten and bruised and bleeding and about to be killed and eaten by her new friends—her *family.*

"*Thy tarnished flesh our souls have eat and here we drink thy sinner's blood; thus we create a nature pure within and form thy soul averse to sin. The holy joys, our Creator, restore and guard thee so that they fall no more.*"

"Abigail!" Ruth yelled. The ropes scraped her skin raw. She hated the desperation in her voice. "Abigail, please! It's me!"

"*Thy flesh is food and physic too, a balm for all our pains; and the red streams of pardon flow from these, thy pierced veins.*"

The whole crowd—sans Abigail—recited these last lines at twice the speed, the syllables running together as if it were all one single word. The deadline must be close. Abigail's father hoisted the dagger higher, the blade cleaned and sharpened.

"How can you be okay with this?" Ruth pleaded, her voice

cracking around the lump in her throat. "How can you just stand there and let them do this? Let them take me from you?"

Abigail still wouldn't look down at Ruth, glancing around the room, but never at the table—at the relics lining the wall, now with noticeable gaps on the shelves, shards lining the floors; at the velvety cloaks around her; at the shining blade; at her father. She seemed almost enamored with the whole process, watching every step intently, like it was a special moment of father-daughter bonding, and not the ritual murder of her girlfriend, who she'd lived with for years—her best friend, the girl she'd grown up with. The girl she once refused to leave. The girl who had fought for hours to get back to her, who had been so close to freedom, but returned because of her deep love.

Ruth's heart dropped. Why wasn't Abigail fighting? Why wouldn't she look at Ruth? Why did it seem like she was enjoying this? Even if she'd finally found her estranged father, how could she put a man she didn't even know, a man who wanted to *kill* and *eat* her girlfriend, over Ruth herself, who had been by her side their whole childhood? Their whole lives? Who had been there during her mom's death, had been there during her grief, who had devoted herself to her?

She understood now why they picked her. She was the perfect sacrifice. Not only did they need a sinner to complete their ritual, but Ruth had an added bonus—they could use her as a way to bring Abigail into the fold. Get rid of Ruth, and it'd be easy to seduce Abigail, who'd be left with no one. A family reunion, estranged daughter meeting estranged father, was all it would take for Abigail to forget Ruth entirely.

Had it really been just this morning that Abigail had been so concerned about leaving this place, worried that they'd be targeted? So worried that she'd nearly been in tears over it? Willing to leave Ruth over it?

Unless—

A terrible thought wormed its way into Ruth's head. She didn't want it to be true, but the thought wedged itself into the front of her mind anyway. Any fight left in her disappeared as the realization settled in: that Abigail, too, had been in on it. Maybe not for the entirety of their relationship, but, like the police, she must have been playing a part too. Maybe her fear and worry this morning was all an act, a performance to push Ruth to accept the early deadline for that commission that had been made by one of the cult members. The whole thing was a setup.

James had probably been grooming her since they met at Judy's funeral when he showed up unannounced. He must have recognized Judy—and, by proxy, Abigail, his long-lost daughter who had been just a couple miles away, all this time.

Ruth's heart couldn't take it. She gave up, releasing her muscles. There was no point in continuing to fight if they'd already ensnared Abigail, if she had been part of this the whole time. Ruth was so tired. She didn't have anything left to fight for. Not even herself. She couldn't foresee a future without Abigail in it.

So fuck it.

They'd won.

She relaxed on the table, waiting for the dagger to drop.

Chapter 29

Gideon held the dagger above Ruth, ready to plunge it into her flesh, ready to complete the rites at last. It hovered above her, the sharp blade waiting to carve into her body and dole out the pieces like birthday cake. Ruth imagined the hierarchy, specific portions going to specific people or ranks, like how the birthday girl always got the first slice, the corner with a big buttercream rose. Which parts of Ruth would be the most valuable? Which piece would Abigail get to chew on?

Defeat settled into Ruth's bones, nestling against the lingering pain, the missing chunk of her thigh spilling sticky blood onto the stone table, into the fibers of the oversized shirt. Ruth felt herself fading, even before the dagger broke her skin. She closed her eyes, leaned into her exhaustion. Maybe she could pass out before they made the first cut. Maybe it could at least be painless for her.

Then Abigail spoke.

"Wait," she said.

Ruth's eyes popped open. What was she doing? Was she

having second thoughts?

Confusion settled between the wrinkles on her father's scrunched face, the parts visible beneath his hood.

"What is it, my darling daughter, Elizabeth?" he asked. "Our time is almost up. We must move quickly."

"I just—I feel so bad about my sins," she said.

"I know, my child," he replied. "But you have already completed the atonement ceremony. Your soul is cleansed. Your sins are gone. You wanted to repent, and now you are right with the Creator."

"I know, Father," she continued, blushing, like she was so happy to be able to say that word, "but I still feel like I haven't done enough to atone." She looked at the dagger. Gideon followed her gaze but didn't seem to follow whatever she was thinking.

"Can I make the first cut?" she asked. "I think that would really allow me to atone, even if only within myself. It would be like cutting that dark part of myself away to make a clean slate."

Now her father smiled. He shone with pride, like Abigail had won a major award, as if she were parading on a stage, holding a golden trophy. He'd finally found his daughter and she was truly his now, truly on his side.

Discontented murmurs spread among the cloaks, hissing whispers wondering why a *woman* was present at all, let alone being allowed to perform such an important part of the ritual.

Gideon hissed back, yelling for silence, the complaints cut off at their crescendoed peak. He kissed her on the forehead and handed the dagger to her.

Abigail raised the blade high in the air while her father stood in awe. Ruth braced herself for the incision, now wide awake. The cut would hurt even more than she could have imagined, because it was coming from Abigail.

“Now, my child,” her father instructed.

Chapter 30

Abigail

A sharp knock at the door startled Abigail from sleep.

She groaned. The only people who ever showed up at the door were those pesky missionaries, those starched freaks from the church beyond the trees. They had just been here, when Ruth left. Did they want her to sign off on a ticket to hell?

Still trapped in the groggy grips of sleep, she plucked gunk from the corners of her eyes and checked the time on her phone. It was late, the tiny sliver of sky between the bedroom curtains dark. Had it really been that long since Ruth had gone? Shouldn't she be back by now? A tightness formed in Abigail's chest, bony fingers stretching up from the acid boiling in her stomach to squeeze her heart, to cease its endless beating.

The fingers clenched tighter when she slid the metal disk away from the peephole and glanced through it. Distorted in the fishbowl lens were two uniformed police officers, their badges centered inside the funhouse effect. Abigail worked quickly to undo the column of locks, the metal ephemera leftover from her mother. *Looks like Ruth went and got herself caught*, she thought, just like she'd warned her when she left. She loved Ruth, but damn if she wasn't stubborn.

The last lock slid out of its holster and she cracked the door, her hand secure on the knob, only her face peering out. An old habit.

"Can I help you?" she asked.

"Are you Abigail Hobbs?" one of the officers asked.

"Yes. What's going on?"

"Your roommate, Ruth Bishop, was apprehended for shop-lifting at the New Creations store. We need you to come with us."

Abigail did not budge, did not inch the door open any further. She hadn't received a phone call from Ruth, from anyone at all. Since when did the police personally escort your emergency contact to the precinct?

"Is she okay?"

"Yes, she's fine," the other replied. Both officers seemed to inch closer to the sliver of open door. Their hands rested on their belts, their fingers twitchy and jerky, as if they were pondering which handy little gadget they would deploy for this situation. As though Abigail herself were complicit, too, and they were at the doorstep of a perp who needed to be subdued with handcuffs and batons and Tasers and who knew what else.

"We need you to come with us," the other said, his toes

scooting forward, the rubber scratching against the splintering wood beneath. His fingers danced against the tools at his waist.

Abigail hesitated, wondering what might happen if she just closed the door and snapped all the locks back into place. Something inside her screamed. Something deep in her gut was stabbed by premonition. Something told her they would not accept that response, that there would suddenly be a whole army of shrill sirens and spinning lights and screeching tires and bullhorns at their dead-end street. Or maybe they'd be more covert—maybe they'd try breaking a window or knocking down the back door, breaking through the same number and arrangement of locks there. Either way, something told her she'd end up in the back of their cruiser.

"I know this is unusual," the first said, seeming to read her thoughts. "Usually you'd just get a phone call, but our lines are down—for maintenance, squirrel chewed through the wire outside, and it's a slow day for us, and she seemed really distraught and worried about you, that you wouldn't know where she was and would be frantic looking for her. The charge really isn't that big, either, and we felt bad, so we just decided to come ourselves."

"She's diabetic," Abigail replied, still clutching the doorknob, still ready to drag her head inside and slam it shut, "and hasn't had her medicine in a while, so I'll need to get a medical package together. I'll head up to the station when I'm finished. Thanks for taking the time to stop by and let me know."

She started to close the door when meaty fingers wrapped around the edge, just above the first lock, almost as if he knew their arrangement, as if he knew the exact right place for his fingers to fall.

"It will be better if you come with us," he said. His fingernails were white from the pressure of his grip. "That way we can take you straight to her, and you can give her the medicine without having to deal with waiting in the lobby for the secretary to call back to us."

"I thought it was a slow day."

"For us, it is," he said, his tone twinged with irritation and anxiety. "But she's always got a million things to do. The paperwork never ends. Get the go bag together, and we'll wait here for you when you're done."

Abigail closed the door behind her, the officer's digits slithering out of the closing gap. Her fingers urged her to snap all the locks shut, to try to hold out until she could figure out what the fuck was going on, if there was anything she could do besides hand herself over. But if they were telling the truth, Ruth needed her. She tried calling, but it went straight to voicemail. She grabbed the small insulated lunch bag from the top of the kitchen cabinets and packed it with Ruth's insulin, syringes, the glucose meter and its ephemera. She even managed to squeeze in some sweets in case Ruth was too low, draping it across her chest with a long strap.

Abigail's heart pounded, slamming against her rib cage, as she locked the door behind her and followed the officers to their cruiser, an unmarked sedan. It felt like the bones in her chest cracked in time with the closing of the door behind her. What had Ruth done? Were these people even cops? Abigail forced herself to exhale, slowly. Whoever they were, they were taking her to Ruth. She had to hold on to that hope, that tiny connective thread. They'd take her to Ruth and they'd figure out what they needed to do, together.

The car rumbled away, down the long stretch of the road, turning right where it connected to the larger strip. Abigail's brain rattled with worry, the whole journey spent forcing herself to breathe between panicked images of Ruth in handcuffs, in a cell, of Ruth fainting or seizing from too-low blood sugar, receiving no help. So she didn't notice when the driver turned right, away from the main roads onto the newly paved stretch that led to the New Creationist church and store. When she finally lifted her head to look out the window, the driver was pivoting into the parking lot of the church.

"Wait," she said, the words tumbling out before she could stop them, "why aren't we at the station?"

"They're holding her here," one of the officers said after a beat.

"Yeah, uh," the other added, "she seemed sick or something, so we had them keep her here. Figured it would be better for her, you know—not to have to deal with all the stress and craziness at the precinct."

"I thought you said it was slow today," Abigail replied.

In the front, one of them grunted. The pair exchanged a tense look that made a ball of lead sink in Abigail's stomach, the sound of their fingers rummaging along their tool belts clear even through the pockmarked steel divider. She needed to shut the fuck up.

"Precincts are always stressful," one of them said finally. "Now, let's get you in there so you can give her medicine."

The pair led her to a set of doors at the side of the church, a massive structure Abigail had never seen up close, had never even seen from the road, her mother always warning her to *stay away from those freaks*. The building was a Frankenstein's monster of a stadium, an office park, a mansion, and a school, with even more wings around back, it looked like. Before she could catch all of the angles and glass walls and architectural features, the officers handed her off to a different pair of men, who pulled her into the yawning mouth of the church, the carpet blue and puffy, like a dead, frozen tongue.

These men wore stiff, starched long-sleeve shirts tucked neatly into belted khakis. Each one held on to her arm with a grip so firm she could feel her own nervous sweat pooling in their palms, the same liquid that also stained the lunch bag clutched between her hands.

The trio followed the tongue of the carpet, curving around a few corners, until they reached a conference room. The men released Abigail's arms and invited her to take a seat at the table, offering her refreshments, as though she were a client to be wooed. More likely a sinner to be converted, a fly to be sweetened with honey and cookies, to be lured in with kindness and false niceties.

"Where's Ruth?" she asked.

"All in due time, dear," one of them said, their words as stiff as their pants.

The other was at the far end of the room, whispering into a telephone. Was she an honored guest or a hostage, a witness or perp to be interrogated? Her palms continued their flash flood, the wetness seeping through the lacquer on the tabletop. She bit her lip, trying to swallow all the words and questions and demands that shoved against her teeth, wanting to escape. These men didn't have a belt full of weapons, but they stood in front of the doors like sentinels. She knew, innately, that these men would not answer her questions; she would not get anywhere with demands.

No, it would be wiser to keep her teeth clamped together. To approach with quiet, observant caution.

A few moments later, another man arrived in the doorway.

"My dear," he said, gesturing for Abigail to stand, opening his arms like a vulture's wings, wanting to embrace, or perhaps to sink his talons into her. He seemed familiar, though she couldn't place how she knew him.

She obliged, her hands limp at her sides.

"My darling," he said, standing back to admire her, as if she were a glittering doll, "I have been looking for you for ages."

"Looking—for me?" she stuttered.

"Sit," he said, gesturing back to the chairs. "We have so much to discuss, and so little time, my daughter."

Abigail's teeth unclamped, her jaw dropping, parting her lips. Yet nothing escaped; no questions or even shrill screams wanting to know what was going on and why she was there. Had he said *daughter*?

He took her hands in his. The man was unassuming. Slicked-back brown hair. Blue eyes, matching hers. He wore a linen button-up shirt with rolled-up sleeves, tucked into plain pants.

"My child, I have been looking for you for so long. Ever since your mother stole you away. What fate that she brought you here, to the ancestral home of the New Creationists, before we were driven away all those centuries ago. What more proof could there be of the Creator's divine hand? Of his great powers and love than to bring you here, waiting for me?"

"Wh-what?" she replied, the only word she could muster.

The man before her nodded at the sentinels, one of whom delivered a box from a cabinet.

"I know this is a lot to take in. But I'll explain everything. My name is James," the man said, pulling the lid from the box. "I am your father. When you were just a baby, your mother stole you from me."

He slid several photographs toward her. Abigail gasped, her breath catching. An ache blossomed inside her chest. Each photograph showed her mother, nearly three decades younger, holding a baby. All standing next to the same man, the same one who sat beside her now, missing only a few wrinkles and gray hairs. All smiles, his teeth gleaming like fangs. In one photo, behind the happy family, stood a small home, matching the house in the only photograph she'd ever seen of her mother and herself as an infant—the only clue she'd ever had to finding her father.

And now, here he was, sitting before her. Her search was over.

"I looked for ages for you," he said, taking her hands again, squeezing them. "I never stopped. But your mother changed your names—to me, you were Elizabeth. It was divine providence, more proof of the Creator's love and power, that the land of our ancestors was for sale at last, and we could finally return home to our sacred temple—but I had no idea you'd been here all this time. I had seen you around town before—I saw the resemblance, I had my suspicions that it was you, my daughter, but I had no proof. I prayed to the Creator for guidance, but received none; and who can blame Him for making me wait on such a selfish endeavor? But it was you who finally made the connection, when you published your mother's obituary with her photograph. It was then that I knew."

"But—she died months ago," Abigail said, her gut churning, boiling with searing doubts. Was this really her father? Or were these doctored photos? "Why now?"

"For that, I do apologize," he said. He brushed his hand through her hair, held it at the back of her head. A warmth spread from his fingers. "Of course, I wanted to reach out to you immediately, but I needed to sort some things out, needed to really make sure, and—well, I wanted it to be the right time."

Tears bubbled in the corners of Abigail's eyes. After years, after her whole life—was her search really over? Was the one person she had always desperately wanted to find sitting right in front of her?

"My darling," he said, cocking his head, pursing his lips as if pitying a child, as though she were still the infant who disappeared. "My sweet girl, we will have years and years now that we have found each other. But for now, it is a very important night."

"Important?"

"Normally, women are not to partake in the ceremony," he said, "but I yearn for you to be a part of it. The Creator has spoken to me, and has granted this exception for my years of sacrifice that I lived without you."

He stood up from the table, her hands still encased in his. His kissed the top of each one, the feeling of his lips soft and tender.

"I need to make arrangements," he said. "I will see you soon."

With a final glance toward her, he slipped between the two starched men, exiting back into the throat of the building.

Abigail's thoughts swirled, each one cascading over the next like crashing waves eroding the wrinkles etched onto her brain. She'd searched for so long. She'd scanned satellite imagery trying to find that house. She'd toiled on ancestry sites for hours, but she couldn't find even her mother or herself. If she'd had the money, she might have tried one of those at-home ancestry DNA tests. All that work and toil, and her father had been just a couple miles away, through the trees. She wasn't sure what she had expected—wasn't sure what to think now, knowing that he was involved with this megachurch, with the starched people who showed up on their doorstep and shoved pamphlets into their doorjamb, pamphlets that had seemed so insane when they'd received them. With the people her mother had told her to stay the hell away from. But now she couldn't quite remember what they'd said that had felt so wrong.

The lunch bag lay forgotten on the table, the long strap still hung around her shoulder.

The sentinels scurried at the other end of the room, retrieving objects from the cabinets set into the walls. "Before you are reunited again," one said, "we need to perform a small ritual."

"It is very simple, just a small ceremony to cleanse your

sins," the other said.

Twisting her hands around, they positioned her wrists toward the sky. Upon each they poured a single drop of dark oil. Another dollop sat on the crown of her scalp. "With this oil, we anoint thee in the name of our Creator," they said, in unison. "We bestow upon you your original name of Elizabeth."

Now cleansed, the ritual ephemera restored inside the cabinets, Abigail sat, her thoughts swirling around and around, an electricity buzzing through her, the photographs of her past still spread on the table before her. She'd finally found her father. He had been right here for years. Her mother must have known, must have done everything she could to keep Abigail away, to keep them separated. Until the day she died, she'd succeeded. Until Abigail printed her photo.

"It's time," one of the sentinels said, breaking her rumination. "We will bring you to your father now. To the ritual." She stood, the lunch bag sliding away from the table and knocking into her hip with a gentle prod. Only then did she remember its presence, remember the guise that had brought her here—remember Ruth.

Chapter 31

The blade landed against the table with a *thwack*. Ruth kept her eyes squeezed shut, waiting for the pain to arrive, for the wound to scream as the air reached deep inside a new part of her. But there was no fresh bloom of agony. It hadn't broken skin. The pressure at one of Ruth's wrists dissipated. Abigail had cut the rope holding her hand to the table. And then, in three quick swipes, she cut the rest of the ties.

Abigail moved quickly, swinging the blade at anyone who tried to stop her, at any cloak who tried to pry it out of her hands. The men were quick to grab Ruth and hold her back, pin her against the slab, but they seemed hesitant to touch Abigail, unsure how to proceed with the leader's daughter. Should they tackle her from behind? Risk being sliced in order to get the knife back? Would laying hands on her draw their leader's ire?

Now reinvigorated, Ruth kicked and bit and scratched—she did anything she could to get the cultists' hands off her, to get off the fucking table and get to Abigail.

Abigail *had* been playing a part, but not the one she'd thought.

Ruth's kicking feet knocked against the little side table, the one that held the precious jar, the little demon condo. Its contents clattered to the floor, bone saws and other metal instruments clanging against the hard stone. The minuscule ceramic jar tottered, weebled, and wobbled, but remained on the table, right in the center.

"The jar!" Ruth yelled to Abigail, still trying to free her arms from the men's grip. "Break it!"

Before the cult members could divert their attention from Ruth, before they could snatch the jar from the table, Abigail rushed to it. As her hand wrapped around it, her father grabbed her wrist, holding it tight.

"Don't do this," he said. "Don't return to your sinful ways."

"Let go or I'll cut you," Abigail hissed, her teeth glinting in the candlelight.

His grip persisted. Perhaps he was still under the illusion that his Creator would protect him, or believed that Abigail wouldn't hurt him because he was her father, even if she still loved Ruth. Even if she was still sinful, she must love her father, surely—because that was how all narcissistic men thought, and this asshole was no different.

"I cannot let you be given to the devil!" he shouted.

"Mom was right to leave you," Abigail replied, sliding the blade across his hand.

His fingers released, an automatic motion, and before he could get a new grip on her, she raised the little ceramic jar and hurled it toward the ground with all her strength.

It didn't shatter like Ruth expected. It hit the stone floor with a heaviness that managed to splinter the stone beneath it, as though an anvil had been dropped there, as if the jar were filled with plutonium. The sound echoed through the narrow room, loud as a gong. Along the side of the jar snaked a crack, a dark hairline curling up from the base.

A newfound chill spread through the cramped space, cutting through the humidity of packed bodies, of sweat and breath, goose bumps rising on every arm. There was a frozen, suspended moment as all eyes turned to the crack on the jar, before the mass of fluttering cloaks rushed toward it, crowding and trampling each other to get to it.

"Bring me a blade!" Charlie cried. "I will sacrifice myself to contain it—my choice has failed us!"

"You despicable worms," Gideon shouted, swiping once more at Abigail. "You've doomed us all!"

Abigail untangled herself from the desperate throng, weaving and slicing her way back to Ruth, the blade clearing the way, carving through any cloaked flesh in its path. There were the sounds of desperation, screams and spilled blood, urgent prayers as the Shepherds attempted to make right with their Creator.

Hand in hand, the pair escaped, pounding up the stairs and down the blue-carpeted throat, spat back out of the church's mouth.

Chapter 32

The pair spilled out into the asphalt sea.

Ruth craned her head skyward. The deadline was very close, if not already here, the moon almost directly overhead, centered in the sky. A deep, blood red.

The cultists didn't have time to catch them and perform all the steps of the ritual anew. And they'd cracked the vessel—that meant something, right, if there truly was a demon? Abigail had spilled plenty of their supposed Pure and True blood on the way out. Had that sufficed as the sacrifice their Creator demanded? Or had the crack ruined everything?

They headed for the trees, running as fast as they could, Ruth having learned her lesson about using the roads. She would have to be careful to avoid the commune, too. But they were together now. She no longer needed to get home. They could hide in the forest until morning, nestled in the loam.

Behind them, flame rose, the spaces between the trees illuminated. In mere minutes, fire engulfed the massive church, the blaze hot enough to warm their skin all the way back into the trees. Exhausted, Ruth and Abigail stopped, holding each other, the dagger dropping down into the dirt by their feet. They no longer needed it. Together, they watched the licking flames devour the church, their eyes wide with awe.

They'd won. All those fuckers were burning, maybe not in the flaming pits of hell, but in the all-too-real fires of their own doing—their own broken building code and lack of emergency exits. Ruth could only grin as the roof collapsed in on itself, as those fucked-up stained-glass windows melted and crashed into the wreckage.

But this wasn't an ordinary fire. Even with all the code-cutting they did, it was devouring the building too quickly. How had it started? Had the candles in the ritual room lit their cloaks ablaze? How had it devoured the whole building in just a few short minutes? Ruth didn't care. Fuck them. A giddy warmth spread through her chest.

The rest of the structure soon followed the roof, each beam and plush stadium seat crashing inward. What lay between the flames resembled red-hot magma, like it had boiled up from the earth's crust, churning and consuming anything in its path. Ruth thought it must be an illusion, a trick of the eyes at their distance. It must have been the embers of the roof falling into the basement, eroding the stone ceiling over the ritual room. It looked like hell.

Through the trees, they spied the final collapse, the last bits of wall and gory stained glass toppling into the fiery pit. Above them, the bright moon peeked through the branches, an orangey haze matching the fire. A roar sounded, cutting through the smoke-heated air, some guttural, primal scream. Too cohesive, too one-note, to be the final, dying agonies of the cultists below, lacking any harmony or discordant tones. Despite the boiling humidity, a chill cascaded along Ruth's spine. Did she really hear an undertone of glee within the cacophonous roar?

From the pit sprang splashes of blistering orange, unmistakably like that of boiling lava. Neither had the opportunity to ponder this vision, to so much as blink and squint for a better view, before the ground beneath them tumbled and shook, rumbling and cracking in a line that started from the spot where the church had once stood. The shattered earth snaked across the fresh pavement, toward the craft store, and a second path slithered through the woods toward them. Ruth and Abigail pushed backward, farther into the trees as the ground before them opened like a massive, yawning jaw.

Inside, the tongue was liquid fire.

Bloodcurdling screams floated between the trees a few seconds later, as the fault line reached the hidden patch of cabins. Above the trees, in front of the bloody moon, a column of smoke rose. For a brief moment, Ruth swore it looked human.

After the dust stilled, Abigail wrapped Ruth in a tight hug. Ruth's nerves protested, but she didn't budge, clinging back with all her remaining strength.

"I'm so sorry, Ruth," she said. "For scaring you like that. I didn't know what else to do. The police came to the house saying you'd been caught shoplifting, and they wanted me to go with them, saying they were taking me to you—my heart was pounding the whole time."

"You saved us," Ruth said, pulling Abigail in for a bloody, wonderful kiss.

"How's your blood sugar?" she asked, pulling a singed bag from her back, uncovering all of Ruth's insulin and gear and pristine candies.

By now the fire had started to spread to the woods, the fault line sputtering lava and spitting out giant embers into the dry trees. The heat was too close, too suddenly, and it was spreading quickly. No more time to embrace.

At their backs, screams rose from the trees, the same blood-curdling, giddy noise they'd heard before, this time mixed with the discordant harmony of human agony.

Ruth and Abigail ran through the woods, their hands clasped together, never letting go. The fire licking at their heels pushed them onward, forcing them to turn and pivot as if it were herding them. In between the silhouettes of the trees, in the dancing flames, Ruth thought she saw the shapes of other bodies, of sprinting women and children.

The heat persisted at their backs until they reached the creek that ran next to their house, watching the world burn, up to their waists in the waters of Hell for Certain.

NEW CREATIONIST CHURCH, STORE DESTROYED IN FIRE, SINKHOLE

KILL DEVIL, KENTUCKY

Early Sunday morning the New Creationist Church complex was destroyed in a fire, which caused a sinkhole to develop.

Local authorities were alerted to the fire around 1:39 a.m. after it had spread to the surrounding forest. By the time firefighters arrived on the scene, the New Creationist church building was entirely demolished. The structure had collapsed and fallen into a sinkhole caused by an unknown system of limestone caves underneath the building. The cause of the fire remains unknown.

"We're still assessing the scene," said police chief Bob Higgins. "At this time we do not suspect foul play."

The extensive damage also included the craft store New Creations, owned by the church, as well as several cabins that were under construction as the church prepared to open its own summer camp as part of its youth programming. Both were destroyed by the sinkhole, because of the expansive nature of the underground cave system.

Though the fire was extremely hot and spread quickly, it was unable to spread to neighboring homes or businesses because of Hell for Certain creek.

Authorities have closed Bethlehem Road at the junction of Hell for Certain Road while they complete their investigation and search for victims or survivors.

It is unknown at this time whether there are any casualties. However, the whereabouts of several prominent church leaders, including the preacher James Atkins, are not known and it is believed they may have been in the building at the time of the fire.

This is a developing story.

ANTIQUITIES DISCOVERED IN CHURCH SINKHOLE

KILL DEVIL, KENTUCKY

Authorities have halted cleanup attempts after the discovery of hundreds of antiquities at the site of the New Creationist Church wreckage.

Archaeologists and experts from the University of Kentucky were called in to authenticate the items.

Experts say the items range in age, though they estimate that nearly all of the objects are genuine antiques. Among the antiquities, the researchers found Roman glass vials, Minoan pottery, Mesopotamian cuneiform tablets, and more.

"How these items came to reside in a sinkhole in the middle of Kentucky is a mystery," archaeologist Dr. Dave Bell said. "Many predate Kentucky's colonization and statehood, and appear to originate from all over the world."

A few weeks ago, a sinkhole destroyed the New Creationist Church, along with New Creations, a craft store owned by the church, and cabins under construction for a summer camp. Authorities believe the sinkhole was prompted by a fire of unknown origin that started in the church.

"It's a wonder that, despite the wreckage from the sinkhole and fire, many of these items are still in pristine condition," Dr. Bell continued. "They were shielded inside a cave that remained intact."

Once authorities extinguished the fire, efforts were made to clear the wreckage, leading to the discovery of the antiquities.

Some of the recovered items were known to be missing, having been reported as stolen from private collections or vanished from archaeological sites. However, authorities do not currently believe there is a connection between the New Creationists and the thefts, as some of the items were known to be missing for decades prior to the church's purchase of the land. Authorities have not been able to trace the pathway of ownership.

Local authorities are working with international agencies to repatriate the known items to their countries of origin. Any artifact unaccounted for will be donated to various museums around the world.

Epilogue

That same night, the fire inching closer and closer to their home, to the house that had been their own sanctuary for so many years, Ruth and Abigail put that town in their rearview.

They landed in a new city far away from Kill Devil, Kentucky. A place where they thrived, where they did not have to pinch their curtains closed or scan the trees for birdwatchers. Where they did not need a money jar, the vessel now bearing flowers instead. The scars lining Ruth's skin, the only evidence of the events of that night, had already begun to fade—or at least they did not cut as deep anymore.

They had not spared a thought for Kill Devil or the New Creationists for months when a knock sang against their door, a *clunk* sounding heavily on the wood while Ruth sat knitting on the sofa, a thin gold band circling her finger.

At the door stood a woman and a young child, a boy. She wore a high-collared, stiff dress, her hair slicked back into a tight bun. The boy wore a miniature button-up tucked into ironed pants.

"Can I help you?" Ruth asked.

The woman shoved a pamphlet into her hands, folded in thirds, the language and design all too familiar. *Lost Sheep of all kinds welcome—come back to the flock!*

"Hello, neighbor," the woman said, grinning, saliva dripping from her incisors. "We'd love for you to join us in service to the Creator. He shall show you many wonders."

THE END

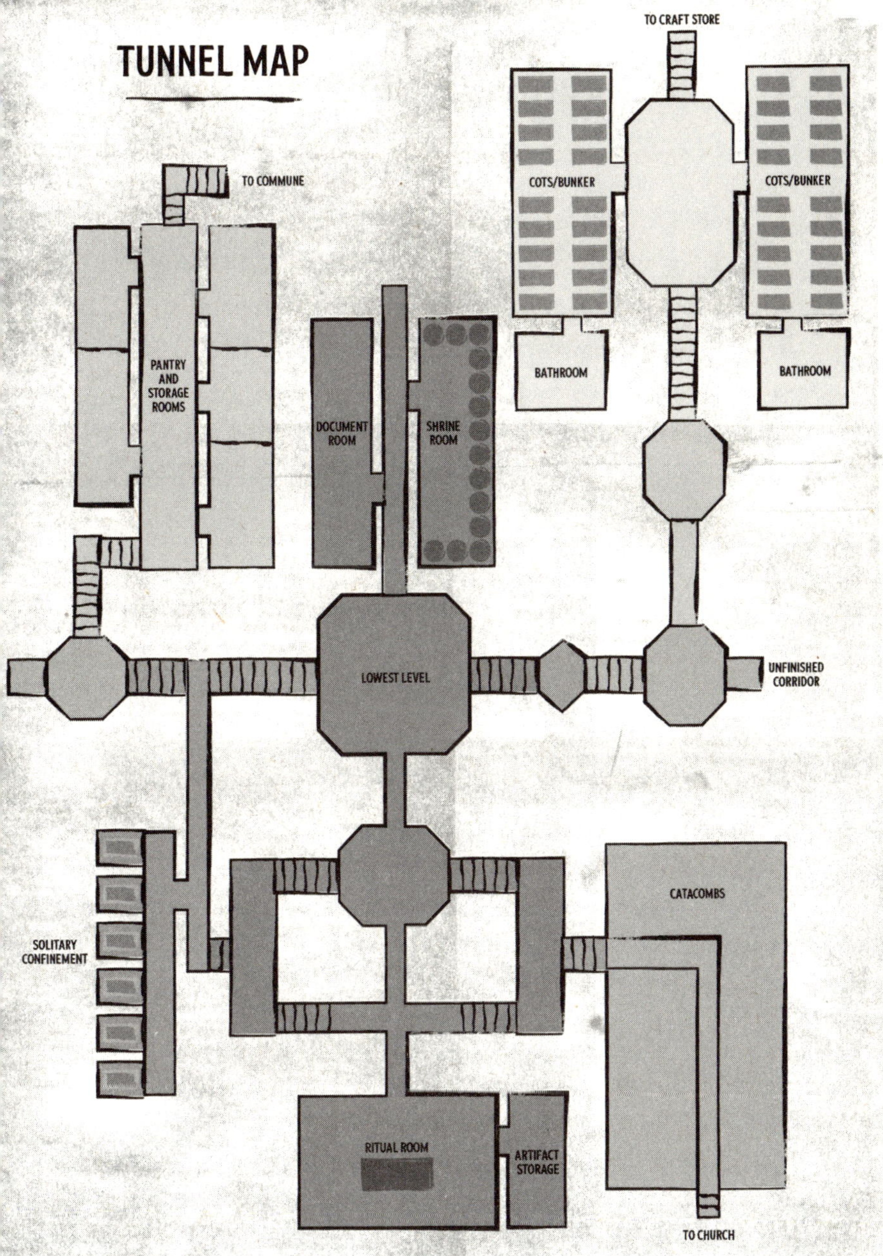
TUNNEL MAP
TO COMMUNE
PANTRY AND STORAGE ROOMS
DOCUMENT ROOM
SHRINE ROOM
TO CRAFT STORE
COTS/BUNKER
COTS/BUNKER
BATHROOM
BATHROOM
LOWEST LEVEL
UNFINISHED CORRIDOR
SOLITARY CONFINEMENT
CATACOMBS
RITUAL ROOM
ARTIFACT STORAGE
TO CHURCH

Acknowledgments

The process of publishing this book has been bittersweet. I'm so happy with how it has turned out, but I was writing it during a rough time. Alongside the writing of this book came the death of the very first dog who was mine alone: Reese. He was tired, and he was ready. I miss him every day.

And now it's being published during a rough time, too. I hope it can do something positive for someone, even if it's just a fun romp through a craft store that takes their mind off things.

Thanks to Rebecca, whose editorial guidance made this book a thousand times better.

Thanks to Lane, for his ever-present support and guidance.

Thanks to Nicole Nikolich for making a real, hand-crocheted piece of art for the cover, and Andie Reid for hand-painting letters and creating the rest of the magic of the cover. (Hell yeah, fuck AI!)

Thanks always to Rob, who continues to support my writing and success.

Thanks to Nichole and Jessica for their support in sharing their personal experiences with diabetes.

Thanks to my mom, Martha, for being my biggest cheerleader and continuing to run Butcher Cabin Books. And to Amanda, who has been invaluable to the store's continued success.

For their friendship and support, thanks to Adria Bailton, Joe Koch, Theodore Hill, Andy Boyle, Michelle Tang, Cynthia

Pelayo, Sasha Brown, Emma Cole, Ryan Ketterer, Clay McLeod Chapman, Laurel Hightower, Kathy Palm, Tony Evans, Andrew Shaffer, and a ton of others in the horror community who have each been a friend, an ear, and a wealth of support and knowledge. Go read their words.

Thanks to my writing haunts: Awry Brewing, Zanzabar, Bean Coffee, Sunergos, Hauck's, and Monnik.

And, as usual, thanks to Rye (and also Rabbit), without whom I would have finished this book much sooner.

Reading Group Guide

Visit quirkbooks.com for more book club resources.

- Have you read Jenny Kiefer's debut novel, *This Wretched Valley*? If so, are there any parallels to draw between these two survival horror novels?

- Kiefer explores the horrors of being trapped in a town that weaponizes religion to reinforce bigoted ideals. Was there anything in her descriptions of Kill Devil that particularly resonated with you?

- How did the use of different media formats in this book (such as forum threads, podcast transcripts, articles, and letters) affect your reading experience and inform the story?

- Did you expect a different fate for Ruth and Abigail? How did you feel about their portrayal as a queer couple in a small town?

- The New Creationists use cult tactics to recruit and convert people. Did their methods remind you of any real-world examples?

- How did you feel about the ending? Do you think the demon was real, or instead served as a metaphor for the horrors humanity can inflict?

- If you were trapped in the craft store like Ruth, how would you escape? Are you a crafter yourself, and do you think that would give you an advantage?

- What are some of the most memorable moments in this book for you?

- Does *Crafting for Sinners* remind you of any other horror media that you've read or watched?

- If you could ask Kiefer any questions about the book or her writing, what would you ask her?

David Borgenicht Chairman and Founder
Nicole De Jackmo EVP, Deputy Publisher
Andie Reid Creative Director
Jane Morley Managing Editor
Mandy Sampson Production Director
Shaquona Crews Principal, Contracts and Rights
Katherine McGuire Assistant Director of Subsidiary Rights

CREATIVE

Alex Arnold Editorial Director, Children's
Jess Zimmerman Editor
Rebecca Gyllenhaal Associate Editor
Jessica Yang Assistant Editor
Elissa Flanigan Senior Designer
Paige Graff Junior Designer
Kassie Andreadis Managing Editorial Assistant

SALES, MARKETING, AND PUBLICITY

Kate Brown Senior Sales Manager
Christina Tatulli Digital Marketing Manager
Ivy Weir Senior Publicity and Marketing Manager
Gaby Iori Publicist and Marketing Coordinator
Kim Ismael Digital Marketing Design Associate
Scott MacLean Publicity and Marketing Assistant
Jesse Mendez Sales Assistant

OPERATIONS

Caprianna Anderson Business Associate
Robin Wright Production and Sales Assistant

PRAISE FOR *CRAFTING FOR SINNERS*

"*Crafting for Sinners* is a relentless, grueling survival story, one that displays the horrors that too many of our hateful and ignorant neighbors are capable of perpetrating. You will compulsively turn these pages well into the dead of night."—**PAUL TREMBLAY, *New York Times* best-selling author of *Horror Movie* and *The Cabin at the End of the World***

"*Crafting for Sinners* is like a deranged, hellish variant of *Die Hard* except instead it's a gay woman trapped inside a craft store run by an evangelical nightmare cult. It's surreal, terrifying, and thrilling and looks right down the barrel at the cultural horrors at the center of our current era. I loved this. You will love this. This is excellent stuff from Jenny Kiefer."—**CHUCK WENDIG, *New York Times* best-selling author of *The Book of Accidents* and *The Staircase in the Woods***

"*Crafting for Sinners* is a crafty yarn crocheted from the same skein as Grady Hendrix's *Horrorstör* and Rachel Harrison's *Cackle*. Jenny Kiefer sure has spun herself a gloriously gory, bisexual MacGyver of the Damned and it absolutely fits this particular sinner like the comfiest blood-soaked sweater."—**CLAY McLEOD CHAPMAN, author of *Wake Up and Open Your Eyes***

"Devilishly clever. Every page of *Crafting for Sinners* is packed with scathing satire, unique horrors, and stunning honesty. With surprising twists and turns from beginning to end, Kiefer has crafted a delight of a novel."—**ERIN E. ADAMS, author of *Jackal* and *One of You***

"A crafty cat-and-mouse thriller."—**JOHNNY COMPTON, author of *Devils Kills Devils* and *The Spite House***

"Suspenseful, of the moment, and bloodthirsty as all hell, Jenny Kiefer's *Crafting for Sinners* is the kind of book we need these days."
—**NICK CUTTER, author of *The Troop* and *The Deep***

PRAISE FOR *THIS WRETCHED VALLEY*

A January 2024 Indie Next List Pick

One of *Esquire*'s Best Horror Books of 2024 (So Far)

A *Library Journal* Best Horror Book of 2024

"A hallucinatory nightmare of a novel that blends adventure, horror, and historical fiction and isn't shy about violence or strangeness."
—***New York Times***

"Kiefer's debut heralds the arrival of a major new horror talent. Through vivid descriptions of the creepy setting and thoughtful character portraits, Kiefer maintains a feeling of unease and nail-biting tension throughout. Devotees of daylight horror will be entranced."—***Publishers Weekly*, starred review**

"A terrifying debut, rendered with the intensity and skill of Scott Smith's cult favorite *The Ruins* and touches of *The Hunger* by Alma Katsu and *Echo* by Thomas Olde Heuvelt. The novel announces Kiefer's intentions to boldly begin her climb to the top of the genre."—***Library Journal*, starred review**

"Kiefer's gory and intense debut centers on a doomed rock-climbing expedition beset by horrors both human and supernatural. Kiefer, a climber herself, utilizes her knowledge of the sport to deliver an evocative and pulse-pounding survival horror novel inspired by the Dyatlov Pass incident. This disturbing outing marks her as a writer to watch and will appeal to fans of Scott Smith's *The Ruins* (2006) and the Showtime series *Yellowjackets*."—***Booklist***

"A master class in both suspense and gore, *This Wretched Valley* is a treat for climbers and horror lovers alike."—**Laura Hubbard, *BookPage***

"Despite being the author's debut novel, *This Wretched Valley* is a glittering contender for Best Horror of 2024 . . . this book is unshakeable."—***Cemetery Dance***